The Princess F
Fortnig

Elizabeth Von Arnim

Alpha Editions

This edition published in 2024

ISBN 9789362090423

Design and Setting By
Alpha Editions
www.alphaedis.com
Email - info@alphaedis.com

Contents

I	- 1 -
II	- 12 -
III	- 22 -
IV	- 27 -
V	- 32 -
VI	- 42 -
VII	- 50 -
VIII	- 57 -
IX	- 64 -
X	- 77 -
XI	- 85 -
XII	- 93 -
XIII	- 101 -
XIV	- 112 -
XV	- 119 -
XVI	- 125 -
XVII	- 132 -
XVIII	- 138 -
XIX	- 147 -
XX	- 156 -
XXI	- 165 -
XXII	- 173 -
XXIII	- 178 -
CONCLUSION	- 188 -

I

Her Grand Ducal Highness the Princess Priscilla of Lothen-Kunitz was up to the age of twenty-one a most promising young lady. She was not only poetic in appearance beyond the habit of princesses but she was also of graceful and appropriate behaviour. She did what she was told; or, more valuable, she did what was expected of her without being told. Her father, in his youth and middle age a fiery man, now an irritable old gentleman who liked good food and insisted on strictest etiquette, was proud of her on those occasions when she happened to cross his mind. Her mother, by birth an English princess of an originality uncomfortable and unexpected in a royal lady that continued to the end of her life to crop up at disconcerting moments, died when Priscilla was sixteen. Her sisters, one older and one younger than herself, were both far less pleasing to look upon than she was, and much more difficult to manage; yet each married a suitable prince and each became a credit to her House, while as for Priscilla,—well, as for Priscilla, I propose to describe her dreadful conduct.

But first her appearance. She was well above the average height of woman; a desirable thing in a princess, who, before everything, must impress the public with her dignity. She had a long pointed chin, and a sweet mouth with full lips that looked most kind. Her nose was not quite straight, one side of it being the least bit different from the other,—a slight crookedness that gave her face a charm absolutely beyond the reach of those whose features are what is known as chiselled. Her skin was of that fairness that freckles readily in hot summers or on winter days when the sun shines brightly on the snow, a delicate soft skin that is seen sometimes with golden eyelashes and eyebrows, and hair that is more red than gold. Priscilla had these eyelashes and eyebrows and this hair, and she had besides beautiful grey-blue eyes—calm pools of thought, the court poet called them, when her having a birthday compelled him to official raptures; and because everybody felt sure they were not really anything of the kind the poet's utterance was received with acclamations. Indeed, a princess who should possess such pools would be most undesirable—in Lothen-Kunitz nothing short of a calamity; for had they not had one already? It was what had been the matter with the deceased Grand Duchess; she would think, and no one could stop her, and her life in consequence was a burden to herself and to everybody else at her court. Priscilla, however, was very silent. She had never expressed an opinion, and the inference was that she had no opinion to express. She had not criticized, she had not argued, she had been tractable, obedient, meek. Yet her sisters, who had often criticized and argued, and who had rarely been obedient and never meek, became as I have said the wives of appropriate princes, while Priscilla,—well, he who runs may read what it was that Priscilla became.

But first as to where she lived. The Grand Duchy of Lothen-Kunitz lies in the south of Europe; that smiling region of fruitful plains, forest-clothed hills, and broad rivers. It is one of the first places Spring stops at on her way up from Italy; and Autumn, coming down from the north sunburnt, fruit-laden, and blest, goes slowly when she reaches it, lingering there with her serenity and ripeness, her calm skies and her windless days long after the Saxons and Prussians have lit their stoves and got out their furs. There figs can be eaten off the trees in one's garden, and vineyards glow on the hillsides. There the people are Catholics, and the Protestant pastor casts no shadow of a black gown across life. There as you walk along the white roads, you pass the image of the dead Christ by the wayside; mute reminder to those who would otherwise forget of the beauty of pitifulness and love. And there, so near is Kunitz to the soul of things, you may any morning get into the train after breakfast and in the afternoon find yourself drinking coffee in the cool colonnades of the Piazza San Marco at Venice.

Kunitz is the capital of the duchy, and the palace is built on a hill. It is one of those piled-up buildings of many windows and turrets and battlements on which the tourist gazes from below as at the realization of a childhood's dream. A branch of the river Loth winds round the base of the hill, separating the ducal family from the red-roofed town along its other bank. Kunitz stretches right round the hill, lying clasped about its castle like a necklet of ancient stones. At the foot of the castle walls the ducal orchards and kitchen gardens begin, continuing down to the water's edge and clothing the base of the hill in a garment of blossom and fruit. No fairer sight is to be seen than the glimpse of these grey walls and turrets rising out of a cloud of blossom to be had by him who shall stand in the market place of Kunitz and look eastward up the narrow street on a May morning; and if he who gazes is a dreamer he could easily imagine that where the setting of life is so lovely its days must of necessity be each like a jewel, of perfect brightness and beauty.

The Princess Priscilla, however, knew better. To her unfortunately the life within the walls seemed of a quite blatant vulgarity; pervaded by lacqueys, by officials of every kind and degree, by too much food, too many clothes, by waste, by a feverish frittering away of time, by a hideous want of privacy, by a dreariness unutterable. To her it was a perpetual behaving according to the ideas officials had formed as to the conduct to be expected of princesses, a perpetual pretending not to see that the service offered was sheerest lip-service, a perpetual shutting of the eyes to hypocrisy and grasping selfishness. Conceive, you tourist full of illusions standing free down there in the market place, the frightfulness of never being alone a moment from the time you get out of bed to the time you get into it again. Conceive the deadly patience needed to stand passive and be talked to, amused, taken care of, all day long for years. Conceive the intolerableness, if you are at all sensitive, of being watched by eyes so sharp and prying, so eager to note the least change of expression and to use the conclusions drawn for personal ends that nothing, absolutely nothing, escapes them. Priscilla's sisters took all these things as a matter of course, did not care in the least how keenly they were watched and talked over, never wanted to be alone, liked being fussed over by their ladies-in-waiting. They, happy girls, had thick skins. But Priscilla was a dreamer of dreams, a poet who never wrote poems, but whose soul though inarticulate was none the less saturated with the desires and loves from which poems are born. She, like her sisters, had actually known no other states; but then she dreamed of them continuously, she desired them continuously, she read of them continuously; and though there was only one person who knew she did these things I suppose one person is enough in the way of encouragement if your mind is bent on rebellion. This old person, cause of all the mischief that followed, for without his help I do not see what Priscilla could have done, was the ducal librarian—*Hofbibliothekar*, head, and practically master of the wonderful collection of books and manuscripts whose mere catalogue made learned mouths in distant parts of Europe water and learned lungs sigh in hopeless envy. He too had officials under him, but they were unlike the others: meek youths, studious and short-sighted, whose business as far as Priscilla could see was to bow themselves out silently whenever she and her lady-in-waiting came in. The librarian's name was Fritzing; plain Herr Fritzing originally, but gradually by various stages at last arrived at the dignity and sonorousness of Herr Geheimarchivrath Fritzing. The Grand Duke indeed had proposed to ennoble him after he had successfully taught Priscilla English grammar, but Fritzing, whose spirit dwelt among the Greeks, could not be brought to see any desirability in such a step. Priscilla called him Fritzi when her lady-in-waiting dozed; dearest Fritzi sometimes even, in the heat of protest or persuasion. But afterwards, leaving the room as solemnly as she had come in, followed by her wide-awake attendant, she would nod a formally gracious "Good afternoon, Herr Geheimrath," for all the world as though she had been talking that way the whole time. The Countess (her lady-in-waiting was the Countess Irmgard von Disthal, an ample slow lady, the unmarried daughter of a noble house, about fifty at this time, and luckily—or unluckily—for Priscilla, a great lover of much food and its resultant deep slumbers) would bow in her turn in as stately a manner as her bulk permitted, and with a frigidity so pronounced that in any one less skilled in shades of deportment it would have resembled with a singular completeness a sniff of scorn. Her frigidity was perfectly justified. Was she not a *hochgeboren*, a member of an ancient house, of luminous pedigree as far back as one could possibly see? And was he not the son of an obscure Westphalian farmer, a person who in his youth had sat barefoot watching pigs? It is true he had learning, and culture, and a big head with plenty of brains in it, and the Countess Disthal had a small head, hardly any brains, no soul to speak of, and no education. This, I say, is true; but it is also neither here nor there. The Countess was the Countess, and Fritzing was a nobody, and the condescension she showed him was far more grand ducal than anything in that way that Priscilla could or ever did produce.

Fritzing, unusually gifted, and enterprising from the first—which explains the gulf between pig-watching and *Hofbibliothekar*—had spent ten years in Paris and twenty in England in various capacities, but always climbing higher in the world of intellect, and had come during this climbing to speak English quite as well as most Englishmen, if in a statelier, Johnsonian manner. At fifty he began his career in Kunitz, and being a lover of children took over the English education of the three princesses; and now that they had long since learned all they cared to know, and in Priscilla's case all of grammar at least that he had to teach, he invented a talent for drawing in Priscilla, who could not draw a straight line, much less a curved one, so that she should still be able to come to the library as often as she chose on the pretext of taking a drawing-lesson. The Grand Duke's idea about his daughters was that they should know a little of everything and nothing too well; and if Priscilla had said she wanted to study Shakespeare with the librarian he would have angrily forbidden it. Had she not had ten years for studying Shakespeare? To go on longer than that would mean that she was eager, and the Grand Duke loathed an eager woman.

But he had nothing to say against a little drawing; and it was during the drawing-lessons of the summer Priscilla was twenty-one that the Countess Disthal slept so peacefully. The summer was hot, and the vast room cool and quiet. The time was three o'clock—immediately, that is, after luncheon. Through the narrow open windows sweet airs and scents came in from the bright world outside. Sometimes a bee would wander up from the fruit-gardens below, and lazily drone round shady corners. Sometimes a flock of pigeons rose swiftly in front of the windows, with a flash of shining wings. Every quarter of an hour the cathedral clock down in the town sent up its slow chime. Voices of people boating on the river floated up too, softened to melodiousness. Down at the foot of the hill the red roofs of the town glistened in the sun. Beyond them lay the sweltering cornfields. Beyond them forests and villages. Beyond them a blue line of hills. Beyond them, said Priscilla to herself, freedom. She sat in her white dress at a table in one of the deep windows, her head on its long slender neck, where the little rings of red-gold hair curled so prettily, bent over the drawing-board, her voice murmuring ceaselessly, for time was short and she had a great many things to say. At her side sat Fritzing, listening and answering. Far away in the coolest, shadiest corner of the room slumbered the Countess. She was lulled by the murmured talk as sweetly as by the drone of the bee.

"Your Grand Ducal Highness receives many criticisms and much advice on the subject of drawing from the Herr Geheimrath?" she said one day, after a lesson during which she had been drowsily aware of much talk.

"The Herr Geheimrath is most conscientious," said Priscilla in the stately, it-has-nothing-to-do-with-you sort of tone she found most effectual with the Countess; but she added a request under her breath that the *lieber Gott* might forgive her, for she knew she had told a fib.

Indeed, the last thing that Fritzing was at this convulsed period of his life was what his master would have called conscientious. Was he not encouraging the strangest, wickedest, wildest ideas in the Princess? Strange and wicked and wild that is from the grand ducal point of view, for to Priscilla they seemed all sweetness and light. Fritzing had a perfect horror of the Grand Duke. He was everything that Fritzing, lean man of learning, most detested. The pleasantest fashion of describing the Grand Duke will be simply to say that he was in all things, both of mind and body, the exact opposite of Fritzing. Fritzing was a man who spent his time ignoring his body and digging away at his mind. You know the bony aspect of such men. Hardly ever is there much flesh on them; and though they are often ugly enough, their spirit blazes at you out of wonderful eyes. I call him old Fritzing, for he was sixty. To me he seemed old; to Priscilla at twenty he seemed coeval with pyramids and kindred hoarinesses; while to all those persons who were sixty-one he did not seem old at all. Only two things could have kept this restless soul chained to the service of the Grand Duke, and those two things were the unique library and Priscilla. For the rest, his life at Kunitz revolted him. He loathed the etiquette and the fuss and the intrigues of the castle. He loathed each separate lady-in-waiting, and every one of the male officials. He loathed the vulgar abundance and inordinate length and frequency of the meals, when down in the town he knew there were people a-hungered. He loathed the lacqueys with a quite peculiar loathing, scowling at them from under angry eyebrows as he passed from his apartment to the library; yet such is the power of an independent and scornful spirit that though they had heard all about Westphalia and the pig-days never once had they, who made insolence their study, dared be rude to him.

Priscilla wanted to run away. This, I believe, is considered an awful thing to do even if you are only a housemaid or somebody's wife. If it were not considered awful, placed by the world high up on its list of Utter Unforgivablenesses, there is, I suppose, not a woman who would not at some time or other have run. She might come back, but she would surely have gone. So bad is it held to be that even a housemaid who runs is unfailingly pursued by maledictions more or less definite according to the education of those she has run from; and a wife who runs is pursued by social ruin, it being taken for granted that she did not run alone. I know at least two wives who did run alone. Far from wanting yet another burden added to them by adding to their lives yet another man, they were anxiously endeavouring to get as far as might be from the man they had got already. The world, foul hag with the downcast eyes and lascivious lips, could not believe it possible, and was quick to draw its dark mantle of disgrace over their shrinking heads. One of them, unable to bear this, asked her husband's pardon. She was a weak spirit, and now lives prostrate days, crushed beneath the unchanging horror of a husband's free forgiveness. The other took a cottage and laughed at the world. Was she not happy at last, and happy in the right way? I go to see her sometimes, and we eat the cabbages she has grown herself. Strange how the disillusioned find their peace in cabbages.

Priscilla, then, wanted to run away. What is awful in a housemaid and in anybody's wife became in her case stupendous. The spirit that could resolve it, decide to do it without being dragged to it by such things as love or passion, calmly looking the risks and losses in the face, and daring everything to free itself, was, it must be conceded, at least worthy of respect. Fritzing thought it worthy of adoration; the divinest spirit that had ever burned within a woman. He did not say so. On the contrary, he was frightened, and tried angrily, passionately, to dissuade. Yet he knew that if she wavered he would never forgive her; she would drop at once from her high estate into those depths in his opinion where the dull average of both sexes sprawled for ever in indiscriminate heaps. Priscilla never dreamed of wavering. She, most poetic of princesses, made apparently of ivory and amber, outwardly so cool and serene and gentle, was inwardly on fire. The fire, I should add, burnt with a very white flame. Nothing in the shape of a young man had ever had the stoking of it. It was that whitest of flames that leaps highest at the thought of abstractions—freedom, beauty of life, simplicity, and the rest. This, I would remark, is a most rare light to find burning in a woman's breast. What she was, however, Fritzing had made her. True the material had been extraordinarily good, and for ten years he had done as he liked with it. Beginning with the simpler poems of Wordsworth—he detested them, but they were better than soiling her soul with Longfellow and Mrs. Hemans—those lessons in English literature, meant by the authorities to be as innocuous to her as to her sisters, had opened her eyes in a way nothing else could have done to the width of the world and the littleness of Kunitz. With that good teacher, as eager to lead as she to follow, she wandered down the splendid walks of culture, met there the best people of all ages, communed with mighty souls, heard how they talked, saw how they lived, and none, not one, lived and talked as they lived and talked at Kunitz.

Imagine a girl influenced for ten years, ten of her softest most wax-like years, by a Fritzing, taught to love freedom, to see the beauty of plain things, of quietness, of the things appertaining to the spirit, taught to see how ignoble it is, how intensely, hopelessly vulgar to spend on one's own bodily comforts more than is exactly necessary, taught to see a vision of happiness possible only to those who look to their minds for their joys and not to their bodies, imagine how such a girl, hearing these things every afternoon almost of her life, would be likely to regard the palace mornings and evenings, the ceremonies and publicity, all those hours spent as though she were a celebrated picture, forced everlastingly to stand in an attitude considered appropriate and smile while she was being looked at.

"No one," she said one day to Fritzing, "who hasn't himself been a princess can have the least idea of what it is like."

"Ma'am, it would be more correct to say herself in place of himself."

"Well, they can't," said Priscilla.

"Ma'am, to begin a sentence with the singular and continue it with the plural is an infraction of all known rules."

"But the sentiments, Fritzi—what do you think of the sentiments?"

"Alas, ma'am, they too are an infraction of rules."

"What is not in this place, I should like to know?" sighed Priscilla, her chin on her hand, her eyes on that distant line of hills beyond which, she told herself, lay freedom.

She had long ago left off saying it only to herself. I think she must have been about eighteen when she took to saying it aloud to Fritzing. At first, before he realized to what extent she was sick for freedom, he had painted in glowing colours the delights that lay on the other side of the hills, or for that matter on this side of them if you were alone and not a princess. Especially had he dwelt on the glories of life in England, glories attainable indeed only by the obscure such as he himself had been, and for ever impossible to those whom Fate obliges to travel in state carriages and special trains. Then he had come to scent danger and had grown wary; trying to put her off with generalities, such as the inability of human beings to fly from their own selves, and irrelevancies such as the amount of poverty and wretchedness to be observed in the east of London; refusing to discuss France, which she was always getting to as the first step towards England, except in as far as it was a rebellious country that didn't like kings; pointing out with no little temper that she had already seen England; and finishing by inquiring very snappily when her Grand Ducal Highness intended to go on with her drawing.

Now what Priscilla had seen of England had been the insides of Buckingham Palace and Windsor Castle; of all insides surely the most august. To and from these she had been conveyed in closed carriages and royal trains, and there was so close a family likeness between them and Kunitz that to her extreme discomfort she had felt herself completely at home. Even the presence of the Countess Disthal had not been wanting. She therefore regarded this as not seeing England at all, and said so. Fritzing remarked tartly that it was a way of seeing it most English people would envy her; and she was so unable to believe him that she said Nonsense.

But lately her desires had taken definite shape so rapidly that he had come to dread the very word hill and turn cold at the name of England. He was being torn in different directions; for he was, you see, still trying to do what other people had decided was his duty, and till a man gives up doing that he will certainly be torn. How great would be the temptation to pause here and consider the mangled state of such a man, the wounds and weakness he will suffer from, and how his soul will have to limp through life, if it were not that I must get on with Priscilla.

One day, after many weeks of edging nearer to it, of going all round it yet never quite touching it, she took a deep breath and told him she had determined to run away. She added an order that he was to help her. With her most grand ducal air she merely informed, ordered, and forbade. What she forbade, of course, was the betrayal of her plans. "You may choose," she said, "between the Grand Duke and myself. If you tell him, I have done with you for ever."

Of course he chose Priscilla.

His agonies now were very great. Those last lacerations of conscience were terrific. Then, after nights spent striding, a sudden calm fell upon him. At length he could feel what he had always seen, that there could not be two duties for a man, that no man can serve two masters, that a man's one clear duty is to be in the possession of his soul and live the life it approves: in other and shorter words, instead of leading Priscilla, Priscilla was now leading him.

She did more than lead him; she drove him. The soul he had so carefully tended and helped to grow was now grown stronger than his own; for there was added to its natural strength the tremendous daring of absolute inexperience. What can be more inexperienced than a carefully guarded young princess? Priscilla's ignorance of the outside world was pathetic. He groaned over her plans—for it was she who planned and he who listened—and yet he loved them. She was a divine woman, he said to himself; the sweetest and noblest, he was certain, that the world would ever see.

Her plans were these:

First, that having had twenty-one years of life at the top of the social ladder she was now going to get down and spend the next twenty-one at the bottom of it. (Here she gave her reasons, and I will not stop to describe Fritzing's writhings as his own past teachings grinned at him through every word she said.)

Secondly, that the only way to get to the bottom being to run away from Kunitz, she was going to run.

Thirdly, that the best and nicest place for living at the bottom would be England. (Here she explained her conviction that beautiful things grow quite naturally round the bottom of ladders that cannot easily reach the top; flowers of self-sacrifice and love, of temperance, charity, godliness— delicate things, with roots that find their nourishment in common soil. You could not, said Priscilla, expect soil at the top of ladders, could you? And as she felt that she too had roots full of potentialities, she must take them down to where their natural sustenance lay waiting.)

Fourthly, they were to live somewhere in the country in England, in the humblest way.

Fifthly, she was to be his daughter.

"Daughter?" cried Fritzing, bounding in his chair. "Your Grand Ducal Highness forgets I have friends in England, every one of whom is aware that I never had a wife."

"Niece, then," said Priscilla.

He gazed at her in silence, trying to imagine her his niece. He had two sisters, and they had stopped exactly at the point they were at when they helped him, barefoot, to watch Westphalian pigs. I do not mean that they had not ultimately left the little farm, gone into stockings, and married. It is their minds I am thinking of, and these had never budged. They were like their father, a doomed dullard; while Fritzing's mother, whom he resembled, had been a rather extraordinary woman in a rough and barbarous way. He found himself wholly unable to imagine either of his sisters the mother of this exquisite young lady.

These, then, baldly, were Priscilla's plans. The carrying of them out was left, she informed him, altogether to Fritzing. After having spent several anxious days, she told him, considering whether she ought to dye her hair black in order to escape recognition, or stay her own colour but disguise herself as a man and buy a golden beard, she had decided that these were questions Fritzing would settle better than she could. "I'd dye my hair at once," she said, "but what about my wretched eyelashes? Can one dye eyelashes?"

Fritzing thought not, and anyhow was decidedly of opinion that her eyelashes should not be tampered with; I think I have said that they were very lovely. He also entirely discouraged the idea of dressing as a man. "Your Grand Ducal Highness would only look like an extremely conspicuous boy," he assured her.

"I could wear a beard," said Priscilla.

But Fritzing was absolutely opposed to the beard.

As for the money part, she never thought of it. Money was a thing she never did think about. It also, then, was to be Fritzing's business. Possibly things might have gone on much longer as they were, with a great deal of planning and talking, and no doing, if an exceedingly desirable prince had not signified his intention of marrying Priscilla. This had been done before by quite a number of princes. They had, that is, not signified, but implored. On their knees would they have implored if their knees could have helped them. They were however all poor, and Priscilla and her sisters were rich; and how foolish, said the Grand Duke, to marry poor men unless you are poor yourself. The Grand Duke, therefore, took these young men aside and crushed them, while Priscilla, indifferent, went on with her drawing. But now came this one who was so eminently desirable that he had no need to do more than merely signify. There had been much trouble and a great deal of delay in finding him a wife, for he had insisted on having a princess who should be both pretty and not his cousin. Europe did not seem to contain such a thing. Everybody was his cousin, except two or three young women whom he was rude enough to call ugly. The Kunitz princesses had been considered in their turn and set aside, for they too were cousins; and it seemed as if one of the most splendid thrones in Europe would either have to go queen-less or be sat upon by somebody plain, when fate brought the Prince to a great public ceremony in Kunitz, and he saw Priscilla and fell so violently in love with her that if she had been fifty times his cousin he would still have married her.

That same evening he signified his intention to the delighted Grand Duke, who immediately fell to an irrelevant praising of God.

"Bosh," said the Prince, in the nearest equivalent his mother-tongue provided.

This was very bad. Not, I mean, that the Prince should have said Bosh, for he was so great that there was not a Grand Duke in Europe to whom he might not have said it if he wanted to; but that Priscilla should have been in imminent danger of marriage. Among Fritzing's many preachings there had been one, often repeated in the strongest possible language, that of all existing contemptibilities the very most contemptible was for a woman to marry any one she did not love; and the peroration, also extremely forcible, had been an announcement that the prince did not exist who was fit to tie her shoestrings. This Priscilla took to be an exaggeration, for she had no very great notion of her shoestrings; but she did agree with the rest. The subject however was an indifferent one, her father never yet having asked her to marry anybody; and so long as he did not do so she need not, she thought, waste time thinking about it. Now the peril was upon her, suddenly, most unexpectedly, very menacingly. She knew there was no hope from the moment she saw her father's face quite distorted by delight. He took her hand and kissed it. To him she was already a queen. As usual she gave him the impression of behaving exactly as he could have wished. She certainly said very little, for she had long ago learned the art of being silent; but her very silences were somehow exquisite, and the Grand Duke thought her perfect. She gave him to understand almost without words that it was a great surprise, an immense honour, a huge compliment, but so sudden that she would be grateful to both himself and the Prince if nothing more need be said about it for a week or two—nothing, at least, till formal negotiations had been opened. "I saw him yesterday for the first time," she pleaded, "so naturally I am rather overwhelmed."

Privately she had thought, his eyes, which he had never taken off her, kind and pleasant; and if she had known of his having said Bosh who knows but that he might have had a chance? As it was, the moment she was alone she sent flying for Fritzing. "What," she said, "do you say to my marrying this man?"

"If you do, ma'am," said Fritzing, and his face seemed one blaze of white conviction, "you will undoubtedly be eternally lost."

II

They fled on bicycles in the dusk. The goddess Good Luck, who seems to have a predilection for sinners, helped them in a hundred ways. Without her they would certainly not have got far, for both were very ignorant of the art of running away. Once flight was decided on Fritzing planned elaborately and feverishly, got things thought out and arranged as well as he, poor harassed man, possibly could. But what in this law-bound world can sinners do without the help of Luck? She, amused and smiling dame, walked into the castle and smote the Countess Disthal with influenza, crushing her down helpless into her bed, and holding her there for days by the throat. While one hand was doing this, with the other she gaily swept the Grand Duke into East Prussia, a terrific distance, whither, all unaware of how he was being trifled with, he thought he was being swept by an irresistible desire to go, before the business of Priscilla's public betrothal should begin, and shoot the roebucks of a friend.

The Countess was thrust into her bed at noon of a Monday in October. At three the Grand Duke started for East Prussia, incognito in a motor—you know the difficulty news has in reaching persons in motors. At four one of Priscilla's maids, an obscure damsel who had been at the mercy of the others and was chosen because she hated them, tripped out of the castle with shining eyes and pockets heavy with bribes, and caused herself to be whisked away by the afternoon express to Cologne. At six, just as the castle guard was being relieved, two persons led their bicycles through the archway and down across the bridge. It was dark, and nobody recognized them. Fritzing was got up sportingly, almost waggishly—heaven knows his soul was not feeling waggish—as differently as possible from his usual sober clothes. Somehow he reminded Priscilla of a circus, and she found it extremely hard not to laugh. On his head he had a cap with ear-pieces that hid his grey hair; round his neck a gaudy handkerchief muffled well about his face; immense goggles cloaked the familiar overhanging eyebrows and deep-set eyes, goggles curiously at variance with the dapper briskness of his gaitered legs. The Princess was in ordinary blue serge, short and rather shabby, it having been subjected for hours daily during the past week to rough treatment by the maid now travelling to Cologne. As for her face and hair, they were completely hidden in the swathings of a motor-veil.

The sentinels stared rather as these two figures pushed their bicycles through the gates, and undoubtedly did for some time afterwards wonder who they could have been. The same thing happened down below on the bridge; but once over that and in the town all they had to do was to ride straight ahead. They were going to bicycle fifteen miles to Rühl, a small town with a railway station on the main line between Kunitz and Cologne. Express trains do not stop at Rühl, but there was a slow train at eight which would get them to Gerstein, the capital of the next duchy, by midnight. Here they would change into the Cologne express; here they would join the bribed maid; here luggage had been sent by Fritzing,—a neat bag for himself, and a neat box for his niece. The neat box was filled with neat garments suggested to him by the young lady in the shop in Gerstein where he had been two days before to buy them. She told him of many other articles which, she said, no lady's wardrobe could be considered complete without; and the distracted man, fearing the whole shop would presently be put into trunks and sent to the station to meet them, had ended by flinging down two notes for a hundred marks each and bidding her keep strictly within that limit. The young lady became very scornful. She told him that she had never heard of any one being clothed from head to foot inside and out, even to brushes, soap, and an umbrella, for two hundred marks. Fritzing, in dread of conspicuous masses of luggage, yet staggered by the girl's conviction, pulled out a third hundred mark note, but added words in his extremity of so strong and final a nature, that she, quailing, did keep within this limit, and the box was packed. Thus Priscilla's outfit cost almost exactly fifteen pounds. It will readily be imagined that it was neat.

Painfully the two fugitives rode through the cobbled streets of Kunitz. Priscilla was very shaky on a bicycle, and so was Fritzing. Some years before this, when it had been the fashion, she had bicycled every day in the grand ducal park on the other side of the town. Then, tired of it, she had given it up; and now for the last week or two, ever since Fritzing had told her that if they fled it would have to be on bicycles, she had pretended a renewed passion for it, riding every day round and round a circle of which the chilled and astonished Countess Disthal, whose duty it was to stand and watch, had been the disgusted central point. But the cobbles of Kunitz are very different from those smooth places in the park. All who bicycle round Kunitz know them as trying to the most skilful. Naturally, then, the fugitives advanced very slowly, Fritzing's heart in his mouth each time they passed a brightly-lit shop or a person who looked at them. Conceive how nearly this poor heart must have jumped right out of his mouth, leaving him dead, when a policeman who had been watching them strode suddenly into the middle of the street, put up his hand, and said, "Halt."

Fritzing, unstrung man, received a shock so awful that he obeyed by falling off. Priscilla, wholly unused to being told to halt and absorbed by the difficulties of the way, did not grasp that the order was meant for her and rode painfully on. Seeing this, the policeman very gallantly removed her from her bicycle by putting his arms round her and lifting her off. He set her quite gently on her feet, and was altogether a charming policeman, as unlike those grim and ghastly eyes of the law that glare up and down the streets of, say, Berlin, as it is possible to imagine.

But Priscilla was perfectly molten with rage, insulted as she had never been in her life. "How dare you—how dare you," she stammered, suffocating; and forgetting everything but an overwhelming desire to box the giant's ears she had actually raised her hand to do it, which would of course have been the ruin of her plan and the end of my tale, when Fritzing, recovering his presence of mind, cried out in tones of unmistakable agony, "Niece, be calm."

She calmed at once to a calm of frozen horror.

"Now, sir," said Fritzing, assuming an air of brisk bravery and guiltlessness, "what can we do for you?"

"Light your lamps," said the policeman, laconically.

They did; or rather Fritzing did, while Priscilla stood passive.

"I too have a niece," said the policeman, watching Fritzing at work; "but I light no lamps for her. One should not wait on one's niece. One's niece should wait on one."

Fritzing did not answer. He finished lighting the lamps, and then held Priscilla's bicycle and started her.

"I never did that for my niece," said the policeman.

"Confound your niece, sir," was on the tip of Fritzing's tongue; but he gulped it down, and remarking instead as pleasantly as he could that being an uncle did not necessarily prevent your being a gentleman, picked up his bicycle and followed Priscilla.

The policeman shook his head as they disappeared round the corner. "One does not light lamps for one's niece," he repeated to himself. "It's against nature. Consequently, though the peppery Fräulein may well be somebody's niece she is not his."

"Oh," murmured Priscilla, after they had ridden some way without speaking, "I'm deteriorating already. For the first time in my life I've wanted to box people's ears."

"The provocation was great, ma'am," said Fritzing, himself shattered by the spectacle of his Princess being lifted about by a policeman.

"Do you think—" Priscilla hesitated, and looked at him. Her bicycle immediately hesitated too, and swerving across the road taught her it would have nothing looked at except its handles. "Do you think," she went on, after she had got herself straight again, "that the way I'm going to live now will make me want to do it often?"

"Heaven forbid, ma'am. You are now going to live a most noble life—the only fitting life for the thoughtful and the earnest. It will be, once you are settled, far more sheltered from contact with that which stirs ignoble impulses than anything your Grand Ducal Highness has hitherto known."

"If you mean policemen by things that stir ignoble impulses," said Priscilla, "I was sheltered enough from them before. Why, I never spoke to one. Much less"—she shuddered—"much less ever touched one."

"Ma'am, you do not repent?"

"Heavens, no," said Priscilla, pressing onward.

Outside Rühl, about a hundred yards before its houses begin, there is a pond by the wayside. Into this, after waiting a moment peering up and down the dark road to see whether anybody was looking, Fritzing hurled the bicycles. He knew the pond was deep, for he had studied it the day he bought Priscilla's outfit; and the two bicycles one after the other were hurled remorsely into the middle of it, disappearing each in its turn with a tremendous splash and gurgle. Then they walked on quickly towards the railway station, infinitely relieved to be on their own feet again, and between them, all unsuspected, walked the radiant One with the smiling eyes, she who was half-minded to see this game through, giving the players just so many frights as would keep her amused, the fickle, laughing goddess Good Luck.

They caught the train neatly at Rühl. They only had to wait about the station for ten minutes before it came in. Hardly any one was there, and nobody took the least notice of them. Fritzing, after a careful look round to see if it contained people he knew, put the Princess into a second-class carriage labelled *Frauen*, and then respectfully withdrew to another part of the train. He had decided that second-class was safest. People in that country nearly always travel second-class, especially women,—at all times in such matters more economical than men; and a woman by herself in a first-class carriage would have been an object of surmise and curiosity at every station. Therefore Priscilla was put into the carriage labelled *Frauen*, and found herself for the first time in her life alone with what she had hitherto only heard alluded to vaguely as the public.

She sat down in a corner with an odd feeling of surprise at being included in the category *Frauen*, and giving a swift timid glance through her veil at the public confronting her was relieved to find it consisted only of a comfortable mother and her child.

I know not why the adjective comfortable should so invariably be descriptive of mothers in Germany. In England and France though you may be a mother, you yet, I believe, may be so without being comfortable. In Germany, somehow, you can't. Perhaps it is the climate; perhaps it is the food; perhaps it is simply want of soul, or that your soul does not burn with a fire sufficiently consuming. Anyhow it is so. This mother had all the good-nature that goes with amplitude. Being engaged in feeding her child with *belegte Brödchen*—that immensely satisfying form of sandwich—she at once offered Priscilla one.

"No thank you," said Priscilla, shrinking into her corner.

"Do take one, Fräulein," said the mother, persuasively.

"No thank you," said Priscilla, shrinking.

"On a journey it passes the time. Even if one is not hungry, thank God one can always eat. Do take one."

"No thank you," said Priscilla.

"Why does she wear that black thing over her face?" inquired the child. "Is she a witch?"

"Silence, silence, little worthless one," cried the mother, delightedly stroking his face with half a *Brödchen*. "You see he is clever, Fräulein. He resembles his dear father as one egg does another."

"Does he?" said Priscilla, immediately conceiving a prejudice against the father.

"Why don't she take that black thing off?" said the child.

"Hush, hush, small impudence. The Fräulein will take it off in a minute. The Fräulein has only just got in."

"Mutti, is she a witch? Mutti, Mutti, is she a witch, Mutti?"

The child, his eyes fixed anxiously on Priscilla's swathed head, began to whimper.

"That child should be in bed," said Priscilla, with a severity born of her anxiety lest, to calm him, humanity should force her to put up her veil. "Persons who are as intelligent as that should never be in trains at night. Their brains cannot bear it. Would he not be happier if he lay down and went to sleep?"

"Yes, yes; that is what I have been telling him ever since we left Kunitz"—Priscilla shivered—"but he will not go. Dost thou hear what the Fräulein says, Hans-Joachim?"

"Why don't she take that black thing off?" whimpered the child.

But how could the poor Princess, however anxious to be kind, take off her veil and show her well-known face to this probable inhabitant of Kunitz?

"Do take it off, Fräulein," begged the mother, seeing she made no preparations to do so. "When he gets ideas into his head there is never peace till he has what he wants. He does remind me so much of his father."

"Did you ever," said Priscilla, temporizing, "try him with a little—just a little slap? Only a little one," she added hastily, for the mother looked at her oddly, "only as a sort of counter-irritant. And it needn't be really hard, you know—"

"*Ach*, she's a witch—Mutti, she's a witch!" shrieked the child, flinging his face, butter and all, at these portentous words, into his mother's lap.

"There, there, poor tiny one," soothed the mother, with an indignant side-glance at Priscilla. "Poor tiny man, no one shall slap thee. The Fräulein does not allude to thee, little son. The Fräulein is thinking of bad children such as the sons of Schultz and thy cousin Meyer. Fräulein, if you do not remove your veil I fear he will have convulsions."

"Oh," said the unhappy Priscilla, getting as far into her corner as she could, "I'm so sorry—but I—but I really can't."

"She's a witch, Mutti!" roared the child, "I tell it to thee again— therefore is she so black, and must not show her face!"

"Hush, hush, shut thy little eyes," soothed the mother, putting her hand over them. To Priscilla she said, with an obvious dawning of distrust, "But Fräulein, what reason can you have for hiding yourself?"

"Hiding myself?" echoed Priscilla, now very unhappy indeed, "I'm not hiding myself. I've got—I've got—I'm afraid I've got a—an affection of the skin. That's why I wear a veil."

"*Ach*, poor Fräulein," said the mother, brightening at once into lively interest. "Hans-Joachim, sleep," she added sharply to her son, who tried to raise his head to interrupt with fresh doubts a conversation grown thrilling. "That is indeed a misfortune. It is a rash?"

"Oh, it's dreadful," said Priscilla, faintly.

"*Ach*, poor Fräulein. When one is married, rashes no longer matter. One's husband has to love one in spite of rashes. But for a Fräulein every spot is of importance. There is a young lady of my acquaintance whose life-happiness was shipwrecked only by spots. She came out in them at the wrong moment."

"Did she?" murmured Priscilla.

"You are going to a doctor?"

"Yes—that is, no—I've been."

"Ah, you have been to Kunitz to Dr. Kraus?"

"Y—es. I've been there."

"What does he say?"

"That I must always wear a veil."

"Because it looks so bad?"

"I suppose so."

There was a silence. Priscilla lay back in her corner exhausted, and shut her eyes. The mother stared fixedly at her, one hand mechanically stroking Hans-Joachim, the other holding him down.

"When I was a girl," said the mother, so suddenly that Priscilla started, "I had a good deal of trouble with my skin. Therefore my experience on the subject is great. Show me your face, Fräulein—I might be able to tell you what to do to cure it."

"Oh, on no account—on no account whatever," cried Priscilla, sitting up very straight and speaking with extraordinary emphasis. "I couldn't think of it—I really positively couldn't."

"But my dear Fräulein, why mind a woman seeing it?"

"But what do you want to see it for?"

"I wish to help you."

"I don't want to be helped. I'll show it to nobody—to nobody at all. It's much too—too dreadful."

"Well, well, do not be agitated. Girls, I know, are vain. If any one can help you it will be Dr. Kraus. He is an excellent physician, is he not?"

"Yes," said Priscilla, dropping back into her corner.

"The Grand Duke is a great admirer of his. He is going to ennoble him."

"Really?"

"They say—no doubt it is gossip, but still, you know, he is a very handsome man—that the Countess von Disthal will marry him."

"Gracious!" cried Priscilla, startled, "what, whether he wants to or not?"

"No doubt he will want to. It would be a brilliant match for him."

"But she's at least a hundred. Why, she looks like his mother. And he is a person of no birth at all."

"Birth? He is of course not noble yet, but his family is excellent. And since it is not possible to have as many ailments as she has and still be alive, some at least must be feigned. Why, then, should she feign if it is not in order to see the doctor? They were saying in Kunitz that she sent for him this very day."

"Yes, she did. But she's really ill this time. I'm afraid the poor thing caught cold watching—dear me, only see how sweetly your little boy sleeps. You should make Levallier paint him in that position."

"Ah, he looks truly lovely, does he not. Exactly thus does his dear father look when asleep. Sometimes I cannot sleep myself for joy over the splendid picture. What is the matter with the Countess Disthal? Did Dr. Kraus tell you?"

"No, no. I—I heard something—a rumour."

"Ah, something feigned again, no doubt. Well, it will be a great match for him. You know she is lady-in-waiting to the Princess Priscilla, the one who is so popular and has such red hair? The Countess has an easy life. The other two Princesses have given their ladies a world of trouble, but Priscilla—oh, she is a model. Kunitz is indeed proud of her. They say in all things she is exactly what a Princess should be, and may be trusted never to say or do anything not entirely fitting her station. You have seen her? She often drives through the town, and then the people all run and look as pleased as if it were a holiday. We in Gerstein are quite jealous. Our duchy has no such princess to show. Do you think she is so beautiful? I have often seen her, and I do not think she is. People exaggerate everything so about a princess. My husband does not admire her at all. He says it is not what he calls classic. Her hair, for instance—but that one might get over. And people who are really beautiful always have dark eyelashes. Then her nose—my husband often laughs, and says her nose—"

"Oh," said Priscilla, faintly, "I've got a dreadful headache. I think I'll try to sleep a little if you would not mind not talking."

"Yes, that hot thing round your face must be very trying. Now if you were not so vain—what does a rash matter when only women are present?

Well, well, I will not tease you. Do you know many of the Kunitzers? Do you know the Levisohns well?"

"Oh," sighed Priscilla, laying her distracted head against the cushions and shutting her eyes, "who are they?"

"Who are they? Who are the Levisohns? But dearest Fräulein if you know Kunitz you must know the Levisohns. Why, the Levisohns *are* Kunitz. They are more important far than the Grand Duke. They lend to it, and they lead it. You must know their magnificent shop at the corner of the Heiligengeiststrasse? Perhaps," she added, with a glance at the Princess's shabby serge gown, "you have not met them socially, but you must know the magnificent shop. We visit."

"Do you?" said Priscilla wearily, as the mother paused.

"And you know her story, of course?"

"Oh, oh," sighed Priscilla, turning her head from side to side on the cushions, vainly seeking peace.

"It is hardly a story for the ears of Fräuleins."

"Please don't tell it, then."

"No, I will not. It is not for Fräuleins. But one still sees she must have been a handsome woman. And he, Levisohn, was clever enough to see his way to Court favour. The Grand Duke—"

"I don't think I care to hear about the Levisohns," said Priscilla, sitting up suddenly and speaking with great distinctness. "Gossip is a thing I detest. None shall be talked in my presence."

"Hoity-toity," said the astonished mother; and it will easily be believed that no one had ever said hoity-toity to Priscilla before.

She turned scarlet under her veil. For a moment she sat with flashing eyes, and the hand lying in her lap twitched convulsively. Is it possible she was thinking of giving the comfortable mother that admonition which the policeman had so narrowly escaped? I know not what would have happened if the merry goddess, seeing things rushing to this dreadful climax, had not stopped the train in the nick of time at a wayside station and caused a breathless lady, pushing parcels before her, to clamber in. The mother's surprised stare was of necessity diverted to the new-comer. A parcel thrust into Priscilla's hands brought her back of necessity to her senses.

"*Danke, Danke,*" cried the breathless lady, though no help had been offered; and hoisting herself in she wished both her fellow-passengers a boisterous good evening. The lady, evidently an able person, arranged her parcels swiftly and neatly in the racks, pulled up the windows, slammed the ventilators, stripped off her cloak, flung back her veil, and sitting down with a sigh of vast depth and length stared steadily for five minutes without wavering at the other two. At the end of that time she and the mother began, as with a common impulse, to talk. And at the end of five minutes more they had told each other where they were going, where they had been, what their husbands were, the number, age, and girth of their children, and all the adjectives that might most conveniently be used to describe their servants. The adjectives, very lurid ones, took some time. Priscilla shut her eyes while they were going on, thankful to be left quiet, feeling unstrung to the last degree; and she gradually dropped into an uneasy doze whose chief feature was the distressful repetition, like hammer-strokes on her brain, of the words, "You're deteriorating—deteriorating—deteriorating."

"*Lieber Gott*," she whispered at last, folding her hands in her lap, "don't let me deteriorate too much. Please keep me from wanting to box people's ears. *Lieber Gott*, it's so barbarous of me. I never used to want to. Please stop me wanting to now."

And after that she dropped off quite, into a placid little slumber.

III

They crossed from Calais in the turbine. Their quickest route would have been Cologne-Ostend-Dover, and every moment being infinitely valuable Fritzing wanted to go that way, but Priscilla was determined to try whether turbines are really as steady as she had heard they were. The turbine was so steady that no one could have told it was doing anything but being quiescent on solid earth; but that was because, as Fritzing explained, there was a dead calm, and in dead calms—briefly, he explained the conduct of boats in dead calms with much patience, and Priscilla remarked when he had done that they might then, after all, have crossed by Ostend.

"We might, ma'am, and we would be in London now if we had," said Fritzing.

They had, indeed, lost several hours and some money coming by Calais, and Fritzing had lost his temper as well.

Fritzing, you remember, was sixty, and had not closed his eyes all night. He had not, so far as that goes, closed his eyes for nights without number; and what his soul had gone through during those nights was more than any soul no longer in its first youth should be called upon to bear. In the train between Cologne and Calais he had even, writhing in his seat, cursed every single one of his long-cherished ideals, called them fools, shaken his fist at them; a dreadful state of mind to get to. He did not reveal anything of this to his dear Princess, and talking to her on the turbine wore the clear brow of the philosopher; but he did feel that he was a much-tried man, and he behaved to the maid Annalise exactly in the way much-tried men do behave when they have found some one they think defenceless. Unfortunately Annalise was only apparently defenceless. Fritzing would have known it if he had been more used to running away. He did, in his calmer moments, dimly opine it. The plain fact was that Annalise held both him and Priscilla in the hollow of her hand.

At this point she had not realized it. She still was awestruck by her promotion, and looked so small and black and uncertain among her new surroundings on the turbine that if not clever of him it was at least natural that he should address her in a manner familiar to those who have had to do with men when they are being tried. He behaved, that is, to Annalise, as he had behaved to his ideals in the night; he shook his fist at her, and called her fool. It was because she had broken the Princess's umbrella. This was the new umbrella bought by him with so much trouble in Gerstein two days before, and therefore presumably of a sufficient toughness to stand any reasonable treatment for a time. There was a mist and a drizzle at Calais, and Priscilla, refusing to go under shelter, had sent Fritzing to fetch her umbrella, and when he demanded it of Annalise, she offered it him in two pieces. This alone was enough to upset a wise man, because wise men are easily upset; but Annalise declared besides that the umbrella had broken itself. It probably had. What may not one expect of anything so cheap? Fritzing, however, was maddened by this explanation, and wasted quite a long time pointing out to her in passionate language that it was an inanimate object, and that inanimate objects have no initiative and never therefore break themselves. To which Annalise, with a stoutness ominous as a revelation of character, replied by repeating her declaration that the umbrella had certainly broken itself. Then it was that he shook his fist at her and called her fool. So greatly was he moved that, after walking away and thinking it over, he went to her a second time and shook his fist at her and called her knave.

I will not linger over this of the umbrella; it teems with lessons.

While it was going on the Princess was being very happy. She was sitting unnoticed in a deck-chair and feeling she was really off at last into the Ideal. Some of us know the fascination of that feeling, and all of us know the fascination of new things; and to be unnoticed was for her of a most thrilling newness. Nobody looked at her. People walked up and down the deck in front of her as though she were not there. One hurried passenger actually tripped over her feet, and passed on with the briefest apology. Everywhere she saw indifferent faces, indifferent, oblivious faces. It was simply glorious. And she had had no trials since leaving Gerstein. There Fritzing had removed her beyond the range of the mother's eyes, grown at last extremely cold and piercing; Annalise, all meek anxiety to please, had put her to bed in the sleeping-car of the Brussels express; and in the morning her joy had been childish at having a little tray with bad coffee on it thrust in by a busy attendant, who slammed it down on the table and hurried out without so much as glancing at her. How delicious that was. The Princess laughed with delight and drank the coffee, grits and all. Oh, the blessed freedom of being insignificant. It was as good, she thought, as getting rid of your body altogether and going about an invisible spirit. She sat on the deck of the apparently motionless turbine and thought gleefully of past journeys, now for ever done with; of the grand ducal train, of herself drooping inside it as wearily as the inevitable bouquets drooping on the tables, of the crowds of starers on every platform, of the bowing officials wherever your eye chanced to turn. The Countess Disthal, of course, had been always at her elbow, and when she had to go to the window and do the gracious her anxiety lest she should bestow one smile too few had only been surpassed by the Countess's anxiety lest she should bestow one smile too many. Well, that was done with now; as much done with as a nightmare, grisly staleness, is done with when you wake to a fair spring morning and the smell of dew. And she had no fears. She was sure, knowing him as she did, that when the Grand Duke found out she had run away he would make no attempt to fetch her back, but would simply draw a line through his remembrance of her, rub her out of his mind, (his heart, she knew, would need no rubbing, because she had never been in it,) and after the first fury was over, fury solely on account of the scandal, he would be as he had been before, while she—oh wonderful new life!—she would be born again to all the charities.

Now how can I, weak vessel whose only ballast is a cargo of interrogations past which life swirls with a thunder of derisively contradictory replies, pretend to say whether Priscilla ought to have had conscience-qualms or not? Am I not deafened by the roar of answers, all seemingly so right yet all so different, that the simplest question brings? And would not the answering roar to anything so complicated as a question about conscience-qualms deafen me for ever? I shall leave the Princess, then, to run away from her home and her parent if she chooses, and make no effort to whitewash any part of her conduct that may seem black. I shall chronicle, and not comment. I shall try to, that is, for comments are very dear to me. Indeed I see I cannot move on even now till I have pointed out that though Priscilla was getting as far as she could from the Grand Duke she was also getting as near as she could to the possession of her soul; and there are many persons who believe this to be a thing so precious that it is absolutely the one thing worth living for.

The crossing to Dover, then, was accomplished quite peacefully by Priscilla. Not so, however, by Fritzing. He, tormented man, chief target for the goddess's darts, spent his time holding on to the rail along the turbine's side in order to steady himself; and as there was a dead calm that day the reader will at once perceive that the tempest must have been inside Fritzing himself. It was; and it had been raised to hurricane pitch by some snatches of the talk of two Englishmen he had heard as they paced up and down past where he was standing.

The first time they passed, one was saying to the other, "I never heard of anything so infamous."

This ought not to have made Fritzing, a person of stainless life and noble principles, start, but it did. He started; and he listened anxiously for more.

"Yes," said the other, who had a newspaper under his arm, "they deserve about as bad as they'll—"

He was out of ear-shot; but Fritzing mechanically finished the sentence himself. Who had been infamous? And what were they going to get? It was at this point that he laid hold of the handrail to steady himself till the two men should pass again.

"You can tell, of course, what steps our Government will take," was the next snatch.

"I shall be curious to see the attitude of the foreign papers," was the next.

"Anything more wanton I never heard of," was the next.

"Of all the harmless, innocent creatures—" was the next.

And the last snatch of all—for though they went on walking Fritzing heard no more after it—was the brief and singular expression "Devils."

Devils? *What* were they talking about? Devils? Was that, then, how the public stigmatized blameless persons in search of peace? Devils? What, himself and—no, never Priscilla. She was clearly the harmless innocent creature, and he must be the other thing. But why plural? He could only suppose that he and Annalise together formed a sulphurous plural. He clung very hard to the rail. Who could have dreamed it would get so quickly into the papers? Who could have dreamed the news of it would call forth such blazing words? They would be confronted at Dover by horrified authorities. His Princess was going to be put in a most impossible position. What had he done? Heavens and earth, what had he done?

He clung to the rail, staring miserably over the side into the oily water. Some of the passengers lingered to watch him, at first because they thought he was going to be seasick with so little provocation that it amounted to genius, and afterwards because they were sure he must want to commit suicide. When they found that time passed and he did neither, he became unpopular, and they went away and left him altogether and contemptuously alone.

"Fritzi, are you worried about anything?" asked Priscilla, coming to where he still stood staring, although they had got to Dover.

Worried! When all Europe was going to be about their ears? When he was in the eyes of the world a criminal—an aider, abettor, lurer-away of youth and impulsiveness? He loved the Princess so much that he cared nothing for his own risks, but what about hers? In an agony of haste he rushed to his ideals and principles for justification and comfort, tumbling them over, searching feverishly among them. They had forsaken him. They were so much lifeless rubbish. Nowhere in his mind could he find a rag of either comfort or justification with which to stop up his ears against the words of the two Englishmen and his eyes against the dreadful sight he felt sure awaited them on the quay at Dover—the sight of incensed authorities ready to pounce on him and drag him away for ever from his Princess.

Priscilla gazed at him in astonishment. He was taking no notice of her, and was looking fearfully up and down the row of faces that were watching the turbine's arrival.

"Fritzi, if you are worried it must be because you've not slept," said Priscilla, laying her hand with a stroking little movement on his sleeve; for what but overwrought nerves could make him look so odd? It was after all Fritzing who had behaved with the braveness of a lion the night before in that matter of the policeman; and it was he who had asked in stern tones of rebuke, when her courage seemed aflicker, whether she repented. "You do not repent?" she asked, imitating that sternness.

"Ma'am—" he began in a low and dreadful voice, his eyes ceaselessly ranging up and down the figures on the quay.

"Sh—sh—Niece," interrupted Priscilla, smiling.

He turned and looked at her as a man may look for the last time at the thing in life that has been most dear to him, and said nothing.

IV

But nobody was waiting for them at Dover. Fritzing's agonies might all have been spared. They passed quite unnoticed through the crowd of idlers to the train, and putting Priscilla and her maid into it he rushed at the nearest newspaper-boy, pouncing on him, tearing a handful of his papers from him, and was devouring their contents before the astonished boy had well finished his request that he should hold hard. The boy, who had been brought up in the simple faith that one should pay one's pennies first and read next, said a few things under his breath about Germans—crude short things not worth repeating—and jerking his thumb towards the intent Fritzing, winked at a detective who was standing near. The detective did not need the wink. His bland, abstracted eyes were already on Fritzing, and he was making rapid mental notes of the goggles, the muffler, the cap pulled down over the ears. Truly it is a great art, that of running away, and needs incessant practice.

And after all there was not a word about the Princess in the papers. They were full, as the Englishmen on the turbine had been full, of something the Russians, who at that time were always doing something, had just done—something that had struck England from end to end into a blaze of indignation and that has nothing to do with my story. Fritzing dropped the papers on the platform, and had so little public spirit that he groaned aloud with relief.

"Shilling and a penny 'alfpenny, please, sir," said the newspaper-boy glibly. "*Westminster Gazette*, sir, *Daily Mail*, *Sporting and Dramatic*, one *Lady*, and two *Standards*." From which it will be seen that Fritzing had seized his handful very much at random.

He paid the boy without heeding his earnest suggestions that he should try *Tit-Bits*, the *Saturday Review*, and *Mother*, to complete, said the boy, in substance if not in words, his bird's-eye view over the field of representative English journalism, and went back to the Princess with a lighter heart than he had had for months. The detective, apparently one of Nature's gentlemen, picked up the scattered papers, and following Fritzing offered them him in the politest way imaginable just as Priscilla was saying she wanted to see what tea-baskets were like.

"Sir," said the detective, taking off his hat, "I believe these are yours."

"Sir," said Fritzing, taking off his cap in his turn and bowing with all the ceremony of foreigners, "I am much obliged to you."

"Pray don't mention it, sir," said the detective, on whose brain the three were in that instant photographed—the veiled Priscilla, the maid sitting on the edge of the seat as though hardly daring to sit at all, and Fritzing's fine head and mop of grey hair.

Priscilla, as she caught his departing eye, bowed and smiled graciously. He withdrew to a little distance, and fell into a reverie: where had he seen just that mechanically gracious bow and smile? They were very familiar to him.

As the train slowly left the station he saw the lady in the veil once more. She was alone with her maid, and was looking out of the window at nothing in particular, and the station-master, who was watching the train go, chanced to meet her glance. Again there was the same smile and bow, quite mechanical, quite absent-minded, distinctly gracious. The station-master stared in astonishment after the receding carriage. The detective roused himself from his reverie sufficiently to step forward and neatly swing himself into the guard's van: there being nothing to do in Dover he thought he would go to London.

I believe I have forgotten, in the heat of narration, to say that the fugitives were bound for Somersetshire. Fritzing had been a great walker in the days when he lived in England, and among other places had walked about Somersetshire. It is a pleasant county; fruitful, leafy, and mild. Down in the valleys myrtles and rhododendrons have been known to flower all through the winter. Devonshire junkets and Devonshire cider are made there with the same skill precisely as in Devonshire; and the parts of it that lie round Exmoor are esteemed by those who hunt.

Fritzing quite well remembered certain villages buried among the hills, miles from the nearest railway, and he also remembered the farmhouses round about these villages where he had lodged. To one of these he had caused a friend in London to write engaging rooms for himself and his niece, and there he proposed to stay till they should have found the cottage the Princess had set her heart on.

This cottage, as far as he could gather from the descriptions she gave him from time to time, was going to be rather difficult to find. He feared also that it would be a very insect-ridden place, and that their calm pursuits would often be interrupted by things like earwigs. It was to be ancient, and much thatched and latticed and rose-overgrown. It was, too, to be very small; the smallest of labourers' cottages. Yet though so small and so ancient it was to have several bathrooms—one for each of them, so he understood; "For," said the Princess, "if Annalise hasn't a bathroom how can she have a bath? And if she hasn't had a bath how can I let her touch me?"

"Perhaps," said Fritzing, bold in his ignorance of Annalise's real nature, "she could wash at the pump. People do, I believe, in the country. I remember there were always pumps."

"But do pumps make you clean enough?" inquired the Princess, doubtfully.

"We can try her with one. I fancy, ma'am, it will be less difficult to find a cottage that has only two bathrooms than one that has three. And I know there are invariably pumps."

Searching his memory he could recollect no bathrooms at all, but he did not say so, and silently hoped the best.

To the Somerset village of Symford and to the farm about a mile outside it known as Baker's, no longer, however, belonging to Baker, but rented by a Mr. Pearce, they journeyed down from Dover without a break. Nothing alarming happened on the way. They were at Victoria by five, and the Princess sat joyfully making the acquaintance of a four-wheeler's inside for twenty minutes during which Fritzing and Annalise got the luggage through the customs. Fritzing's goggles and other accessories of flight inspired so much interest in the customs that they could hardly bear to let him go and it seemed as if they would never tire of feeling about in the harmless depths of Priscilla's neat box. They had however ultimately to part from him, for never was luggage more innocent; and rattling past Buckingham Palace on the way to Paddington Priscilla blew it a cheerful kiss, symbolic of a happiness too great to bear ill-will. Later on Windsor Castle would have got one too, if it had not been so dark that she could not see it. The detective, who felt himself oddly drawn towards the trio, went down into Somersetshire by the same train as they did, but parted from them at Ullerton, the station you get out at when you go to Symford. He did not consider it necessary to go further; and taking a bedroom at Ullerton in the same little hotel from which Fritzing had ordered the conveyance that was to drive them their last seven miles he went to bed, it being close on midnight, with Mr. Pearce's address neatly written in his notebook.

This, at present, is the last of the detective. I will leave him sleeping with a smile on his face, and follow the dog-cart as it drove along that beautiful road between wooded hills that joins Ullerton to Symford, on its way to Baker's Farm.

At the risk of exhausting Priscilla Fritzing had urged pushing on without a stop, and Priscilla made no objection. This is how it came about that the ostler attached to the Ullerton Arms found himself driving to Symford in the middle of the night. He could not recollect ever having done such a thing before, and the memory of it would be quite unlikely to do anything but remain fixed in his mind till his dying day. Fritzing was a curiously conspicuous fugitive.

It was a clear and beautiful night, and the stars twinkled brightly over the black tree-tops. Down in the narrow gorge through which the road runs they could not feel the keen wind that was blowing up on Exmoor. The waters of the Sym, whose windings they followed, gurgled over their stones almost as quietly as in summer. There was a fresh wet smell, consoling and delicious after the train, the smell of country puddles and country mud and dank dead leaves that had been rained upon all day. Fritzing sat with the Princess on the back seat of the dog-cart, and busied himself keeping the rug well round her, the while his soul was full of thankfulness that their journey should after all have been so easy. He was weary in body, but very jubilant in mind. The Princess was so weary in body that she had no mind at all, and dozed and nodded and threatened to fall out, and would have fallen out a dozen times but for Fritzing's watchfulness. As for Annalise, who can guess what thoughts were hers while she was being jogged along to Baker's? That they were dark I have not a doubt. No one had told her this was to be a journey into the Ideal; no one had told her anything but that she was promoted to travelling with the Princess and that she would be well paid so long as she held her tongue. She had never travelled before, yet there were some circumstances of the journey that could not fail to strike the most inexperienced. This midnight jogging in the dog-cart, for instance. It was the second night spent out of bed, and all day long she had expected every moment would end the journey, and the end, she had naturally supposed, would be a palace. There would be a palace, and warmth, and light, and food, and welcome, and honour, and appreciative lacqueys with beautiful white silk calves—alas, Annalise's ideal, her one ideal, was to be for ever where there were beautiful white silk calves. The road between Ullerton and Symford conveyed to her mind no assurance whatever of the near neighbourhood of such things; and as for the dog-cart—"*Himmel,*" said Annalise to herself, whenever she thought of the dog-cart.

Their journey ended at two in the morning. Almost exactly at that hour they stopped at the garden gate of Baker's Farm, and a woman came out with a lantern and helped them down and lighted them up the path to the porch. The Princess, who could hardly make her eyes open themselves, leaned on Fritzing's arm in a sort of confused dream, got somehow up a little staircase that seemed extraordinarily steep and curly, and was sound asleep in a knobbly bed before Annalise realized she had done with her. Priscilla had forgotten all about the Ideal, all about her eager aspirations. Sleep, dear Mother with the cool hand, had smoothed them all away, the whole rubbish of those daylight toys, and for the next twelve hours sat tenderly by her pillow, her finger on her lips.

V

No better place than Symford can be imagined for those in search of a spot, picturesque and with creepers, where they may spend quiet years guiding their feet along the way of peace. It is one of the prettiest of English villages. It does and has and is everything the ideal village ought to. It nestles, for instance, in the folds of hills; it is very small, and far away from other places; its cottages are old and thatched; its little inn is the inn of a story-book, with a quaint signboard and an apparently genial landlord; its church stands beautifully on rising ground among ancient trees, besides being hoary; its vicarage is so charming that to see it makes you long to marry a vicar; its vicar is venerable, with an eye so mild that to catch it is to receive a blessing; pleasant little children with happy morning faces pick butter-cups and go a-nutting at the proper seasons and curtsey to you as you pass; old women with clean caps and suitable faces read their Bibles behind latticed windows; hearths are scrubbed and snowy; appropriate kettles simmer on hobs; climbing roses and trim gardens are abundant; and it has a lady bountiful of so untiring a kindness that each of its female inhabitants gets a new flannel petticoat every Christmas and nothing is asked of her in return but that she shall, during the ensuing year, be warm and happy and good. The same thing was asked, I believe, of the male inhabitants, who get comforters, and also that they should drink seltzer-water whenever their lower natures urged them to drink rum; but comforters are so much smaller than petticoats that the men of Symford's sense of justice rebelled, and since the only time they ever felt really warm and happy and good was when they were drinking rum they decided that on the whole it would be more in accordance with their benefactress's wishes to go on doing it.

Lady Shuttleworth, the lady from whom these comforters and petticoats proceeded, was a just woman who required no more of others than she required of herself, and who was busy and kind, and, I am sure happy and good, on cold water. But then she did not like rum; and I suppose there are few things quite so easy as not to drink rum if you don't like it. She lived at Symford Hall, two miles away in another fold of the hills, and managed the estate of her son who was a minor—at this time on the very verge of ceasing to be one—with great precision and skill. All the old cottages in Symford were his, and so were the farms dotted about the hills. Any one, therefore, seeking a cottage would have to address himself to the Shuttleworth agent, Mr. Dawson, who too lived in a house so picturesque that merely to see it made you long either to poison or to marry Mr. Dawson—preferably, I think, to poison him.

These facts, stripped of the redundances with which I have garnished them, were told Fritzing on the day after his arrival at Baker's Farm by Mrs. Pearce the younger, old Mr. Pearce's daughter-in-law, a dreary woman with a rent in her apron, who brought in the bacon for Fritzing's solitary breakfast and the chop for his solitary luncheon. She also brought in a junket so liquid that the innocent Fritzing told her politely that he always drank his milk out of a glass when he did drink milk, but that, as he never did drink milk, she need not trouble to bring him any.

"Sir," said Mrs. Pearce in her slow sad voice, after a glance at his face in search of sarcasm, "'tisn't milk. 'Tis a junket that hasn't junked."

"Indeed?" said Fritzing, bland because ignorant.

Mrs. Pearce fidgeted a little, wrestling perhaps with her conscience, before she added defiantly, "It wouldn't."

"Indeed?" said Fritzing once more; and he looked at the junket through his spectacles with that air of extreme and intelligent interest with which persons who wish to please look at other people's babies.

He was desirous of being on good terms with Symford, and had been very pleasant all the morning to Mrs. Pearce. That mood in which, shaken himself to his foundations by anxiety, he had shaken his fist to Annalise, was gone as completely as yesterday's wet mist. The golden sunshine of October lay beautifully among the gentle hills and seemed to lie as well in Fritzing's heart. He had gone through so much for so many weeks that merely to be free from worries for the moment filled him with thankfulness. So may he feel who has lived through days of bodily torture in that first hour when his pain has gone: beaten, crushed, and cowed by suffering, he melts with gratitude because he is being left alone, he gasps with a relief so utter that it is almost abject praise of the Cruelty that has for a little loosened its hold. In this abjectly thankful mood was Fritzing when he found his worst agonies were done. What was to come after he really for the moment did not care. It was sufficient to exist untormented and to let his soul stretch itself in the privacy and peace of Baker's. He and his Princess had made a great and noble effort towards the realization of dreams that he felt were lofty, and the gods so far had been with them. All that first morning in Symford he had an oddly restful, unburdened feeling, as of having been born again and born aged twenty-five; and those persons who used to be twenty-five themselves will perhaps agree that this must have been rather nice. He did not stir from the parlour lest the Princess should come down and want him, and he spent the waiting hours getting information from Mrs. Pearce and informing her mind in his turn with just that amount of knowledge about himself and his niece that he wished Symford to possess. With impressive earnestness he told her his name was Neumann, repeating it three times, almost as if in defiance of contradiction; that his niece was his deceased brother's child; that her Christian name— here he was swept away by inspiration—was Maria-Theresa; that he had saved enough as a teacher of German in London to retire into the country; and that he was looking for a cottage in which to spend his few remaining years.

It all sounded very innocent. Mrs. Pearce listened with her head on one side and with something of the air of a sparrow who doesn't feel well. She complimented him sadly on the fluency of his English, and told him with a sigh that in no cottage would he ever again find the comforts with which Baker's was now surrounding him.

Fritzing was surprised to hear her say so, for his impressions had all been the other way. As far as he, inexperienced man, could tell, Baker's was a singularly draughty and unscrubbed place. He smelt that its fires smoked, he heard that its windows rattled, he knew that its mattresses had lumps in them, and he saw that its food was inextricably mixed up with objects of a black and gritty nature. But her calm face and sorrowful assurance shook the evidence of his senses, and gazing at her in silence over his spectacles a feeling crept dimly across his brain that if the future held many dealings with women like Mrs. Pearce he was going to be very helpless.

Priscilla appeared while he was gazing. She was dressed for going out and came in buttoning her gloves, and I suppose it was a long time since Baker's had seen anything quite so radiant in the way of nieces within its dusty walls. She had on the clothes she had travelled in, for a search among the garments bought by Fritzing had resulted in nothing but a sitting on the side of the bed and laughing tears, so it was clearly not the clothes that made her seem all of a sparkle with lovely youth and blitheness. Kunitz would not have recognized its ivory Princess in this bright being. She was the statue come to life, the cool perfection kissed by expectation into a bewitching living woman. I doubt whether Fritzing had ever noticed her beauty while at Kunitz. He had seen her every day from childhood on, and it is probable that his attention being always riveted on her soul he had never really known when her body left off being lanky and freckled. He saw it now, however; he would have been blind if he had not; and it set him vibrating with the throb of a new responsibility. Mrs. Pearce saw it too, and stared astonished at this oddly inappropriate niece. She stared still more when Fritzing, jumping up from his chair, bent over the hand Priscilla held out and kissed it with a devotion and respect wholly absent from the manner of Mrs. Pearce's own uncles. She, therefore, withdrew into her kitchen, and being a person of little culture crudely expressed her wonder by thinking "Lor." To which, after an interval of vague meanderings among saucepans, she added the elucidation, "Foreigners."

Half an hour later Lady Shuttleworth's agent, Mr. Dawson, was disturbed at his tea by the announcement that a gentleman wished to speak to him. Mr. Dawson was a bluff person, and something of a tyrant, for he reigned supreme in Symford after Lady Shuttleworth, and to reign supreme over anybody, even over a handful of cottagers, does bring out what a man may have in him of tyrant. Another circumstance that brings this out is the possession of a meek wife; and Mr. Dawson's wife was really so very meek that I fear when the Day of Reckoning comes much of this tyranny will be forgiven him and laid to her account. Mr. Dawson, in fact, represented an unending series of pitfalls set along his wife's path by Fate, into every one of which she fell; and since we are not supposed, on pain of punishment, to do anything but keep very upright on our feet as we trudge along the dusty road of life, no doubt all those amiable stumblings will be imputed to her in the end for sin. "This man was handed over to you quite nice and kind," one can imagine Justice saying in an awful voice; "his intentions to start with were beyond reproach. Do you not remember, on the eve of your wedding, how he swore with tears he would be good to you? Look, now, what you have made of him. You have prevented his being good to you by your own excessive goodness to him. You have spent your time nourishing his bad qualities. Though he still swears, he never does it with tears. Do you not know the enormous, the almost insurmountable difficulty there is in not bullying meekness, in not responding to the cringer with a kick? Weak and unteachable woman, away with you."

Certainly it is a great responsibility taking a man into one's life. It is also an astonishment to me that I write thus in detail of Mrs. Dawson, for she has nothing whatever to do with the story.

"Who is it?" asked Mr. Dawson; immediately adding, "Say I'm engaged."

"He gave no name, sir. He says he wishes to see you on business."

"Business! I don't do business at tea time. Send him away."

But Fritzing, for he it was, would not be sent away. Priscilla had seen the cottage of her dreams, seen it almost at once on entering the village, fallen instantly and very violently in love with it regardless of what its inside might be, and had sent him to buy it. She was waiting while he bought it in the adjoining churchyard sitting on a tombstone, and he could neither let her sit there indefinitely nor dare, so great was her eagerness to have the thing, go back without at least a hope of it. Therefore he would not be sent away. "Your master's in," he retorted, when the maid suggested he should depart, "and I must see him. Tell him my business is pressing."

"Will you give me your card, sir?" said the maid, wavering before this determination.

Fritzing, of course, had no card, so he wrote his new name in pencil on a leaf of his notebook, adding his temporary address.

"Tell Mr. Dawson," he said, tearing it out and giving it to her, "that if he is so much engaged as to be unable to see me I shall go direct to Lady Shuttleworth. My business will not wait."

"Show him in, then," growled Mr. Dawson on receiving this message; for he feared Lady Shuttleworth every bit as much as Mrs. Dawson feared him.

Fritzing was accordingly shown into the room used as an office, and was allowed to cool himself there while Mr. Dawson finished his tea. The thought of his Princess waiting on a tombstone that must be growing colder every moment, for the sun was setting, made him at last so impatient that he rang the bell.

"Tell your master," he said when the maid appeared, "that I am now going to Lady Shuttleworth." And he seized his hat and was making indignantly for the door when Mr. Dawson appeared.

Mr. Dawson was wiping his mouth. "You seem to be in a great hurry," he said; and glancing at the slip of paper in his hand added, "Mr. Newman."

"Sir," said Fritzing, bowing with a freezing dignity, "I am."

"Well, so am I. Sit down. What can I do for you? Time's money, you know, and I'm a busy man. You're German, ain't you?"

"I am, sir. My name is Neumann. I am here—"

"Oh, Noyman, is it? I thought it was Newman." And he glanced again at the paper.

"Sir," said Fritzing, with a wave of his hand, "I am here to buy a cottage, and the sooner we come to terms the better. I will not waste valuable moments considering niceties of pronunciation."

Mr. Dawson stared. Then he said, "Buy a cottage?"

"Buy a cottage, sir. I understand that practically the whole of Symford is the property of the Shuttleworth family, and that you are that family's accredited agent. I therefore address myself in the first instance to you. Now, sir, if you are unable, either through disinclination or disability, to do business with me, kindly state the fact at once, and I will straightway proceed to Lady Shuttleworth herself. I have no time to lose."

"I'm blessed if I have either, Mr."—he glanced again at the paper—"Newman."

"Neumann, sir," corrected Fritzing irritably.

"All right—Noyman. But why don't you write it then? You've written Newman as plain as a doorpost."

"Sir, I am not here to exercise you in the proper pronunciation of foreign tongues. These matters, of an immense elementariness I must add, should be and generally are acquired by all persons of any education in their childhood at school."

Mr. Dawson stared. "You're a long-winded chap," he said, "but I'm blessed if I know what you're driving at. Suppose you tell me what you've come for, Mr."—he referred as if from habit to the paper—"Newman."

"*Neu*mann, sir," said Fritzing very loud, for he was greatly irritated by Mr. Dawson's manner and appearance.

"*Noy*mann, then," said Mr. Dawson, equally loudly; indeed it was almost a shout. And he became possessed at the same instant of what was known to Fritzing as a red head, which is the graphic German way of describing the glow that accompanies wrath. "Look here," he said, "if you don't say what you've got to say and have done with it you'd better go. I'm not the chap for the fine-worded game, and I'm hanged if I'll be preached to in my own house. I'll be hanged if I will, do you hear?" And he brought his fist down on the table in a fashion very familiar to Mrs. Dawson and the Symford cottagers.

"Sir, your manners—" said Fritzing, rising and taking up his hat.

"Never mind my manners, Mr. Newman."

"*Neu*mann, sir!" roared Fritzing.

"Confound you, sir," was Mr. Dawson's irrelevant reply.

"Sir, confound *you*," said Fritzing, clapping on his hat. "And let me tell you that I am going at once to Lady Shuttleworth and shall recommend to her most serious consideration the extreme desirability of removing you, sir."

"Removing me! Where the deuce to?"

"Sir, I care not whither so long as it is hence," cried Fritzing, passionately striding to the door.

Mr. Dawson lay back in his chair and gasped. The man was plainly mad; but still Lady Shuttleworth might—you never know with women— "Look here—hie, you! Mr. Newman!" he called, for Fritzing had torn open the door and was through it.

"*Neu*mann, sir," Fritzing hurled back at him over his shoulder.

"Lady Shuttleworth won't see you, Mr. Noyman. She won't on principle."

Fritzing wavered.

"Everything goes through my hands. You'll only have your walk for nothing. Come back and tell me what it is you want."

"Sir, I will only negotiate with you," said Fritzing down the passage— and Mrs. Dawson hearing him from the drawing-room folded her hands in fear and wonder—"if you will undertake at least to imitate the manners of a gentleman."

"Come, come, you musn't misunderstand me," said Mr. Dawson getting up and going to the door. "I'm a plain man, you know—"

"Then, sir, all I can say is that I object to plain men."

"I say, who are you? One would think you were a duke or somebody, you're so peppery. Dressed up"—Mr. Dawson glanced at the suit of pedagogic black into which Fritzing had once more relapsed—"dressed up as a street preacher."

"I am not dressed up as anything, sir," said Fritzing coming in rather hurriedly. "I am a retired teacher of the German tongue, and have come down from London in search of a cottage in which to spend my remaining years. That cottage I have now found here in your village, and I have come to inquire its price. I wish to buy it as quickly as possible."

"That's all very well, Mr.—oh all right, all right, I won't say it. But why on earth don't you write it properly, then? It's this paper's set me wrong. I was going to say we've got no cottages here for sale. And look here, if that's all you are, a retired teacher, I'll trouble you not to get schoolmastering me again."

"I really think, sir," said Fritzing stretching his hand towards his hat, "that it is better I should try to obtain an interview with Lady Shuttleworth, for I fear you are constitutionally incapable of carrying on a business conversation with the requisite decent self-command."

"Pooh—you'll get nothing out of her. She'll send you back to me. Why, you'd drive her mad in five minutes with that tongue of yours. If you want anything I'm your man. Only let's get at what you do want, without all these confounded dictionary words. Which cottage is it?"

"It is the small cottage," said Fritzing mastering his anger, "adjoining the churchyard. It stands by itself, and is separated from the road by an extremely miniature garden. It is entirely covered by creeping plants which I believe to be roses."

"That's a couple."

"So much the better."

"And they're let. One to the shoemaker, and the other to old mother Shaw."

"Accommodation could no doubt be found for the present tenants in some other house, and I am prepared to indemnify them handsomely. Might I inquire the number of rooms the cottages contain?"

"Two apiece, and a kitchen and attic. Coal-hole and pig-stye in the back yard. Also a pump. But they're not for sale, so what's the use—"

"Sir, do they also contain bathrooms?"

"Bathrooms?" Mr. Dawson stared with so excessively stupid a stare that Fritzing, who heaver could stand stupidity, got angry again.

"I said bathrooms, sir," he said, raising his voice, "and I believe with perfect distinctness."

"Oh, I heard you right enough. I was only wondering if you were trying to be funny."

"Is this a business conversation or is it not?" cried Fritzing, in his turn bringing his fist down on the table.

"Look here, what do you suppose people who live in such places want?"

"I imagine cleanliness and decency as much as anybody else."

"Well, I've never been asked for one with a bathroom in my life."

"You are being asked now," said Fritzing, glaring at him, "but you wilfully refuse to reply. From your manner, however, I conclude that they contain none. If so, no doubt I could quickly have some built."

"Some? Why, how many do you want?"

"I have a niece, sir, and she must have her own."

Mr. Dawson again stared with what seemed to Fritzing so deplorably foolish a stare. "I never heard of such a thing," he said.

"What did you never hear of, sir?"

"I never heard of one niece and one uncle in a labourer's cottage wanting a bathroom apiece."

"Apparently you have never heard of very many things," retorted Fritzing angrily. "My niece desires to have her own bathroom, and it is no one's business but hers."

"She must be a queer sort of girl."

"Sir," cried Fritzing, "leave my niece out of the conversation."

"Oh all right—all right. I'm sure I don't want to talk about your niece. But as for the cottages, it's no good wanting those or any others, for you won't get 'em."

"And pray why not, if I offer a good price?"

"Lady Shuttleworth won't sell. Why should she? She'd only have to build more to replace them. Her people must live somewhere. And she'll never turn out old Shaw and the shoemaker to make room for a couple of strangers."

Fritzing was silent, for his heart was sinking. "Suppose, sir," he said after a pause, during which his eyes had been fixed thoughtfully on the carpet and Mr. Dawson had been staring at him and whistling softly but very offensively, "suppose I informed Lady Shuttleworth of my willingness to build two new cottages—excellent new cottages—for the tenants of these old ones, and pay her a good price as well for these, do you think she would listen to me?"

"I say, the schoolmastering business must be a rattling good one. I'm blessed if I know what you want to live in 'em for if money's so little object with you. They're shabby and uncomfortable, and an old chap like you—I mean, a man of your age, who's made his little pile, and wants luxuries like plenty of bathrooms—ought to buy something tight and snug. Good roof and electric light. Place for horse and trap. And settle down and be a gentleman."

"My niece," said Fritzing, brushing aside these suggestions with an angrily contemptuous wave of his hand, "has taken a fancy—I may say an exceedingly violent fancy—to these two cottages. What is all this talk of traps and horses? My niece wishes for these cottages. I shall do my utmost to secure them for her."

"Well, all I can say is she must be a—"

"Silence, sir!" cried Fritzing.

Mr. Dawson got up and opened the door very wide.

"Look here," he said, "there's no use going on talking. I've stood more from you than I've stood from any one for years. Take my advice and get back home and keep quiet for a bit. I've got no cottages, and Lady Shuttleworth would shut the door in your face when you got to the bathroom part. Where are you staying? At the Cock and Hens? Oh—ah— yes—at Baker's. Well, ask Mrs. Pearce to take great care of you. Tell her I said so. And good afternoon to you, Mr. Noyman. You see I've got the name right now—just as we're going to part."

"Before I go," said Fritzing, glaring down at Mr. Dawson, "let me tell you that I have seldom met an individual who unites in his manner so singularly offensive a combination of facetiousness and hectoring as yourself. I shall certainly describe your conduct to Lady Shuttleworth, and not, I hope, in unconvincing language. Sir, good afternoon."

"By-bye," said Mr. Dawson, grinning and waving a pleasant hand. Several bathrooms indeed! He need have no fears of Lady Shuttleworth. "Good luck to you with Lady S.!" he called after him cheerily. Then he went to his wife and bade her see to it that the servant never let Fritzing in again, explaining that he was not only a foreigner but a lunatic, and that the mixture was so bad that it hardly bore thinking of.

VI

While Fritzing was losing his temper in this manner at the agent's, Priscilla sat up in the churchyard in the sun. The Symford churchyard, its church, and the pair of coveted cottages, are on a little eminence rising like an island out of the valley. Sitting under the trees of this island Priscilla amused herself taking in the quiet scene at her feet and letting her thoughts wander down happy paths. The valley was already in shadow, but the tops of the hills on the west side of it were golden in the late afternoon sunshine. From the cottage chimneys smoke went up straight and blue into the soft sky, rooks came and settled over her head in the branches of the elms, and every now and then a yellow leaf would fall slowly at her feet. Priscilla's heart was filled with peace. She was going to be so good, she was going to lead such a clean and beautiful life, so quiet, so helpful to the poor, so hidden, so cleared of all confusions. Never again would she need to pose; never again be forced into conflict with her soul. She had chosen the better part; she had given up everything and followed after wisdom; and her life would be her justification. Who but knows the inward peace that descends upon him who makes good resolutions and abides with him till he suddenly discovers they have all been broken? And what does the breaking of them matter, since it is their making that is so wholesome, so bracing to the soul, bringing with it moments of such extreme blessedness that he misses much who gives it up for fear he will not keep them? Such blessed moments of lifting up of the heart were Priscilla's as she sat in the churchyard waiting, invisibly surrounded by the most beautiful resolutions it is possible to imagine. The Rev. Edward Morrison, the vicar of whom I have spoken as venerable, coming slowly up the path leaning on his son's arm with the intention of going into the church in search of a mislaid sermon-book, saw Priscilla's thoughtful back under the elm-tree and perceived at once that it was a back unknown to him. He knew all the Symford backs, and tourists hardly ever coming there, and never at that time of the year, it could not, he thought, be the back of a tourist. Nor could it belong to any one staying with the Shuttleworths, for he had been there that very afternoon and had found Lady Shuttleworth rejoicing over the brief period of solitude she and her son were enjoying before the stream of guests for the coming of age festivities began.

"Robin, what girl is that?" asked the vicar of his son.

"I'm sure I don't know," said Robin.

"She'll catch cold," said the vicar.

"I dare say," said Robin.

When they came out of the church ten minutes later Priscilla had not moved.

"She'll certainly catch cold," said the vicar, concerned.

"I should think it very likely," said Robin, locking the door.

"She's sitting on a stone."

"Yes, on old Dawson's slab."

"Unwise," said the vicar.

"Profane," said Robin.

The vicar took his boy's arm again—the boy, head and shoulders taller than his father, was down from Cambridge for the vacation then drawing to its close—and moved, I fear, by the same impulse of pure curiosity they walked together down the path that would take them right in front of the young woman on the slab.

Priscilla was lost in the bright dreams she was weaving, and looked up with the radiance of them still in her eyes at the two figures between her and the sunset.

"My dear young lady," said the vicar kindly, "are you not afraid of catching cold? The evenings are so damp now, and you have chosen a very cold seat."

"I don't feel cold," said Priscilla, smiling at this vision of benevolence.

"But I do think you ought not to linger here," said the vicar.

"I am waiting for my uncle. He's gone to buy a cottage, and ought to be back, really, by now."

"Buy a cottage?" repeated the vicar. "My dear young lady, you say that in the same voice you might use to tell me your uncle had gone to buy a bun."

"What is a bun?" asked Priscilla.

"A bun?" repeated the vicar bewildered, for nobody had ever asked him that before.

"Oh I know—" said Priscilla quickly, faintly flushing, "it's a thing you eat. Is there a special voice for buns?"

"There is for a thing so—well, so momentous as the buying of a cottage."

"Is it momentous? It seems to me so nice and natural."

She looked up at the vicar and his son, calmly scrutinizing first one and then the other, and they stood looking down at her; and each time her eyes rested on Robin they found his staring at her with the frankest expression of surprise and admiration.

"Pardon me," said the vicar, "if I seem inquisitive, but is it one of the Symford cottages your uncle wishes to buy? I did not know any were for sale."

"It's that one by the gate," said Priscilla, slightly turning her head in its direction.

"Is it for sale? Dear me, I never knew Lady Shuttleworth sell a cottage yet."

"I don't know yet if she wants to," said Priscilla; "but Fr—, my uncle, will give any price. And I must have it. I shall—I shall be ill if I don't."

The vicar gazed at her upturned face in perplexity. "Dear me," he said, after a slight pause.

"We must live somewhere," remarked Priscilla.

"Of course you must," said Robin, suddenly and so heartily that she examined his eager face in more detail.

"Quite so, quite so," said the vicar. "Are you staying here at present?"

"Never at the Cock and Hens?" broke in Robin.

"We're at Baker's Farm."

"Ah yes—poor Mrs. Pearce will be glad of lodgers. Poor soul, poor soul."

"She's a very dirty soul," said Robin; and Priscilla's eyes flashed over him with a sudden sparkle.

"Is she the soul with the holes in its apron?" she asked.

"I expect there are some there. There generally are," said Robin.

They both laughed; but the vicar gently shook his head. "Ah well, poor thing," he said, "she has an uphill life of it. They don't seem able—they don't seem to understand the art of making both ends meet."

"It's a great art," said Robin.

"Perhaps they could be helped," said Priscilla, already arranging in her mind to go and do it.

"They do not belong to the class one can help. And Lady Shuttleworth, I am afraid, disapproves of shiftless people too much to do anything in the way of reducing the rent."

"Lady Shuttleworth can't stand people who don't look happy and don't mend their apron," said Robin.

"But it's her own apron," objected Priscilla.

"Exactly," said Robin.

"Well, well, I hope they'll make you comfortable," said the vicar; and having nothing more that he could well say without having to confess to himself that he was inquisitive, he began to draw Robin away. "We shall see you and your uncle on Sunday in church, I hope," he said benevolently, and took off his hat and showed his snow-white hair.

Priscilla hesitated. She was, it is true, a Protestant, it having been arranged on her mother's marriage with the Catholic Grand Duke that every alternate princess born to them was to belong to the Protestant faith, and Priscilla being the alternate princess it came about that of the Grand Duke's three children she alone was not a Catholic. Therefore she could go to church in Symford as often as she chose; but it was Fritzing's going that made her hesitate, for Fritzing was what the vicar would have called a godless man, and never went to church.

"You are a member of the Church of England?" inquired the vicar, seeing her hesitate.

"Why, pater, she's not English," burst out Robin.

"Not English?" echoed the vicar.

"Is my English so bad?" asked Priscilla, smiling.

"It's frightfully good," said Robin; "but the 'r's,' you know—"

"Ah, yes. No, I'm not English. I'm German."

"Indeed?" said the vicar, with all the interest that attaches to any unusual phenomenon, and a German in Symford was of all phenomena the most unusual. "My dear young lady, how remarkable. I don't remember ever having met a German before in these parts. Your English is really surprising. I should never have noticed—my boy's ears are quicker than my old ones. Will you think me unpardonably curious if I ask what made you pitch on Symford as a place to live in?"

"My uncle passed through it years ago and thought it so pretty that he determined to spend his old age here."

"And you, I suppose, are going to take care of him."

"Yes," said Priscilla, "for we only"—she looked from one to the other and thought herself extremely clever—"we only have each other in the whole wide world."

"Ah, poor child—you are an orphan."

"I didn't say so," said Priscilla quickly, turning red; she who had always been too proud to lie, how was she going to lie now to this aged saint with the snow-white hair?

"Ah well, well," said the vicar, vaguely soothing. "We shall see you on Sunday perhaps. There is no reason that I know of why a member of the German Church should not assist at the services of the Church of England." And he took off his hat again, and tried to draw Robin away.

But Robin lingered, and Priscilla saw so much bright curiosity in his eyes that she felt she was giving an impression of mysteriousness; and this being the last thing she wanted to do she thought she had better explain a little—always a dangerous course to take—and she said, "My uncle taught languages for years, and is old now and tired, and we both long for the country and to be quiet. He taught me English—that's why it's as good as it is. His name"—She was carried away by the desire to blow out that questioning light in Robin's eyes—"his name is Schultz."

The vicar bowed slightly, and Robin asked with an air of great politeness but still with that light in his eyes if he were to address her, then, as Miss Schultz.

"I'm afraid so," said Priscilla, regretfully. It really sounded gross. Miss Schultz? She might just as well have chosen something romantic while she was about it, for Fritzing in the hurry of many cares had settled nothing yet with her about a name.

Robin stared at her very hard, her answer seemed to him so odd. He stared still more when she looked up with the air of one who has a happy thought and informed him that her Christian name was Ethel.

"Ethel?" echoed Robin.

"It's a very pretty name, I think," said Priscilla, looking pleased.

"Our housemaid's called Ethel, and so is the little girl that wheels the gardener's baby's perambulator," was Robin's impetuous comment.

"That doesn't make it less pretty," said Priscilla, frowning.

"Surely," interrupted the vicar mildly, "Ethel is not a German name?"

"I was christened after my mother," said Priscilla gently; and this was strictly true, for the deceased Grand Duchess had also been Priscilla. Then a feeling came over her that she was getting into those depths where persons with secrets begin to flounder as a preliminary to letting them out, and seized with panic she got up off the slab.

"You are half English, then," said Robin triumphantly, his bright eyes snapping. He looked very bold and masterful staring straight at her, his head thrown back, his handsome face twinkling with interest. But a person of Priscilla's training could not possibly be discomposed by the stare of any Robin, however masterful; had it not been up to now her chief function in life to endure being stared at with graceful indifference? "I did not say so," she said, glancing briefly at him; and including both father and son in a small smile composed indescribably of graciousness and chill she added, "It really is damp here—I don't think I'll wait for my uncle," and slightly bowing walked away without more ado.

She walked very slowly, her skirts gathered loosely in one hand, every line of her body speaking of the most absolute self-possession and unapproachableness. Never had the two men seen any one quite so calm. They watched her in silence as she went up the path and out at the gate; then Robin looked down at his father and drew his hand more firmly through his arm and said with a slight laugh, "Come on, pater, let's go home. We're dismissed."

"By a most charming young lady," said the vicar, smiling.

"By a very cool one," said Robin, shrugging his shoulders, for he did not like being dismissed.

"Yes—oddly self-possessed for her age," agreed the vicar.

"I wonder if all German teacher's nieces are like that," said Robin with another laugh.

"Few can be so blest by nature, I imagine."

"Oh, I don't mean faces. She is certainly prettier by a good bit than most girls."

"She is quite unusually lovely, young man. Don't quibble."

"Miss Schultz—Ethel Schultz," murmured Robin; adding under his breath, "Good Lord."

"She can't help her name. These things are thrust upon one."

"It's a beastly common name. Macgrigor, who was a year in Dresden, told me everybody in Germany is called Schultz."

"Except those who are not."

"Now, pater, you're being clever again," said Robin, smiling down at his father.

"Here comes some one in a hurry," said the vicar, his attention arrested by the rapidly approaching figure of a man; and, looking up, Robin beheld Fritzing striding through the churchyard, his hat well down over his eyes as if clapped on with unusual vigour, both hands thrust deep in his pockets, the umbrella, without which he never, even on the fairest of days, went out, pressed close to his side under his arm, and his long legs taking short and profane cuts over graves and tombstones with the indifference to decency of one immersed in unpleasant thought. It was not the custom in Symford to leap in this manner over its tombs; and Fritzing arriving at a point a few yards from the vicar, and being about to continue his headlong career across the remaining graves to the tree under which he had left Priscilla, the vicar raised his voice and exhorted him to keep to the path.

"Quaint-looking person," remarked Robin. "Another stranger. I say, it can't be—no, it can't possibly be the uncle?" For he saw he was a foreigner, yet on the other hand never was there an uncle and a niece who had less of family likeness.

Fritzing was the last man wilfully to break local rules or wound susceptibilities; and pulled out of his unpleasant abstraction by the vicar's voice he immediately desisted from continuing his short cut, and coming onto the path removed his hat and apologized with the politeness that was always his so long as nobody was annoying him.

"My name is Neumann, sir," he said, introducing himself after the German fashion, "and I sincerely beg your pardon. I was looking for a lady, and"—he gave his spectacles a little adjusting shove as though they were in fault, and gazing across to the elm where he had left Priscilla sitting added with sudden anxiety—"I fear I do not see her."

"Do you mean Miss Schultz?" asked the vicar, looking puzzled.

"No, sir, I do not mean Miss Schultz," said Fritzing, peering about him at all the other trees in evident surprise and distress.

"A lady left about five minutes ago," said Robin.

"A tall young lady in a blue costume?"

"Yes. Miss Schultz."

Fritzing looked at him with some sternness. "Sir, what have I to do with Miss Schultz?" he inquired.

"Oh come now," said the cheerful Robin, "aren't you looking for her?"

"I am in search of my niece, sir."

"Yes. Miss Schultz."

"No sir," said Fritzing, controlling himself with an effort, "not Miss Schultz. I neither know Miss Schultz nor do I care a—"

"Sir, sir," interposed the vicar, hastily.

"I do not care a *pfenning* for any Miss Schultz."

The vicar looked much puzzled. "There was a young lady," he said, "waiting under that tree over there for her uncle who had gone, she said, to see Lady Shuttleworth's agent about the cottage by the gate. She said her uncle's name was Schultz."

"She said she was Miss Ethel Schultz," said Robin.

"She said she was staying at Baker's Farm," said the vicar.

Fritzing stared for a moment from one to the other, then clutching his hat mechanically half an inch into the air turned on his heel without another word and went with great haste out of the churchyard and down the hill and away up the road to the farm.

"Quaint, isn't he," said Robin as they slowly followed this flying figure to the gate.

"I don't understand it," said the vicar.

"It does seem a bit mixed."

"Did he not say his name was Neumann?"

"He did. And he looked as if he'd fight any one who said it wasn't."

"It is hardly credible that there should be two sets of German uncles and nieces in Symford at one and the same time," mused the vicar. "Even one pair is a most unusual occurrence."

"If there are," said Robin very earnestly, "pray let us cultivate the Schultz set and not the other."

"I don't understand it," repeated the vicar, helplessly.

VII

Symford, innocent village, went to bed very early; but early as it went long before it had got there on this evening it contained no family that had not heard of the arrivals at Baker's Farm. From the vicarage the news had filtered that a pretty young lady called Schultz was staying there with her uncle; from the agent's house the news that a lunatic called Neumann was staying there with his niece; and about supper-time, while it was still wondering at this sudden influx of related Germans, came the postmistress and said that the boy from Baker's who fetched the letters knew nothing whatever of any one called Schultz. He had, said the postmistress, grown quite angry and forgotten the greater and by far the better part of his manners when she asked him how he could stand there and say such things after all the years he had attended Sunday-school and if he were not afraid the earth would open and swallow him up, and he had stuck to it with an obstinacy that had at length convinced her that only one uncle and niece were at Baker's, and their name was Neumann. He added that there was another young lady there whose name he couldn't catch, but who sat on the edge of her bed all day crying and refusing sustenance. Appeased by the postmistress's apologies for her first unbelief he ended by being anxious to give all the information in his power, and came back quite a long way to tell her that he had forgotten to say that his mother had said that the niece's Christian name was Maria-Theresa.

"But what, then," said the vicar's wife to the vicar when this news had filtered through the vicarage walls to the very sofa where she sat, "has become of the niece called Ethel?"

"I don't know," said the vicar, helplessly.

"Perhaps she is the one who cried all day."

"My dear, we met her in the churchyard."

"Perhaps they are forgers," suggested the vicar's wife.

"My dear?"

"Or anarchists."

"Kate?"

The vicar's wife said no more, but silently made up her mind to go the very next day and call at Baker's. It would be terrible if a bad influence got into Symford, her parish that she had kept in such good order for so long. Besides, she had an official position as the wife of the vicar and could and ought to call on everybody. Her call would not bind her, any more than the call of a district visitor would, to invite the called-upon to her house. Perhaps they were quite decent, and she could ask the girl up to the Tuesday evenings in the parish-room; hardly to the vicarage, because of her daughter Netta. On the other hand, if they looked like what she imagined anarchists or forgers look like, she would merely leave leaflets and be out when they returned her call.

Robin, all unaware of his mother's thoughts, was longing to ask her to go to Baker's and take him with her as a first step towards the acquaintance after which his soul thirsted, but he refrained for various discreet reasons based on an intimate knowledge of his mother's character; and he spent the evening perfecting a plan that should introduce him into the interior of Baker's without her help. The plan was of a barbarous simplicity: he was going to choose an umbrella from the collection that years had brought together in the stand in the hall, and go boldly and ask the man Neumann if he had dropped it in the churchyard. The man Neumann would repudiate the umbrella, perhaps with secret indignation, but he would be forced to pretend he was grateful, and who knew what luck might not do for him after that?

While Robin was plotting, and his mother was plotting, that the next day would certainly see them inside Baker's, a third person was trying to do exactly the same thing at Symford Hall; and this third person was no other than Augustus, the hope of all the Shuttleworths. Augustus—he was known to his friends briefly as Tussie—had been riding homewards late that afternoon, very slowly, for he was an anxious young man who spent much of his time dodging things like being overheated, when he saw a female figure walking towards him along the lonely road. He was up on the heath above Symford, a solitary place of heather, and gorse bushes, and winding roads that lead with many hesitations and delays to different parts of Exmoor, and he himself with his back to that wild region and the sunset was going, as every sensible person would be going at that time of the evening, in the direction of the village and home. But where could the girl be going? For he now saw it was a girl, and in a minute or two more that it was a beautiful girl. With the golden glow of the sky the sun had just left on her face Priscilla came towards him out of the gathering dusk of approaching evening, and Tussie, who had a poetic soul, gazed at the vision openmouthed. Seeing him, she quickened her steps, and he took off his cap eagerly when she asked him to tell her where Symford was. "I've lost it," she said, looking up at him.

"I'm going through it myself," he answered. "Will you let me show you the way?"

"Thank you," said Priscilla; and he got off his horse and she turned and walked beside him with the same unruffled indifference with which she would have walked beside the Countess Disthal or in front of an attending lacquey. Nor did she speak, for she was busy thinking of Fritzing and hoping he was not being too anxious about her, and Tussie (God defend his innocence) thought she was shy. So sure was he as the minutes past that her silence was an embarrassed one that he put an end to it by remarking on the beauty of the evening, and Priscilla who had entirely forgotten Miss Schultz gave him the iciest look as a reminder that it was not his place to speak first. It was lost on Tussie as a reminder, for naturally it did not remind him of anything, and he put it down at first to the girl's being ill at ease alone up there with a strange man, and perhaps to her feeling she had better keep him at arm's length. A glance at her profile however dispelled this illusion once and for ever, for never was profile of a profounder calm. She was walking now with her face in shadow, and the glow behind her played strange and glorious tricks with her hair. He looked at her, and looked, and not by the quiver of an eyelash did she show she was aware of anybody's presence. Her eyes were fixed on the ground, and she was deep in thought tinged with remorsefulness that she should have come up here instead of going straight home to the farm, and by losing her way and staying out so long have given Fritzing's careful heart an unnecessary pang of anxiety. He had had so many, and all because of her. But then it had been the very first time in her life that she had ever walked alone, and if words cannot describe the joy and triumph of it how was it likely that she should have been able to resist the temptation to stray aside up a lovely little lane that lured her on and on from one bend to another till it left her at last high up, breathless and dazzled, on the edge of the heath, with Exmoor rolling far away in purple waves to the sunset and all the splendour of the evening sky in her face? She had gone on, fascinated by the beauty of the place, and when she wanted to turn back found she had lost herself. Then appeared Sir Augustus to set her right, and with a brief thought of him as a useful person on a nice horse she fell into sober meditations as to the probable amount of torture her poor Fritzi was going through, and Augustus ceased to exist for her as completely as a sign-post ceases to exist for him who has taken its advice and passed on.

He looked at her, and looked, and looked again. He had never seen any one quite so beautiful, and certainly never any one with such an air of extreme detachment. He was twenty-one and much inclined to poetry, and he thought as she walked beside him so tall and straight and aloof, with the nimbus of flaming hair and the noble little head and slightly stern brow that she looked like nothing less than a young saint of God.

Tussie was not bold like Robin. He was a gentle youth who loved quiet things, quiet places, placid people, kind dogs, books, canaries even, if they did not sing too loud. He was sensitive about himself, being small and weakly, and took, as I have said, great care of what he had of health, such care indeed that some of his robust friends called him Fussie. He hated the idea of coming of age and of having a great deal of money and a great many active duties and responsibilities. His dream was to be left in peace to write his verses; to get away into some sweet impossible wilderness, and sit there singing with as much of the spirit of Omar Kayyam as could reasonably be expected to descend on a youth who only drank water. He was not bold, I say; and after that one quelling glance from the young saint's eyes did not dare speak again for a long while. But they were getting near Symford; they were halfway down the hill; he could not let her slip away perhaps suddenly from his side into the shadows without at least trying to find out where she was staying. He looked at her soft kind mouth and opened his own to speak. He looked at her stern level brows and shut it again. At last, keeping his eyes on her mouth he blurted out, growing red, "I know every soul in Symford, and every soul for miles round, but I don't know—" He stopped. He was going to say "you," but he stopped.

Priscilla's thoughts were so far away that she turned her head and gazed vaguely at him for a moment while she collected them again. Then she frowned at him. I do not know why Robin should have had at least several smiles and poor Tussie only frowns, unless it was that during this walk the young person Ethel Schultz had completely faded from Priscilla's mind and the Royal Highness was well to the fore. She certainly frowned at Tussie and asked herself what could possess the man to keep on speaking to her. Keep on speaking! Poor Tussie. Aloud she said freezingly, "Did you say something?"

"Yes," said Tussie, his eyes on her mouth—surely a mouth only made for kindness and gentle words. "I was wondering whether you were staying at the vicarage."

"No," said Priscilla, "we're staying at Baker's Farm." And at the mention of that decayed lodging the friendly Schultz expression crept back, smiling into her eyes.

Tussie stopped short. "Baker's Farm?" he said. "Why, then this is the way; down here, to the right. It's only a few yards from here."

"Were you going that way too?"

"I live on the other side of Symford."

"Then good-bye and thank you."

"Please let me go with you as far as the high-road—it's almost dark."

"Oh no—I can't lose myself again if it's only a few yards."

She nodded, and was turning down the lane.

"Are you—are you comfortable there?" he asked hurriedly, blushing. "The Pearces are tenants of ours. I hope they make you comfortable?"

"Oh, we're only going to be there a few days. My uncle is buying a cottage, and we shall leave almost directly."

The girl Ethel nodded and smiled and went away quickly into the dusk; and Tussie rode home thoughtfully, planning elaborate plans for a descent the next day upon Baker's Farm that should have the necessary air of inevitableness.

Fritzing was raging up and down the road in front of the gate when Priscilla emerged, five minutes later, from the shadows of the lane. She ran up to him and put her arm through his, and looked up at him with a face of great penitence. "Dear Fritzi," she said, "I'm so sorry. I've been making you anxious, haven't I? Forgive me—it was the first taste of liberty, and it got into my feet and set them off exploring, and then I lost myself. Have you been worrying?"

He was immensely agitated, and administered something very like a scolding, and he urged the extreme desirability of taking Annalise with her in future wherever she went—("Oh nonsense, Fritzi," interjected Priscilla, drawing away her arm)—and he declared in a voice that trembled that it was a most intolerable thought for him that two strange men should have dared address her in the churchyard, that he would never forgive himself for having left her there alone—("Oh, Fritzi, how silly," interjected Priscilla)—and he begged her almost with tears to tell him exactly what she had said to them, for her Grand Ducal Highness must see that it was of the first importance they should both say the same things to people.

Priscilla declared she had said nothing at all but what was quite diplomatic, in fact quite clever; indeed, she had been surprised at the way ideas had seemed to flow.

"So please," she finished, "don't look at me with such lamentable eyes."

"Ma'am, did you not tell them our name is Schultz?"

"But so it is."

"It is not, ma'am. Our name is Neumann."

Priscilla stared astonished. "Neumann?" she said. "Nonsense, Fritzi. Why should it be Neumann? We're Schultz. I told these people we were. It's all settled."

"Settled, ma'am? I told the woman here as well as the estate agent that you are my brother's child and that we are Neumann."

Priscilla was aghast. Then she said severely, "It was your duty to ask me first. What right have you to christen me?"

"I intended to discuss it during our walk to the village this afternoon. I admit I forgot it. On the other hand I could not suppose your Grand Ducal Highness, left for a moment unprotected, would inform two strange gentlemen that our name was Schultz."

"You should certainly have asked me first," repeated Priscilla with knitted brows. "Why should I have to be Neumann?"

"I might inquire with equal reason why I should have to be Schultz," retorted Fritzing.

"But why Neumann?" persisted Priscilla, greatly upset.

"Ma'am, why not?" said Fritzing, still more upset. Then he added, "Your Grand Ducal Highness might have known that at the agent's I would be obliged to give some name."

"I didn't think any more than you did," said Priscilla stopping in front of the gate as a sign he was to open it for her. He did, and they walked through the garden and into the house in silence. Then she went into the parlour and dropped into a horsehair armchair, and leaning her head against its prickliness she sighed a doleful sigh.

"Shall I send Annalise to you, ma'am?" asked Fritzing, standing in the doorway.

"What can we do?" asked Priscilla, her eyes fixed on the tips of her shoes in earnest thought. "Come in, Fritzi, and shut the door," she added. "You don't behave a bit like an uncle." Then an idea struck her, and looking up at him with sudden gaiety she said, "Can't we have a hyphen?"

"A hyphen?"

"Yes, and be Neumann-Schultz?"

"Certainly we can," said Fritzing, his face clearing; how muddled he must be getting not to have thought of it himself! "I will cause cards to be printed at once, and we will be Neumann-Schultz. Ma'am, your woman's wit—"

"Fritzi, you're deteriorating—you never flattered me at Kunitz. Let us have tea. I invite you to tea with me. If you'll order it, I'll pour it out for you and practice being a niece."

So the evening was spent in harmony; a harmony clouded at intervals, it is true, first by Priscilla's disappointment about the cottage, then by a certain restiveness she showed before the more blatant inefficiencies of the Baker housekeeping, then by a marked and ever recurring incapacity to adapt herself to her new environment, and lastly and very heavily when Fritzing in the course of conversation let drop the fact that he had said she was Maria-Theresa. This was a very black cloud and hung about for a long while; but it too passed away ultimately in a compromise reached after much discussion that Ethel should be prefixed to Maria-Theresa; and before Priscilla went to bed it had been arranged that Fritzing should go next morning directly after a very early breakfast to Lady Shuttleworth and not leave that lady's side and house till he had secured the cottage, and the Princess for her part faithfully promised to remain within the Baker boundaries during his absence.

VIII

Lady Shuttleworth then, busiest and most unsuspecting of women, was whisking through her breakfast and her correspondence next morning with her customary celerity and method, when a servant appeared and offered her one of those leaves from Fritzing's note-book which we know did duty as his cards.

Tussie was sitting at the other end of the table very limp and sad after a night of tiresome tossing that was neither wholly sleep nor wholly wakefulness, and sheltered by various dishes with spirit-lamps burning beneath them worked gloomily at a sonnet inspired by the girl he had met the day before while his mother thought he was eating his patent food. The girl, it seemed, could not inspire much, for beyond the fourth line his muse refused to go; and he was beginning to be unable to stop himself from an angry railing at the restrictions the sonnet form forces upon poets who love to be vague, which would immediately have concentrated his mother's attention on himself and resulted in his having to read her what he had written—for she sturdily kept up the fiction of a lively interest in his poetic tricklings—when the servant came in with Fritzing's leaf.

"A gentleman wishes to see you on business, my lady," said the servant.

"Mr. Neumann-Schultz?" read out Lady Shuttleworth in an inquiring voice. "Never heard of him. Where's he from?"

"Baker's Farm, my lady."

At that magic name Tussie's head went up with a jerk.

"Tell him to go to Mr. Dawson," said Lady Shuttleworth.

The servant disappeared.

"Why do you send him away, mother?" asked Tussie.

"Why, you know things must go through Dawson," said Lady Shuttleworth pouncing on her letters again. "I'd be plagued to death if they didn't."

"But apparently this is the stranger within our gates. Isn't he German?"

"His name is. Dawson will be quite kind to him."

"Dawson's rather a brute I fancy, when you're not looking."

"Dearest, I always am looking."

"He must be one of Pearce's lodgers."

"Poor man, I'm sorry for him if he is. Of all the shiftless women—"

"The gentleman says, my lady," said the servant reappearing with rather an awestruck face, "that he wishes to speak to you most particular."

"James, did I not tell you to send him to Mr. Dawson?"

"I delivered the message, my lady. But the gentleman says he's seen Mr. Dawson, and that he"—the footman coughed slightly—"he don't want to see any more of him, my lady."

Lady Shuttleworth put on her glasses and stared at the servant. "Upon my word he seems to be very cool," she said; and the servant, his gaze fixed on a respectful point just above his mistress's head, reflected on the extreme inapplicability of the adjective to anything so warm as the gentleman at the door.

"Shall I see him for you, mother?" volunteered Tussie briskly.

"You?" said his mother surprised.

"I'm rather a dab at German, you know. Perhaps he can't talk much English"—the footman started—"evidently he wasn't able to say much to Dawson. Probably he wants you to protect him from the onslaughts of old Pearce's cockroaches. Anyhow as he's a foreigner I think it would be kinder to see him."

Lady Shuttleworth was astonished. Was Tussie going to turn over a new leaf after all, now that he was coming of age, and interest himself in more profitable things than verse-making?

"Dearest," she said, quite touched, "he shall be seen if you think it kinder. I'll see him—you haven't done breakfast yet. Show him into the library, James." And she gathered up her letters and went out—she never kept people waiting—and as she passed Tussie she laid her hand tenderly for a moment on his shoulder. "If I find I can't understand him I'll send for you," she said.

Tussie folded up his sonnet and put it in his pocket. Then he ate a few spoonfuls of the stuff warranted to give him pure blood, huge muscles, and a vast intelligence; then he opened a newspaper and stared vacantly at its contents; then he went to the fire and warmed his feet; then he strolled round the table aimlessly for a little; and then, when half an hour had passed and his mother had not returned, he could bear it no longer and marched straight into the library.

"I think the cigarettes must be here," said Tussie, going over to the mantelpiece and throwing a look of eager interest at Fritzing.

Fritzing rose and bowed ceremoniously. Lady Shuttleworth was sitting in a straight-backed chair, her elbows on its arms, the tips of her ten fingers nicely fitted together. She looked very angry, and yet there was a sparkle of something like amusement in her eyes. Having bowed to Tussie Fritzing sat down again with the elaboration of one who means to stay a long while. During his walk from the farm he had made up his mind to be of a most winning amiability and patience, blended with a determination that nothing should shake. At the door, it is true, he had been stirred to petulance by the foolish face and utterances of the footman James, but during the whole of the time he had been alone with Lady Shuttleworth he had behaved, he considered, with the utmost restraint and tact.

Tussie offered him a cigarette.

"My dear Tussie," said his mother quickly, "we will not keep Mr. Neumann-Schultz. I'm sure his time must be quite as valuable as mine is."

"Oh madam," said Fritzing with a vast politeness, settling himself yet more firmly in his chair, "nothing of mine can possibly be of the same value as anything of yours."

Lady Shuttleworth stared—she had stared a good deal during the last halfhour—then began to laugh, and got up. "If you see its value so clearly," she said, "I'm sure you won't care to take up any more of it."

"Nay, madam," said Fritzing, forced to get up too, "I am here, as I explained, in your own interests—or rather in those of your son, who I hear is shortly to attain his majority. This young gentleman is, I take it, your son?"

Tussie assented.

"And therefore the owner of the cottages?"

"What cottages?" asked Tussie, eagerly. He was manifestly so violently interested in Mr. Neumann-Schultz that his mother could only gaze at him in wonder. He actually seemed to hang on that odd person's lips.

"My dear Tussie, Mr. Neumann-Schultz has been trying to persuade me to sell him the pair of cottages up by the church, and I have been trying to persuade him to believe me when I tell him I won't."

"But why won't you, mother?" asked Tussie.

Lady Shuttleworth stared at him in astonishment. "Why won't I? Do I ever sell cottages?"

"Your esteemed parent's reasons for refusing," said Fritzing, "reasons which she has given me with a brevity altogether unusual in one of her sex and which I cannot sufficiently commend, do more credit, as was to be expected in a lady, to her heart than to her head. I have offered to build two new houses for the disturbed inhabitants of these. I have offered to give her any price—any price at all, within the limits of reason. Your interests, young gentleman, are what will suffer if this business is not concluded between us."

"Do you want them for yourself?" asked Tussie.

"Yes, sir, for myself and for my niece."

"Mother, why do you refuse to do a little business?"

"Tussie, are we so poor?"

"As far as I'm concerned," said Tussie airily to Fritzing, "you may have the things and welcome."

"Tussie?"

"But they are not worth more than about fifty pounds apiece, and I advise you not to give more for them than they're worth. Aren't they very small, though? Isn't there any other place here you'd rather have?"

"Tussie?"

"Do you mind telling me why you want them?"

"Young man, to live in them."

"And where are the people to live who are in them now?" asked Lady Shuttleworth, greatly incensed.

"Madam, I promised you to build."

"Oh nonsense. I won't have new red-brick horrors about the place. There's that nice good old Mrs. Shaw in one, so clean and tidy always, and the shoemaker, a very good man except for his enormous family, in the other. I will not turn them out."

"Put 'em in the empty lodge at the north gate," suggested Tussie. "They'd be delighted."

Lady Shuttleworth turned angrily on Fritzing—she was indeed greatly irritated by Tussie's unaccountable behaviour. "Why don't you build for yourself?" she asked.

"My niece has set her heart on these cottages in such a manner that I actually fear the consequences to her health if she does not get them."

"Now, mother, you really can't make Mr. Neumann-Schultz's niece ill."

"Dearest boy, have you suddenly lost your senses?"

"Not unless it's losing them to be ready to do a kindness."

"Well said, well said, young man," said Fritzing approvingly.

"Tussie, have I ever shirked doing a kindness?" asked Lady Shuttleworth, touched on her tenderest point.

"Never. And that's why I can't let you begin now," said Tussie, smiling at her.

"Well said, well said, young man," approved Fritzing. "The woman up to a certain age should lead the youth, and he should in all things follow her counsels with respect and obedience. But she for her part should know at what moment to lay down her authority, and begin, with a fitting modesty, to follow him whom she has hitherto led."

"Is that what your niece does?" asked Lady Shuttleworth quickly.

"Madam?"

"Is she following you into these cottages, or are you following her?"

"You must pardon me, madam, if I decline to discuss my niece."

"Do have a cigarette," said Tussie, delighted.

"I never smoke, young man."

"Something to drink, then?"

"I never drink, young man."

"If I decide to let you have these cottages—*if* I do," said Lady Shuttleworth, divided between astonishment at everything about Fritzing and blankest amazement at her son's behaviour, "you will understand that I only do it because my son seems to wish it."

"Madam, provided I get the cottages I will understand anything you like."

"First that. Then I'd want some information about yourself. I couldn't let a stranger come and live in the very middle of my son's estate unless I knew all about him."

"Why, mother—" began Tussie.

"Is not the willingness to give you your own price sufficient?" inquired Fritzing anxiously.

"Not in the least sufficient," snapped Lady Shuttleworth.

"What do you wish to know, madam?" said Fritzing stiffly.

"I assure you a great deal."

"Come, mother," said Tussie, to whom this was painful, for was not the man, apart from his strange clothes and speeches, of a distinctly refined and intellectual appearance? And even if he wasn't, was he not still the uncle of that divine niece?—"these are things for Dawson to arrange."

Fritzing started at the hated name, and began to frown dreadfully. His frown was always very impressive because of his bushy eyebrows and deep-set eyes. "Dawson, as you call him," he said, "and he certainly has no claim to any prefix of politeness, is not a person with whom I will consent to arrange anything. Dawson is the most offensive creature who ever walked this earth clad in the outer semblance of one of God's creatures."

This was too much for Lady Shuttleworth. "Really—" she said, stretching out her hand to the bell.

"Didn't I tell you so, mother?" cried Tussie triumphantly; and that Tussie, her own dear boy, should in all things second this madman completely overwhelmed her. "I knew he was a brute behind your back. Let's sack him."

"James, show this gentleman out."

"Pardon me, madam, we have not yet arranged—"

"Oh," interrupted Tussie, "the business part can be arranged between you and me without bothering my mother. I'll come part of the way with you and we'll talk it over. You're absolutely right about Dawson. He's an outrageous mixture of bully and brute." And he hurried into the hall to fetch his cap, humming *O dear unknown One with the stern sweet face,* which was the first line of his sonnet in praise of Priscilla, to a cheerful little tune of his own.

"Tussie, it's so damp," cried his anxious mother after him—"you're not really going out in this nasty Scotch mist? Stay in, and I'll leave you to settle anything you like."

"Oh, it's a jolly morning for a walk," called back Tussie gaily, searching about for his cap—"*And eyes all beautiful with strenuous thought*—Come on, sir."

But Fritzing would not skimp any part of his farewell ceremonies.

"Permit me, madam," he said, deeply bowing, "to thank you for your extremely kind reception."

"Kind?" echoed Lady Shuttleworth, unable to stop herself from smiling.

"Yes, madam, kind, and before all things patient."

"Yes, I do think I've been rather patient," agreed Lady Shuttleworth, smiling again.

"And let me," proceeded Fritzing, "join to my thanks my congratulations on your possession of so unusually amiable and promising a son."

"Come on, sir—you'll make me vain," said Tussie, in the doorway—"'*Hair like a web divine wherein is caught*,'"—he hummed, getting more and more shrill and happy.

Lady Shuttleworth put out her hand impulsively. Fritzing took it, bent over it, and kissed it with much respect.

"A most unusually promising young man," he repeated; "and, madam, I can tell you it is not my habit to say a thing I do not mean."

"'*The last reflection of God's daily grace*'"—chirped Tussie, looking on much amused.

"No, that I'm quite certain you don't," said Lady Shuttleworth with conviction.

"Don't say too many nice things about me," advised Tussie. "My mother will swallow positively anything."

But nevertheless he was delighted; for here were his mother and the uncle—the valuable and highly to be cherished uncle—looking as pleased as possible with each other, and apparently in the fairest way to becoming fast friends.

IX

The cheerful goddess who had brought Fritzing and his Princess safely over from Kunitz was certainly standing by them well. She it was who had driven Priscilla up on to the heath and into the acquaintance of Augustus Shuttleworth, without whom a cottage in Symford would have been for ever unattainable. She it was who had sent the Morrisons, father and son, to drive Priscilla from the churchyard before Fritzing had joined her, without which driving she would never have met Augustus. She it was who had used the trifling circumstance of a mislaid sermon-book to take the vicar and Robin into the church at an unaccustomed time, without which sermon-book they would never have met Priscilla in the churchyard and driven her out of it. Thus are all our doings ruled by Chance; and it is a pleasant pastime for an idle hour to trace back big events to their original and sometimes absurd beginnings. For myself I know that the larger lines of my life were laid down once for all by—but what has this to do with Priscilla? Thus, I say, are all our doings ruled by Chance, who loves to use small means for the working of great wonders. And as for the gay goddess's ugly sister, the lady of the shifty eye and lowering brow called variously Misfortune and Ill Luck, she uses the same tools exactly in her hammering out of lives, meanly taking little follies and little weaknesses, so little and so amiable at first as hardly to be distinguished from little virtues, and with them building up a mighty mass that shall at last come down and crush our souls. Of the crushing of souls, however, my story does not yet treat, and I will not linger round subjects so awful. We who are nestling for the moment like Priscilla beneath the warm wing of Good Fortune can dare to make what the children call a face at her grey sister as she limps scowling past. Shall we not too one day in our turn feel her claws? Let us when we do at least not wince; and he who feeling them can still make a face and laugh, shall be as the prince of the fairy tales, transforming the sour hag by his courage into a bright reward, striking his very griefs into a shining shower of blessing.

From this brief excursion into the realm of barren musings, whither I love above all things to wander and whence I have continually to fetch myself back again by force, I will return to the story.

At Tussie's suggestion when the business part of their talk was over—and it took exactly five minutes for Tussie to sell and Fritzing to buy the cottages, five minutes of the frothiest business talk ever talked, so profound was the ignorance of both parties as to what most people demand of cottages—Fritzing drove to Minehead in the postmistress's son's two-wheeled cart in order to purchase suitable furniture and bring back persons who would paper and paint. Minehead lies about twenty miles to the north of Symford, so Fritzing could not be back before evening. By the time he was back, promised Tussie, the shoemaker and Mrs. Shaw should be cleared out and put into a place so much better according to their views that they would probably make it vocal with their praises.

Fritzing quite loved Tussie. Here was a young man full of the noblest spirit of helpfulness, and who had besides the invaluable gift of seeing no difficulties anywhere. Even Fritzing, airy optimist, saw more than Tussie, and whenever he expressed a doubt it was at once brushed aside by the cheerfullest "Oh, that'll be all right." He was the most practical, businesslike, unaffected, energetic young man, thought Fritzing, that he had even seen. Tussie was surprised himself at his own briskness, and putting the wonderful girl on the heath as much as possible out of his thoughts, told himself that it was the patent food beginning at last to keep its promises.

He took Fritzing to the post-office and ordered the trap for him, cautioned the postmistress's son, who was going to drive, against going too fast down the many hills, for the bare idea of the priceless uncle being brought back in bits or in any state but absolutely whole and happy turned him cold, told Fritzing which shops to go to and where to lunch, begged him to be careful what he ate, since hotel luncheons were good for neither body nor soul, ordered rugs and a mackintosh covering to be put in, and behaved generally with the forethought of a mother. "I'd go with you myself," he said,—and the postmistress, listening with both her ears, recognized that the Baker's Farm lodgers were no longer persons to be criticised—"but I can be of more use to you here. I must see Dawson about clearing out the cottages. Of course it is very important you shouldn't stay a moment longer than can be helped in uncomfortable lodgings."

Here was a young man! Sensible, practical, overflowing with kindness. Fritzing had not met any one he esteemed so much for years. They went down the village street together, for Tussie was bound for Mr. Dawson who was to be set to work at once, and Fritzing for the farm whither the trap was to follow him as soon as ready, and all Symford, curtseying to Tussie, recognized, as the postmistress had recognized, that Fritzing was now raised far above their questionings, seated firmly on the Shuttleworth rock.

They parted at Mr. Dawson's gate, Mrs. Dawson mildly watching their warmth over a wire blind. "When we are settled, young man," said Fritzing, after eloquent words of thanks and appreciation, "you must come in the evenings, and together we will roam across the splendid fields of English literature."

"Oh *thanks*," exclaimed Tussie, flushing with pleasure. He longed to ask if the divine niece would roam too, but even if she did not, to roam at all would be a delight, and he would besides be doing it under the very roof that sheltered that bright and beautiful head. "Oh *thanks*," cried Tussie, then, flushing.

His extreme joy surprised Fritzing. "Are you so great a friend of literature?" he inquired.

"I believe," said Tussie, "that without it I'd have drowned myself long ago. And as for the poets—"

He stopped. No one knew what poetry had been to him in his sickly existence—the one supreme interest, the one thing he really cared to live for.

Fritzing now loved him with all his heart. "*Ach Gott, ja*," he ejaculated, clapping him on the shoulder, "the poets—*ja, ja*—'Blessings be with them and eternal praise,' what? Young man," he added enthusiastically, "I could wish that you had been my son. I could indeed." And as he said it Robin Morrison coming down the street and seeing the two together and the expression on Tussie's face instantly knew that Tussie had met the niece.

"Hullo, Tuss," he called across, hurrying past, for it would rather upset his umbrella plan to be stopped and have to talk to the man Neumann thus prematurely. But Tussie neither saw nor heard him, and "By Jove, hasn't he just seen the niece though," said Robin to himself, his eyes dancing as he strode nimbly along on long and bird-like legs. The conviction seized him that when he and his umbrella should descend upon Baker's that afternoon Tussie would either be there already or would come in immediately afterwards. "Who would have thought old Fuss would be so enterprising?" he wondered, thinking of the extreme cordiality of Fritzing's face. "He's given them those cottages, I'll swear."

So Fritzing went to Minehead. I will not follow his painful footsteps as they ranged about that dreary place, nor will I dwell upon his purchases, which resolved themselves at last, after an infinite and soul-killing amount of walking and bewilderment, into a sofa, a revolving bookstand, and two beds. He forgot a bed for Annalise because he forgot Annalise; and he didn't buy things like sheets because he forgot that beds want them. On the other hand he spent quite two hours in a delightful second-hand bookshop on his way to the place where you buy crockery, and then forgot the crockery. He did, reminded and directed by Mr. Vickerton, the postmistress's son, get to a paperhanger's and order him and his men to come out in shoals to Symford the next morning at daybreak, making the paperhanger vow, who had never seen them, that the cottages should be done by nightfall. Then, happening to come to the seashore, he stood for a moment refreshing his nostrils with saltness, for he was desperately worn out, and what he did after that heaven knows. Anyhow young Vickerton found him hours afterwards walking up and down the shingle in the dark, waving his arms about and crying—

"O, qui me gelidis convallibus Haemi
Sistat et ingenti ramorum protegat umbra!"

"Talking German out loud to himself," said young Vickerton to his mother that night; and it is possible that he had been doing it all the time.

And while he was doing these things Priscilla was having calls paid her. Nothing could exceed her astonishment when about four o'clock, as she was sitting deep in thought and bored on the arm of a horsehair chair, Mrs. Pearce opened the door and without the least warning let in Mrs. Morrison. Priscilla had promised Fritzing for that one day to stay quietly at the farm, and for the last two hours, finding the farm of an intolerable dulness, she had been engaged in reflections of an extremely complex nature on subjects such as Duty, Will, and Personality. Her morning in the Baker fields and by the banks of that part of the Sym that meanders through them had tuned her mind to meditation. The food at one o'clock and the manner of its bringing in by Annalise—Priscilla had relieved Mrs. Pearce of that office— tuned it still more. The blended slipperiness and prickliness of all the things she tried to sit on helped surprisingly; and if I knew how far it is allowable to write of linen I could explain much of her state of mind by a description of the garments in which she was clothed that day. They were new garments taken straight from the Gerstein box. They were not even linen,—how could they be for Fritzing's three hundred marks? And their newness had not yet been exposed to the softening influence of any wash- tub. Straight did they come, in all their crackling stiffness, out of the shop and on to the Princess. Annalise had been supposed to wash them or cause them to be washed the day before, but Annalise had been far too busy crying to do anything of the sort; and by four o'clock Priscilla was goaded by them into a condition of mind so unworthy that she was thinking quite hard about the Kunitz fine linen and other flesh-pots and actually finding the recollection sweet. It was a place, Priscilla mused, where her body had been exquisitely cared for. Those delicate meals, served in spotlessness, surely they had been rather of the nature of poems? Those web-like garments, soft as a kiss, how beautiful they had been to touch and wear. True her soul had starved; yes, it had cruelly starved. But was it then—she started at her own thought—was it then being fed at Baker's?

And into the middle of this question, a tremendous one to be asked on the very threshold of the new life, walked Mrs. Morrison.

"How d'y do," said Mrs. Morrison. "The vicar asked me to come and see you. I hope the Pearces make you comfortable."

"Well I never," thought Mrs. Pearce, lingering as was her custom on the door-mat, and shaking her head in sorrow rather than in anger.

Priscilla sat for a moment staring at her visitor.

"You are Miss Schultz, are you not?" asked Mrs. Morrison rather nervously.

Priscilla said she was,—her name, that is, was Neumann-Schultz—and got up. She had the vaguest notion as to how Miss Schultz would behave under these trying circumstances, but imagined she would begin by getting up. So she got up, and the sofa being a low one and her movements leisurely, Mrs. Morrison told her husband afterwards there seemed to be no end to the girl. The girl certainly was long, and when at last unfolded and quite straightened out she towered over Mrs. Morrison, who looked up uneasily at the grave young face. Why, Mrs. Morrison asked herself, didn't the girl smile? It was the duty of a Miss Schultz called upon by the vicar's wife to smile; so profound a gravity on such an occasion was surely almost rude. Priscilla offered her hand and hoped it was all right to do so, but still she did not smile. "Are you Mrs. Morrison?" she asked.

"Yes," said Mrs. Morrison with an immense reserve in her voice.

Then Priscilla suggested she should sit down. Mrs. Morrison was already doing it; and Priscilla sank on to her sofa again and wondered what she had better say next. She wondered so much that she became lost in mazes of wonder, and there was so long a silence that Mrs. Pearce outside the door deplored an inconsiderateness that could keep her there for nothing.

"I didn't know you had a double name," said Mrs. Morrison, staring at Priscilla and trying to decide whether this was not a case for the application of leaflets and instant departure. The girl was really quite offensively pretty. She herself had been pretty—she thanked heaven that she still was so—but never, never pretty—she thanked heaven again—in this glaringly conspicuous fashion.

"My name is Ethel Maria-Theresa Neumann-Schultz," said Priscilla, very clearly and slowly; and though she was, as we know, absolutely impervious to the steadiest staring, she did wonder whether this good lady could have seen her photograph anywhere in some paper, her stare was so very round and bright and piercing.

"What a long name," said Mrs. Morrison.

"Yes," said Priscilla; and as another silence seemed imminent she added, "I have two hyphens."

"Two what?" said Mrs. Morrison, startled; and so full was her head of doubt and distrust that for one dreadful moment she thought the girl had said two husbands. "Oh, hyphens. Yes. Germans have them a good deal, I believe."

"That sounds as if we were talking about diseases," said Priscilla, a faint smile dawning far away somewhere in the depths of her eyes.

"Yes," said Mrs. Morrison, fidgeting.

Odd that Robin should have said nothing about the girl's face. Anyhow she should be kept off Netta. Better keep her off the parish-room Tuesdays as well. What in the world was she doing in Symford? She was quite the sort of girl to turn the heads of silly boys. And so unfortunate, just as Augustus Shuttleworth had taken to giving Netta little volumes of Browning.

"Is your uncle out?" she asked, some of the sharpness of her thoughts getting into her voice.

"He's gone to Minehead, to see about things for my cottage."

"Your cottage? Have you got Mrs. Shaw's, then?"

"Yes. She is being moved out to-day."

"Dear me," said Mrs. Morrison, greatly struck.

"Is it surprising?"

"Most. So unlike Lady Shuttleworth."

"She has been very kind."

"Do you know her?"

"No; but my uncle was there this morning."

"And managed to persuade her?"

"He is very eloquent," said Priscilla, with a demure downward sweep of her eyelashes.

"Just a little more," thought Mrs. Morrison, watching their dusky golden curve, "and the girl would have had scarlet hair and white-eyebrows and masses of freckles and been frightful." And she sighed an impatient sigh, which, if translated into verse, would undoubtedly have come out—

"Oh the little more and how much it is,
And the little less and what worlds away!"

"And poor old Mrs. Shaw—how does she like being turned out?"

"I believe she is being put into something that will seem to her a palace."

"Dear me, your uncle must really be very eloquent."

"I assure you that he is," said Priscilla earnestly.

There was a short pause, during which Mrs. Morrison staring straight into those unfathomable pools, Priscilla's eyes, was very angry with them for being so evidently lovely. "You are very young," she said, "so you will not mind my questions—"

"Don't the young mind questions?" asked Priscilla, for a moment supposing it to be a characteristic of the young of England.

"Not, surely, from experienced and—and married ladies," said Mrs. Morrison tartly.

"Please go on then."

"Oh, I haven't anything particular to go on about," said Mrs. Morrison, offended. "I assure you curiosity is not one of my faults."

"No?" said Priscilla, whose attention had begun to wander.

"Being human I have no doubt many failings, but I'm thankful to say curiosity isn't one of them."

"My uncle says that's just the difference between men and women. He says women might achieve just as much as men if only they were curious about things. But they're not. A man will ask a thousand questions, and never rest till he's found out as much as he can about anything he sees, and a woman is content hardly even to see it."

"I hope your uncle is a Churchman," was Mrs. Morrison's unexpected reply.

Priscilla's mind could not leap like this, and she hesitated a moment and smiled. ("It's the first time she's looked pleasant," thought Mrs. Morrison, "and now it's in the wrong place.")

"He was born, of course, in the Lutheran faith," said Priscilla.

"Oh, a horrid faith. Excuse me, but it really is. I hope he isn't going to upset Symford?"

"Upset Symford?"

"New people holding wrong tenets coming to such a small place do sometimes, you know, and you say he is eloquent. And we are such a simple and God-fearing little community. A few years ago we had a great bother with a Dissenting family that came here. The cottagers quite lost their heads."

"I think I can promise that my uncle will not try to convert anybody," said Priscilla.

"Of course you mean pervert. It would be a pity if he did. It wouldn't last, but it would give us a lot of trouble. We are very good Churchmen here. The vicar, and my son too when he's at home, set beautiful examples. My son is going into the Church himself. It has been his dearest wish from a child. He thinks of nothing else—of nothing else at all," she repeated, fixing her eyes on Priscilla with a look of defiance.

"Really?" said Priscilla, very willing to believe it.

"I assure you it's wonderful how absorbed he is in his studies for it. He reads Church history every spare moment, and he's got it so completely on his mind that I've noticed even when he whistles it's 'The Church's One Foundation.'"

"What is that?" inquired Priscilla.

"Mr. Robin Morrison," announced Mrs. Pearce.

The sitting-room at Baker's was a small, straightforward place, with no screens, no big furniture, no plants in pots, nothing that could for a moment conceal the persons already in it from the persons coming in, and Robin entering jauntily with the umbrella under his arm fell straight as it were into his mother's angry gaze. "Hullo mater, you here?" he exclaimed genially, his face broadening with apparent satisfaction.

"Yes, Robin, I am here," she said, drawing herself up.

"How do you do, Miss Schultz. I seem to have got shown into the wrong room. It's a Mr. Neumann I've come to see; doesn't he live here?"

Priscilla looked at him from her sofa seat and wondered what she had done that she should be scourged in this manner by Morrisons.

"You know my son, I believe?" said Mrs. Morrison in the stiffest voice; for the girl's face showed neither recognition nor pleasure, and though she would have been angry if she had looked unduly pleased she was still angrier that she should look indifferent.

"Yes. I met him yesterday. Did you want my uncle? His name is Neumann. Neumann-Schultz. He's out."

"I only wanted to give him this umbrella," said Robin, with a swift glance at his mother as he drew it from under his arm. Would she recognize it? He had chosen one of the most ancient; the one most appropriate, as he thought, to the general appearance of the man Neumann.

"What umbrella is that, Robin?" asked his mother suspiciously. Really, it was more than odd that Robin, whom she had left immersed in study, should have got into Baker's Farm so quickly. Could he have been expected? And had Providence, in its care for the righteous cause of mothers, brought her here just in time to save him from this girl's toils? The girl's indifference could not be real; and if it was not, her good acting only betrayed the depths of her experience and balefulness. "What umbrella is that?" asked Mrs. Morrison.

"It's his," said Robin, throwing his head back and looking at his mother as he laid it with elaborate care on the table.

"My uncle's?" said Priscilla. "Had he lost it? Oh thank you—he would have been dreadfully unhappy. Sit down." And she indicated with her head the chair she would allow him to sit on.

"The way she tells us to sit down!" thought Mrs. Morrison indignantly. "As though she were a queen." Aloud she said, "You could have sent Joyce round with it"—Joyce being that gardener whose baby's perambulator was wheeled by another Ethel—"and need not have interrupted your work."

"So I could," said Robin, as though much struck by the suggestion. "But it was a pleasure," he added to Priscilla, "to be able to return it myself. It's a frightful bore losing one's umbrella—especially if it's an old friend."

"Uncle Fritzi's looks as if it were a very old friend," said Priscilla, smiling at it.

Mrs. Morrison glanced at it too, and then glanced again. When she glanced a third time and her glance turned into a look that lingered Robin jumped up and inquired if he should not put it in the passage. "It's in the way here," he explained; though in whose way it could be was not apparent, the table being perfectly empty.

Priscilla made no objection, and he at once removed it beyond the reach of his mother's eye, propping it up in a dark corner of the passage and telling Mrs. Pearce, whom he found there that it was Mr. Neumann's umbrella.

"No it ain't," said Mrs. Pearce.

"Yes it is," said Robin.

"No it ain't. He's took his to Minehead," said Mrs. Pearce.

"It is, and he has not," said Robin.

"I see him take it," said Mrs. Pearce.

"You did not," said Robin.

This would have been the moment, Mrs. Morrison felt, for her to go and to carry off Robin with her, but she was held in her seat by the certainty that Robin would not let himself be carried off; and sooner than say good-bye and then find he was staying on alone she would sit there all night. Thus do mothers sacrifice themselves for their children, thought Mrs. Morrison, for their all too frequently thankless children. But though she would do it to any extent in order to guard her boy she need not, she said to herself, be pleasant besides,—she need not, so to speak, be the primroses on his path of dalliance. Accordingly she behaved as little like a primrose as possible, sitting in stony silence while he skirmished in the passage with Mrs. Pearce, and the instant he came in again asked him where he had found the umbrella.

"I found it—not far from the church," said Robin, desiring to be truthful as long as he could. "But mater, bother the umbrella. It isn't so very noble to bring a man back his own. Did you get your cottages?" he asked, turning quickly to Priscilla.

"Robin, are you sure it is his own?" said his mother.

"My dear mother, I'm never sure of anything. Nor are you. Nor is Miss Schultz. Nor is anybody who is really intelligent. But I found the thing, and Mr. Neumann—"

"The name to-day is Neumann-Schultz," said Mrs. Morrison, in a voice heavy with implications.

"Mr. Neumann-Schultz, then, had been that way just before, and so I felt somehow it must be his."

"Your Uncle Cox had one just like it when he stayed with us last time," remarked Mrs. Morrison.

"Had he? I say, mater, what an eye you must have for an umbrella. That must be five years ago."

"Oh, he left it behind, and I see it in the stand every time I go through the hall."

"No! Do you?" said Robin, who was hurled by this statement into the corner where his wits ended and where he probably would have stayed ignominiously, for Miss Schultz seemed hardly to be listening and really almost looked—he couldn't believe it, no girl had ever done it in his presence yet, but she did undoubtedly almost look—bored, if Mrs. Pearce had not flung open the door, and holding the torn portions of her apron bunched together in her hands, nervously announced Lady Shuttleworth.

"Oh," thought Priscilla, "what a day I'm having." But she got up and was gracious, for Fritzing had praised this lady as kind and sensible; and the moment Lady Shuttleworth set her eyes on her the mystery of her son's behaviour flashed into clearness. "Tussie's seen her!" she exclaimed inwardly; instantly adding "Upon my word I can't blame the boy."

"My dear," she said, holding Priscilla's hand, "I've come to make friends with you. See what a wise old woman I am. Frankly, I didn't want you in those cottages, but now that my son has sold them I lose no time in making friends. Isn't that true wisdom?"

"It's true niceness," said Priscilla, smiling down at the little old lady whose eyes were twinkling all over her. "I don't think you'll find us in any way a nuisance. All we want is to be quiet."

Mrs. Morrison sniffed.

"Do you really?" said Lady Shuttleworth. "Then we shall get on capitally. It's what I like best myself. And you've come too," she went on, turning to Mrs. Morrison, "to make friends with your new parishioner? Why, Robin, and you too?"

"Oh, I'm only accidental," said Robin quickly. "Only a restorer of lost property. And I'm just going," he added, beginning to make hasty adieus; for Lady Shuttleworth invariably produced a conviction in him that his clothes didn't fit and wanted brushing badly, and no young man so attentive to his appearance as Robin could be expected to enjoy that. He fled therefore, feeling that even Miss Schultz's loveliness would not make up for Lady Shuttleworth's eyes; and in the passage, from whence Mrs. Pearce had retreated, removing herself as far as might be from the awful lady to whom her father-in-law owed rent and who saw every hole, Robin pounced on his Uncle Cox's umbrella, tucked is once more beneath his arm, and bore it swiftly back to the stand where it had spent five peaceful years. "Really old women are rather terrible things," he thought as he dropped it in again. "I wonder what they're here for."

"Ah, it's there, I see," remarked his mother that night as she passed through the hall on her way to dinner.

"What is?" inquired Robin who was just behind her.

"Your Uncle Cox's umbrella."

"Dear mater, why this extreme interest in my Uncle Cox's umbrella?"

"I'm glad to see it back again, that's all. One gets so used to things."

Lady Shuttleworth and his mother—I shudder to think that it is possible Robin included his mother in the reflection about old women, but on the other hand one never can tell—had stayed on at the farm for another twenty minutes after he left. They would have stayed longer, for Lady Shuttleworth was more interested in Priscilla than she had ever been in any girl before, and Mrs. Morrison, who saw this interest and heard the kind speeches, had changed altogether from ice to amiability, crushing her leaflets in her hand and more than once expressing hopes that Miss Neumann-Schultz would soon come up to tea and learn to know and like Netta—I repeat, they would have stayed much longer, but that an extremely odd thing happened.

Priscilla had been charming; chatting with what seemed absolute frankness about her future life in the cottages, answering little questionings of Lady Shuttleworth's with a discretion and plausibility that would have warmed Fritzing's anxious heart, dwelling most, for here the ground was safest, on her uncle, his work, his gifts and character, and Lady Shuttleworth, completely fascinated, had offered her help of every sort, help in the arranging of her little home, in the planting of its garden, even in the building of those bathrooms about which Tussie had been told by Mr. Dawson. She thought the desire for many bathrooms entirely praiseworthy, and only a sign of lunacy in persons of small means. Fritzing had assured Tussie that he had money enough for the bathrooms; and if his poetic niece liked everybody about her to be nicely washed was not that a taste to be applauded? Perhaps Lady Shuttleworth expatiated on plans and probable building-costs longer than Priscilla was able to be interested; perhaps she was over-explanatory of practical details; anyhow Priscilla's attention began to wander, and she gradually became very tired of her callers. She answered in monosyllables, and her smile grew vague. Then suddenly, at the first full stop Lady Shuttleworth reached in a sentence about sanitation—the entire paragraph was never finished—she got up with her usual deliberate grace, and held out her hand.

"It has been very kind of you to come and see me," she said to the astounded lady, with a little gracious smile. "I hope you will both come again another time."

For an instant Lady Shuttleworth thought she was mad. Then to her own amazement she found her body rising obediently and letting its hand be taken.

Mrs. Morrison did the same. Both had their hands slightly pressed, both were smiled upon, and both went out at once and speechless. Priscilla stood calmly while they walked to the door, with the little smile fixed on her face.

"Is it possible we've been insulted?" burst out Mrs. Morrison when they got outside.

"I don't know," said Lady Shuttleworth, who looked extremely thoughtful.

"Do you think it can possibly be the barbarous German custom?"

"I don't know," said Lady Shuttleworth again.

And all the way to the vicarage, whither she drove Mrs. Morrison, she was very silent, and no exclamations and conjectures of that indignant lady's could get a word out of her.

X

Kunitz meanwhile was keeping strangely quiet. Not a breath, not a whisper, had reached the newspapers from that afflicted little town of the dreadful thing that had happened to it. It will be remembered that the Princess ran away on a Monday, arrived at Baker's in the small hours of Wednesday morning, and had now spent both Wednesday and Thursday in Symford. There had, then, been ample time for Europe to receive in its startled ears the news of her flight; yet Europe, judging from its silence, knew nothing at all about it. In Minehead on the Thursday evening Fritzing bought papers, no longer it is true with the frenzy he had displayed at Dover when every moment seemed packed with peril, but still with eagerness; and not a paper mentioned Kunitz. On the Saturday he did find the laconic information in the London paper he had ordered to be sent him every day that the Grand Duke of Lothen-Kunitz who was shooting in East Prussia had been joined there by that Prince—I will not reveal his august name—who had so badly wanted to marry Priscilla. And on the Sunday—it was of course the paper published in London on Saturday—he read that the Princess Priscilla of Lothen-Kunitz, the second and only unmarried daughter of the Grand Duke, was confined to her bed by a sharp attack of influenza. After that there was utter silence. Fritzing showed Priscilla the paragraph about her influenza, and she was at first very merry over it. The ease with which a princess can shake off her fetters the moment she seriously tries to surprised her, and amused her too, for a little. It surprised Fritzing, but without amusing him, for he was a man who was never amused. Indeed, I am unable to recall any single occasion on which I saw him smile. Other emotions shook him vigorously as we know, but laughter never visited him with its pleasant ticklings under the ribs; it slunk away abashed before a task so awful, and left him at his happiest to a mood of mild contentment. "Your Royal Parent," he remarked to Priscilla, "has chosen that which is ever the better part of valour, and is hushing the incident up."

"He never loved me," said Priscilla, wistfully. On thinking it over she was not quite sure that she liked being allowed to run away so easily. Did nobody care, then, what became of her? Was she of positively no value at all? Running away is all very well, but your pride demands that those runned from shall at least show some sign of not liking it, make some effort, however humble, to fetch you back. If they do not, if they remain perfectly quiescent and resigned, not even sending forth a wail that shall be audible, you are naturally extremely crushed. "My father," said Priscilla bitterly, "doesn't care a bit. He'll give out I'm dangerously ill, and then you'll see, Fritzi—I shall either die, or be sent away for an interminable yachting cruise with the Countess. And so dust will be thrown in people's eyes. My father is very good at that, and the Countess is a perfect genius. You'll see."

But Fritzing never saw, for there was no more mention at all either of Kunitz or of influenza. And just then he was so much taken up by his efforts to get into the cottages as quickly as possible that after a passing feeling of thankfulness that the Grand Duke should be of such a convenient indifference to his daughter's fate it dropped from his mind in the easy fashion in which matters of importance always did drop from it. What was the use, briefly reflected this philosopher, of worrying about what they were or were not thinking at Kunitz? There would be time enough for that when they actually began to do something. He felt very safe from Kunitz in the folds of the Somerset hills, and as the days passed calmly by he felt still safer. But though no dangers seemed to threaten from without there were certain dangers within that made it most desirable for them to get away from Baker's and into their own little home without a moment's unnecessary delay. He could not always be watching his tongue, and he found for instance that it positively refused to call the Princess Ethel. It had an almost equal objection to addressing her as niece; and it had a most fatal habit of slipping out Grand Ducal Highnesses. True, at first they mostly talked German together, but the tendency to talk English grew more marked every day; it was in the air they breathed, and they both could talk it so fatally well. Up at the cottages among the workmen, or when they were joined by Mr. Dawson, grown zealous to help, or by either of the young men Robin and Tussie, who seemed constantly to be passing, the danger too was great. Fritzing was so conscious of it that he used to break out into perspirations whenever Priscilla was with him in public, and his very perspirations were conspicuous. The strain made his manner oddly nervous when speaking to or of his niece, and he became the subject of much conjecture to the observant Robin. Robin thought that in spite of her caressing ways with her uncle the girl must be privately a dreadful tyrant. It seemed difficult to believe, but Robin prided himself on being ready to believe anything at a moment's notice, especially if it was the worst, and he called it having an open mind. The girl was obviously the most spoilt of girls. No one could help seeing that. Her least wish seemed to be for the uncle a command that was not even to be talked about. Yet the uncle was never openly affectionate to her. It almost seemed as though she must have some secret hold over him, be in possession, perhaps, of some fact connected with a guilty past. But then this girl and guilty pasts! Why, from the look in her eyes she could never even have heard of such things. Robin thought himself fairly experienced in knowledge of human nature, but he had to admit that he had never yet met so incomprehensible a pair. He wanted to talk to Tussie Shuttleworth about them, but Tussie would not talk. To Tussie it seemed impossible to talk about Priscilla because she was sacred to him, and she was sacred to him because he adored her so. He adored her to an extent that amazes me to think of, worshipping her beauty with all the headlong self-abasement of a very young man who is also a poet. His soul was as wax within him, softest wax punched all over with little pictures of Priscilla. No mother is happy while her child's soul is in this state, and though he was extremely decent, and hid it and smothered it and choked it with all the energy he possessed, Lady Shuttleworth knew very well what was going on inside him and spent her spare time trying to decide whether to laugh or to cry over her poor Tussie. "When does Robin go back to Cambridge?" she asked Mrs. Morrison the next time she met her, which was in the front garden of a sick old woman's cottage.

Mrs. Morrison was going in with a leaflet; Lady Shuttleworth was going in with a pound of tea. From this place they could see Priscilla's cottage, and Robin was nailing up its creepers in the sight of all Symford.

"Ah—I know what you mean," said Mrs. Morrison quickly.

"It is always such a pity to see emotions wasted," said Lady Shuttleworth slowly, as if weighing each word.

"Wasted? You do think she's an adventuress, then?" said Mrs. Morrison eagerly.

"Sh-sh. My dear, how could I think anything so unkind? But we who are old"—Mrs. Morrison jerked up her chin—"and can look on calmly, do see the pity of it when beautiful emotions are lavished and wasted. So much force, so much time frittered away in dreams. And all so useless, so barren. Nothing I think is so sad as waste, and nothing is so wasteful as a one-sided love."

Mrs. Morrison gave the pink tulle bow she liked to wear in the afternoons at her throat an agitated pat, and tried to conceal her misery that Augustus Shuttleworth should also have succumbed to Miss Neumann-Schultz. That he had done so was very clear from Lady Shuttleworth's portentous remarks, for it was not in human nature for a woman to be thus solemn about the wasted emotions of other people's sons. His doing so might save Robin's future, but it would ruin Netta's. We all have our little plans for the future—dear rosy things that we dote on and hug to our bosoms with more tenderness even than we hug the babies of our bodies, and the very rosiest and best developed of Mrs. Morrison's darling plans was the marriage of her daughter Netta with the rich young man Augustus. It was receiving a rude knock on its hopeful little head at this moment in old Mrs. Jones's front garden, and naturally the author of its being winced.

Augustus, she feared, must be extremely far gone in love, and it was not likely that the girl would let such a chance go. It was a consolation that the marriage would be a scandal,—this person from nowhere, this niece of a German teacher, carrying off the wealthiest young man in the county. The ways of so-called Providence were quite criminally inscrutable, she thought, in stark defiance of what a vicar's wife should think; but then she was greatly goaded.

Priscilla herself came out of Mrs. Jones's door at that moment with a very happy face. She had succeeded in comforting the sick woman to an extent that surprised her. The sick woman had cheered up so suddenly and so much that Priscilla, delighted, had at once concluded that work among the sick poor was her true vocation. And how easy it had been! A few smiles, a few kind words, a five-pound note put gently into the withered old hands, and behold the thing was done. Never was sick woman so much comforted as Mrs. Jones. She who had been disinclined to speak above a whisper when Priscilla went in was able at the end of the visit to pour forth conversation in streams, and quite loud conversation, and even interspersed with chuckles. All Friday Priscilla had tried to help in the arranging of her cottage, and had made herself and Fritzing so tired over it that on Saturday she let him go up alone and decided that she would, for her part, now begin to do good to the people in the village. It was what she intended to do in future. It was to be the chief work of her new life. She was going to live like the poor and among them, smooth away their sorrows and increase their joys, give them, as it were, a cheery arm along the rough path of poverty, and in doing it get down herself out of the clouds to the very soil, to the very beginnings and solid elementary facts of life. And she would do it at once, and not sit idle at the farm. It was on such idle days as the day Fritzing went to Minehead that sillinesses assailed her soul—shrinkings of the flesh from honest calico, disgust at the cooking, impatience at Annalise's swollen eyes. Priscilla could have cried that night when she went to bed, if she had not held tears in scorn, at the sickliness of her spirit, her spirit that she had thought more than able to keep her body in subjection, that she had hoped was unalterably firm and brave. But see the uses of foolishness,—the reaction from it is so great that it sends us with a bound twice as far again along the right road as we were while we were wise and picking our way with clean shoes slowly among the puddles. Who does not know that fresh impulse, so strong and gracious, towards good that surges up in us after a period of sitting still in mud? What an experience it is, that vigorous shake and eager turning of our soiled face once more towards the blessed light. "I will arise and go to my Father"—of all the experiences of the spirit surely this is the most glorious; and behold the prudent, the virtuous, the steadfast—dogged workers in the vineyard in the heat of the day—are shut out from it for ever.

Priscilla had not backslided much; but short as her tarrying had been among the puddles she too sprang forward after it with renewed strength along the path she had chosen as the best, and having completed the second of her good works—the first had been performed just previously, and had been a warm invitation made personally from door to door to all the Symford mothers to send their children to tea and games at Baker's Farm the next day, which was Sunday—she came away very happy from the comforted Mrs. Jones, and met the two arriving comforters in the front garden.

Now Priscilla's and Mrs. Jones's last words together had been these:

"Is there anything else I can do for you?" Priscilla had asked, leaning over the old lady and patting her arm in farewell.

"No, deary—you've done enough already, God bless your pretty face," said Mrs. Jones, squeezing the five-pound note ecstatically in her hands.

"But isn't there anything you'd like? Can't I get you anything? See, I can run about and you are here in bed. Tell me what I can do."

Mrs. Jones blinked and worked her mouth and blinked again and wheezed and cleared her throat. "Well, I do know of something would comfort me," she said at last, amid much embarrassed coughing.

"Tell me," said Priscilla.

"I don't like," coughed Mrs. Jones.

"Tell me," said Priscilla.

"I'll whisper it, deary."

Priscilla bent down her head, and the old lady put her twitching mouth to her ear.

"Why, of course," said Priscilla smiling, "I'll go and get you some at once."

"Now God for ever bless your beautiful face, darlin'!" shrilled Mrs. Jones, quite beside herself with delight. "The Cock and 'Ens, deary—that's the place. And the quart bottles are the best; one gets more comfort out of them, and they're the cheapest in the end."

And Priscilla issuing forth on this errand met the arriving visitors in the garden.

"How do you do," she said in a happy voice, smiling gaily at both of them. She had seen neither since she had dismissed them, but naturally she had never given that strange proceeding a thought.

"Oh—how do you do," said Lady Shuttleworth, surprised to see her there, and with a slight and very unusual confusion of manner.

Mrs. Morrison said nothing but stood stiffly in the background, answering Priscilla's smile with a stern, reluctant nod.

"I've been talking to poor old Mrs. Jones. Your son"—she looked at Mrs. Morrison—"told me how ill she was."

"Did he?" said Mrs. Morrison, hardly raising her eyes a moment from the ground. This girl was her double enemy: bound, whatever she did, to make either a fool of her son or of her daughter.

"So I went in and tried to cheer her up. And I really believe I did."

"Well that was very kind of you," said Lady Shuttleworth, smiling in spite of herself, unable to withstand the charm of Priscilla's personality. How supremely ridiculous of Mrs. Morrison to think that this girl was an adventuress. Such are the depths of ignorance one can descend to if one is buried long enough in the country.

"Now," said Priscilla cheerfully, "she wants rum, and I'm just going to buy her some."

"Rum?" cried Lady Shuttleworth in a voice of horror; and Mrs. Morrison started violently.

"Is it bad for her?" said Priscilla, surprised.

"Bad!" cried Lady Shuttleworth.

"It is," said Mrs. Morrison with her eyes on the ground, "poison for both body and soul."

"Dear me," said Priscilla, her face falling. "Why, she said it would comfort her."

"It will poison both her body and her soul," repeated Mrs. Morrison grimly.

"My dear," said Lady Shuttleworth, "our efforts are all directed towards training our people to keep from drinking."

"But she doesn't want to drink," said Priscilla. "She only wants to taste it now and then. I'm afraid she's dying. Mustn't she die happy?"

"It is our duty," said Mrs. Morrison, "to see that our parishioners die sober."

"But I've promised," said Priscilla.

"Did she—did she ask for it herself?" asked Lady Shuttleworth, a great anxiety in her voice.

"Yes, and I promised."

Both the women looked very grave. Mrs. Jones, who was extremely old and certainly dying—not from any special disease but from mere inability to go on living—had been up to this a shining example to Symford of the manner in which Christian old ladies ought to die. As such she was continually quoted by the vicar's wife, and Lady Shuttleworth had felt an honest pride in this ordered and seemly death-bed. The vicar went every day and sat with her and said that he came away refreshed. Mrs. Morrison read her all those of her leaflets that described the enthusiasm with which other good persons behave in a like case. Lady Shuttleworth never drove through the village without taking her some pleasant gift—tea, or fruit, or eggs, or even little pots of jam, to be eaten discreetly and in spoonfuls. She also paid a woman to look in at short intervals during the day and shake up her pillow. Kindness and attention and even affection could not, it will be admitted, go further; all three had been heaped on Mrs. Jones with generous hands; and in return she had expressed no sentiments that were not appropriate, and never, never had breathed the faintest suggestion to any of her benefactors that what she really wanted most was rum. It shocked both the women inexpressibly, and positively pained Lady Shuttleworth. Mrs. Morrison privately believed Priscilla had put the idea into the old lady's head, and began to regard her in something of the light of a fiend.

"Suppose," said Priscilla, "we look upon it as medicine."

"But my dear, it is not medicine," said Lady Shuttleworth.

"It is poison," repeated Mrs. Morrison.

"How can it be if it does her so much good? I must keep my promise. I wouldn't disappoint her for the world. If only you'd seen her delight"—they quivered—"you'd agree that she mustn't be disappointed, poor old dying thing. Why, it might kill her. But suppose we treat it as a medicine, and I lock up the bottle and go round and give her a little myself three or four times a day—wouldn't that be a good plan? Surely it couldn't hurt?"

"There is no law to stop you," said Mrs. Morrison; and Lady Shuttleworth stared at the girl in silent dismay.

"I can try it at least," said Priscilla; "and if I find it's really doing her harm I'll leave off. But I promised, and she's expecting it now every minute. I can't break my promise. Do tell me—is the Cock and Hens that inn round the corner? She told me it was best there."

"But you cannot go yourself to the Cock and Hens and buy rum," exclaimed Lady Shuttleworth, roused to energy; and her voice was full of so determined a protest that the vicar's wife, who thought it didn't matter at all where such a young woman went, received a fresh shock.

"Why not?" inquired Priscilla.

"My dear, sooner than you should do that I'll—I'll go and buy it myself," cried Lady Shuttleworth.

"Gracious heavens," thought Mrs. Morrison, perfectly staggered by this speech. Had Lady Shuttleworth suddenly lost her reason? Or was she already accepting the girl as her son's wife? Priscilla looked at her a moment with grave eyes. "Is it because I'm a girl that I mustn't?" she asked.

"Yes. For one thing. But—" Lady Shuttleworth shut her mouth.

"But what?" asked Priscilla.

"Oh, nothing."

"If it's not the custom of the country for a girl to go I'll send Mr. Morrison," said Priscilla.

"Send Mr. Morrison?" gasped the vicar's wife.

"What, the vicar?" exclaimed Lady Shuttleworth.

"No, no," said Priscilla smiling, "young Mr. Morrison. I see him over there tying up my creepers. He's so kind. He'll go. I'll ask him."

And nodding good-bye she hurried out of the garden and over to her cottage, almost running in her desire not to keep Mrs. Jones any longer in suspense.

The two women, rooted to the ground, watched her as if fascinated, saw her speak to Robin on his ladder, saw how he started and dropped his nails, saw how nimbly he clambered down, and how after the shortest parley the infatuated youth rushed away at once in the direction of the Cock and Hens. The only thing they did not see from where they stood was the twinkle in his eye.

"I don't think," murmured Lady Shuttleworth, "I don't think, my dear, that I quite care to go in to Mrs. Jones to-day. I—I think I'll go home."

"So shall I," said Mrs. Morrison, biting her lips to keep them steady. "I shall go and speak to the vicar."

XI

What she meant by speaking to the vicar was a vigorous stirring of him up to wrath; but you cannot stir up vicars if they are truly good. The vicar was a pious and patient old man, practiced in forgiveness, in overlooking, in waiting, in trying again. Always slow to anger, as the years drew him more and more apart into the shadows of old age and he watched from their clear coolness with an ever larger comprehension the younger generations striving together in the heat, he grew at last unable to be angered at all. The scriptural injunction not to let the sun go down upon your wrath had no uses for him, for he possessed no wrath for the sun to go down upon. He had that lovable nature that sees the best in everything first, and then prefers to look no further. He took for granted that people were at bottom good and noble, and the assumption went a long way towards making them so. Robin, for instance, was probably saved by his father's unclouded faith in him. Mrs. Morrison, a woman who had much trouble with herself, having come into the world with the wings of the angel in her well glued down and prevented from spreading by a multitude of little defects, had been helped without her knowing it by his example out of many a pit of peevishness and passion. Who shall measure the influence of one kind and blameless life? His wife, in her gustier moments, thought it sheer weakness, this persistent turning away from evil, this refusal to investigate and dissect, to take sides, to wrestle. The evil was there, and it was making an ostrich or a vegetable of one's self to go on being calm in the face of it. With the blindness of wives, who are prevented from seeing clearly by the very closeness of the object—the same remark exactly applies to husbands—she did not see that the vicar was the candle shining in a naughty world, that he was the leaven that leaveneth the whole lump. And just as leaven leavens by its mere presence in the lump, by merely passively being there, and will go on doing it so long as there is a lump to leaven, so had the vicar, more than his hardworking wife, more than the untiring Lady Shuttleworth, more than any district visitor, parish nurse, or other holy person, influenced Symford by simply living in it in a way that would have surprised him had he known. There is a great virtue in sweeping out one's own house and trimming its lamps before starting on the house and lamps of a neighbour; and since new dust settles every day, and lamps, I believe, need constant trimming, I know not when the truly tidy soul will have attained so perfect a spotlessness as to justify its issuing forth to attack the private dust of other people. And if it ever did, lo, it would find the necessity no longer there. Its bright untiringness would unconsciously have done its work, and every dimmer soul within sight of that cheerful shining been strengthened and inspired to go and do likewise.

But Mrs. Morrison, who saw things differently, was constantly trying to stir up storms in the calm waters of the vicar's mind; and after the episode in Mrs. Jones's front garden she made a very determined effort to get him to rebuke Priscilla. Her own indignation was poured out passionately. The vicar was surprised at her heat, he who was so beautifully cool himself, and though he shook his head over Mrs. Jones's rum he also smiled as he shook it. Nor was he more reasonable about Robin. On the contrary, he declared that he would think mightily little of a young man who did not immediately fall head over ears in love with such a pretty girl.

"You don't mind our boy's heart being broken, then?" questioned his wife bitterly; of her plans for Netta she had never cared to speak.

"My dear, if it is to be broken there is no young lady I would sooner entrust with the job."

"You don't mind his marrying an adventuress, then?"

"My dear, I know of no adventuress."

"You rather like our old people to be tempted to drink, to have it thrust upon them on their very dying beds?"

"Kate, are you not bitter?"

"Psha," said his wife, drumming her foot.

"Psha, Kate?" inquired the vicar mildly; and it is not always that the saintly produce a soothing effect on their wives.

It really seemed as if the girl were to have her own way in Symford, unchecked even by Lady Shuttleworth, whose attitude was entirely incomprehensible. She was to be allowed to corrupt the little hamlet that had always been so good, to lead it astray, to lure it down paths of forbidden indulgence, to turn it topsy turvy to an extent not even reached by the Dissenting family that had given so much trouble a few years before. It was on the Sunday morning as the church bells were ringing, that Mrs. Morrison, prayer-book in hand, looked in at Mrs. Jones's on her way to service and discovered the five-pound note.

The old lady was propped up in bed with her open Bible on her lap and her spectacles lying in it, and as usual presented to her visitor the perfect realization of her ideal as to the looks and manners most appropriate to ailing Christians. There was nowhere a trace of rum, and the only glass in the room was innocently filled with the china roses that flowered so profusely in the garden at Baker's Farm. But Mrs. Morrison could not for all that dissemble the disappointment and sternness of her heart, and the old lady glanced up at her as she came in with a kind of quavering fearfulness, like that of a little child who is afraid it may be going to be whipped, or of a conscientious dog who has lapsed unaccountably from rectitude.

"I have come to read the gospel for the day to you," said Mrs. Morrison, sitting down firmly beside her.

"Thank you mum," said Mrs. Jones with meekness.

"My prayer-book has such small print—give me your Bible."

A look of great anxiety came into Mrs. Jones's eyes, but the Bible was drawn from between her trembling old hands, and Mrs. Morrison began to turn its pages. She had not turned many before she came to the five-pound note. "What is this?" she asked, in extreme surprise.

Mrs. Jones gave a little gasp, and twisted her fingers about.

"A five-pound note?" exclaimed Mrs. Morrison, holding it up. "How did it come here?"

"It's mine, mum," quavered Mrs. Jones.

"Yours? Do you mean to say you have money hidden away and yet allow Lady Shuttleworth to pay everything for you?"

"It's the first I ever 'ad, mum," faintly murmured the old lady, her eyes following every movement of Mrs. Morrison's hands with a look of almost animal anxiety.

"Where did it come from?"

"The young lady give it me yesterday, mum."

"The young lady?" Mrs. Morrison's voice grew very loud. "Do you mean the person staying at the Pearces'?"

Mrs. Jones gulped, and feebly nodded.

"Most improper. Most wrong. Most dangerous. You cannot tell how she came by it, and I must say I'm surprised at you, Mrs. Jones. It probably is not a real one. It is unlikely a chit like that should be able to give so large a sum away—" And Mrs. Morrison held up the note to the light and turned it round and round, scrutinizing it from every point of view, upside down, back to front, sideways, with one eye shut; but it refused to look like anything but a good five-pound note, and she could only repeat grimly "Most dangerous."

The old lady watched her, a terrible anxiety in her eyes. Her worst fears were fulfilled when the vicar's wife folded it up and said decidedly, "For the present I shall take care of it for you. You cannot lie here with so much money loose about the place. Why, if it got round the village you might have some one in who'd murder you. People have been murdered before now for less than this. I shall speak to the vicar about it." And she put it in her purse, shut it with a snap, and took up the Bible again.

Mrs. Jones made a little sound between a gasp and a sob. Her head rolled back on the pillow, and two tears dropped helplessly down the furrows of her face. In that moment she felt the whole crushing misery of being weak, and sick, and old,—so old that you have outlived your claims to everything but the despotic care of charitable ladies, so old that you are a mere hurdy-gurdy, expected each time any one in search of edification chooses to turn your handle to quaver out tunes of immortality. It is a bad thing to be very old. Of all the bad things life forces upon us as we pass along it is the last and worst—the bitterness at the bottom of the cup, the dregs of what for many was after all always only medicine. Mrs. Jones had just enough of the strength of fear left to keep quite still while the vicar's wife read the Gospel in a voice that anger made harsh; but when she had gone, after a parting admonition and a dreadful assurance that she would come again soon, the tears rolled unchecked and piteous, and it was a mercy that Priscilla also took it into her head to look in on her way to church, for if she had not I don't know who would have dried them for this poor baby of eighty-five. And I regret to say that Priscilla's ideas of doing good were in such a state of crudeness that she had no sooner mastered the facts brokenly sobbed out than she ran to the cupboard and gave Mrs. Jones a tablespoonful of rum for the strengthening of her body and then took out her purse and gave her another five-pound note for the comforting of her soul. And then she wiped her eyes, and patted her, and begged her not to mind. Such conduct was, I suppose, what is called indiscriminate charity and therefore blameworthy, but its effect was great. Priscilla went to church with the reflection of the old lady's wonder and joy shining in her own face. "Hide it," had been her last words at the door, her finger on her lips, her head nodding expressively in the direction of the vicarage; and by this advice she ranged herself once and for all on the opposite side to Mrs. Morrison and the followers of obedience and order. Mrs. Jones would certainly have taken her for an angel working miracles with five-pound notes and an inexhaustible pocket if it had not been for the rum; even in her rapture she did feel that a genuine angel would be incapable of any really harmonious combination with rum. But so far had she fallen from the kind of thinking that the vicar's wife thought proper in a person so near her end that she boldly told herself she preferred Priscilla.

Now this was the day of Priscilla's children's party, and though all Symford had been talking of it for twenty-four hours the news of it had not yet reached Mrs. Morrison's ears. The reason was that Symford talked in whispers, only too sure that the authorities would consider it wrong for it to send its children a-merrymaking on a Sunday, and desperately afraid lest the forbidden cup should be snatched from its longing lips. But the news did get to Mrs. Morrison's ears, and it got to them in the porch of the church as she was passing in to prayer. She had it from an overgrown girl who was waiting outside for her father, and who was really much too big for children's parties but had got an invitation by looking wistful at the right moment.

"Emma," said Mrs. Morrison in passing, "you have not returned the book I lent you. Bring it up this afternoon."

"Please mum, I'll bring it to-morrow, mum," said the girl, curtseying and turning red.

"No, Emma, you will do as I direct. One can never be too particular about returning books. You have kept it an unconscionable time. You will bring it to the vicarage at four o'clock."

"Please mum, I—I can't at four o'clock."

"And pray, Emma, what is to prevent you?"

"I—I'm going to Baker's, mum."

"Going to Baker's? Why are you going to Baker's, Emma?"

So it all came out.

The bells were just stopping, and Mrs. Morrison, who played the organ, was forced to hurry in without having told Emma her whole opinion of those who gave and those who attended Sunday parties, but the prelude she played that day expressed the tumult of her mind very well, and struck Tussie Shuttleworth, who had sensitive ears, quite cold. He was the only person in the church acutely sensitive to sound, and it was very afflicting to him, this plunging among the pedals, this angry shrieking of stops no man ever yet had heard together. The very blower seemed frightened, and blew in gasps; and the startled Tussie, comparing the sounds to the clamourings of a fiend in pain, could not possibly guess they were merely the musical expression of the state of a just woman's soul.

Mrs. Morrison's anger was perfectly proper. It had been the conscientious endeavour of twenty-five solid years of her life to make of Symford a model parish, and working under Lady Shuttleworth, whose power was great since all the cottages were her son's and were lived in by his own labourers, it had been kept in a state of order so nearly perfect as to raise it to the position of an example to the adjoining parishes. The church was full, the Sunday-school well attended, the Sabbath was kept holy, the women were one and all sober and thrifty, the men were fairly satisfactory except on Saturday nights, there was no want, little sickness, and very seldom downright sin. The expression downright sin is Mrs. Morrison's own,—heaven forbid that I should have anything to do with such an expression—and I suppose she meant by it thieving, murder, and other grossnesses that would bring the sinner, as she often told her awe-struck Dorcas class, to infallible gallows, and the sinner's parents' grey hairs to sorrowful graves. "Please mum, will the parents go too?" asked a girl one day who had listened breathlessly, an inquiring-minded girl who liked to get to the root of things.

"Go where, Bessie?"

"With the grey hairs, mum."

Mrs. Morrison paused a moment and fixed a searching gaze on Bessie's face. Then she said with much dignity, "The parents, Bessie, will naturally follow the hairs." And to a girl bred in the near neighbourhood of Exmoor it sounded very sporting.

Into this innocent, frugal, well-managed hamlet Priscilla dropped suddenly from nowhere, trailing with her thunder-clouds of impulsive and childish ideas about doing good, and holding in her hands the dangerous weapon of wealth. It is hard to stand by and see one's life-work broken up before one's eyes by an irresponsible stranger, a foreigner, a girl, a young girl, a pretty girl; especially hard if one was born with an unbending character, tough and determined, ambitious and vain. These are not reproaches being piled up on the vicar's wife; who shall dare reproach another? And how could she help being born so? We would all if we could be born good and amiable and beautiful, and remain so perpetually during our lives; and she too was one of God's children, and inside her soul, behind the crust of failings that hindered it during these years from coming out, sat her bright angel, waiting. Meanwhile she was not a person to watch the destruction of her hopes without making violent efforts to stop it; and immediately she had played the vicar into the vestry after service that Sunday she left the congregation organless and hurried away into the churchyard. There she stood and waited for the villagers to question them about this unheard of thing; and it was bad to see how they melted away in other directions,—out at unused gates, making detours over the grass, visiting the long-neglected graves of relatives, anywhere rather than along the ordinary way, which was the path where the vicar's wife stood. At last came Mrs. Vickerton the postmistress. She was deep in conversation with the innkeeper's wife, and did not see the figure on the path in time to melt away herself. If she had she certainly would have melted, for though she had no children but her grown-up son she felt very guilty; for it was her son who had been sent the afternoon before to Minehead by Priscilla with a list as long as his arm of the cakes and things to be ordered for the party. "Oh Mrs. Morrison, I didn't see you," she exclaimed, starting and smiling and turning red. She was a genteel woman who called no one mum.

The innkeeper's wife slipped deftly away among graves.

"Is it true that the children are going to Baker's Farm this afternoon?" asked Mrs. Morrison, turning and walking grimly by Mrs. Vickerton.

"I did hear something about it, Mrs. Morrison," said Mrs. Vickerton, hiding her agitation behind a series of smiles with sudden endings.

"All?"

"I did hear they pretty well all thought of it," said Mrs. Vickerton, coughing. "Beautiful weather, isn't it, Mrs. Morrison."

"They are to have tea there?"

Mrs. Vickerton gazed pleasantly at the clouds and the tree-tops. "I should think there might be tea, Mrs. Morrison," she said; and the vision of that mighty list of cakes rising before her eyes made her put up her hand and cough again.

"Have the parents lost their senses?"

"I couldn't say—I really couldn't say, Mrs. Morrison."

"Have they forgotten the commandments?"

"Oh I 'ope not, Mrs. Morrison."

"And the vicar's teaching? And the good habits of years?"

"Oh, Mrs. Morrison."

"I never heard of anything more disgraceful. Disgraceful to the giver and to those who accept. Wicked, scandalous, and unscriptural."

"We all 'oped you'd see no harm in it, Mrs. Morrison. It's a fine day, and they'll just have tea, and perhaps—sing a little, and they don't get treats often this time of year."

"Why, it's disgraceful—disgraceful anywhere to have a treat on a Sunday; but in a parish like this it is scandalous. When Lady Shuttleworth hears of it I quite expect she'll give everybody notice to quit."

"Notice to quit? Oh I hope not, Mrs. Morrison. And she do know about it. She heard it last night. And Sir Augustus himself has promised the young lady to go and help."

"Sir Augustus?"

"And we all think it so kind of him, and so kind of the young lady too," said Mrs. Vickerton, gathering courage.

"Sir Augustus?" repeated Mrs. Morrison. Then a horrid presentiment laid cold fingers on her heart. "Is any one else going to help?" she asked quickly.

"Only the young lady's uncle, and—"

Mrs. Vickerton hesitated, and looked at the vicar's wife with a slightly puzzled air.

"And who?"

"Of course Mr. Robin."

XII

It is the practice of Providence often to ignore the claims of poetic justice. Properly, the Symford children ought to have been choked by Priscilla's cakes; and if they had been, the parents who had sent them merrymaking on a Sunday would have been well punished by the undeniable awfulness of possessing choked children. But nobody was choked; and when in the early days of the following week there were in nearly every cottage pangs being assuaged, they were so naturally the consequence of the strange things that had been eaten that only Mrs. Morrison was able to see in them weapons being wielded by Providence in the cause of eternal right. She, however, saw it so plainly that each time during the next few days that a worried mother came and asked advice, she left her work or her meals without a murmur, and went to the castor-oil cupboard with an alacrity that was almost cheerful; and seldom, I suppose, have such big doses been supplied and administered as the ones she prescribed for suffering Symford.

But on this dark side of the picture I do not care to look; the party, anyhow, had been a great success, and Priscilla became at one stroke as popular among the poor of Symford as she had been in Lothen-Kunitz. Its success it is true was chiefly owing to the immense variety of things to eat she had provided; for the conjuror, merry-go-round, and cocoa-nuts to be shied at that she had told young Vickerton to bring with him from Minehead, had all been abandoned on Tussie's earnest advice, who instructed her innocent German mind that these amusements, undoubtedly admirable in themselves and on week days, were looked upon askance in England on Sundays.

"Why?" asked Priscilla, in great surprise.

"It's not keeping the day holy," said Tussie, blushing.

"How funny," said Priscilla.

"Oh, I don't know."

"Why," said Priscilla, "in Kun—" but she pulled herself up just as she was about to give him a description of the varied nature of Sunday afternoons in Kunitz.

"You must have noticed," said Tussie, "as you have lived so long in London, that everything's shut on Sundays. There are no theatres and things—certainly no cocoa-nuts."

"No, I don't remember any cocoa-nuts," mused Priscilla, her memory going over those past Sundays she had spent in England.

Tussie tried to make amends for having obstructed her plans by exerting himself to the utmost to entertain the children as far as decorum allowed. He encouraged them to sing, he who felt every ugliness in sound like a blow; he urged them to recite for prizes of sixpences, he on whose soul Casabianca and Excelsior had much the effect of scourges on a tender skin; he led them out into a field between tea and supper and made them run races, himself setting the example, he who caught cold so easily that he knew it probably meant a week in bed. Robin helped too, but his exertions were confined to the near neighbourhood of Priscilla. His mother had been very angry with him, and he had been very angry with his mother for being angry, and he had come away from the vicarage with a bad taste in his mouth and a great defiance in his heart. It was the first time he had said hard things to her, and it had been a shocking moment,—a moment sometimes inevitable in the lives of parents and children of strong character and opposed desires. He had found himself quite unable in his anger to clothe his hard sayings in forms of speech that would have hidden their brutal force, and he had turned his back at last on her answering bitterness and fled to Baker's, thankful to find when he got there that Priscilla's beauty and the interest of the mystery that hung about her wiped out every other remembrance.

Priscilla was in the big farm kitchen, looking on at the children having tea. That was all she did at her party, except go round every now and then saying pleasant little things to each child; but this going round was done in so accomplished a manner, she seemed so used to it, was so well provided with an apparently endless supply of appropriate remarks, was so kind, and yet so—what was the word? could it be mechanical?—that Robin for the hundredth time found himself pondering over something odd, half-remembered, elusive about the girl. Then there was the uncle; manifestly a man who had never before been required to assist at a school-treat, manifestly on this occasion an unhappy man, yet look how he worked while she sat idly watching, look how he laboured round with cakes and bread-and-butter, clumsily, strenuously, with all the heat and anxiety of one eager to please and obey. Yes, that was what he did; Robin had hit on it at last. This extraordinary uncle obeyed his niece; and Robin knew very well that Germany was the last country in the world to produce men who did that. Had he not a cousin who had married a German officer? A whilom gay and sprightly cousin, who spent her time, as she dolefully wrote, having her mind weeded of its green growth of little opinions and gravelled and rolled and stamped with the opinions of her male relations-in-law. "And I'd rather have weeds than gravel," she wrote at the beginning of this process when she was still restive under the roller, "for they at least are green." But long ago she had left off complaining, long ago she too had entered into the rest that remaineth for him who has given up, who has become what men praise as reasonable and gods deplore as dull, who is tired of bothering, tired of trying, tired of everything but sleep. Then there was the girl's maid. This was the first time Robin had seen her; and while she was helping Mrs. Pearce pour out cups of chocolate and put a heaped spoonful of whipped cream on the top of each cup in the fashion familiar to Germans and altogether lovely in the eyes of the children of Symford, Robin went to her and offered help.

Annalise looked at him with heavy eyes, and shook her head.

"She don't speak no English, sir," explained Mrs. Pearce. "This one's pure heathen."

"No English," echoed Annalise drearily, who had at least learned that much, "no English, no English."

Robin gathered up his crumbs of German and presented them to her with a smile. Immediately on hearing her own tongue she flared into life, and whipping out a little pocket-book and pencil asked him eagerly where she was.

"Where you are?" repeated Robin, astonished.

"*Ja, Ja.* The address. This address. What is it? Where am I?"

"What, don't you know?"

"Tell me—quick," begged Annalise.

"But why—I don't understand. You must know you are in England?"

"England! Naturally I know it is England. But this—where is it? What is its address? For letters to reach me? Quick—tell me quick!"

Robin, however, would not be quick. "Why has no one told you?" he asked, with an immense curiosity.

"*Ach*, I have not been told. I know nothing. I am kept in the dark like—like a prisoner." And Annalise dragged her handkerchief out of her pocket, and put it to her eyes just in time to stop her ready tears from falling into the whipped cream and spoiling it.

"There she goes again," sniffed Mrs. Pearce. "It's cry, cry, from morning till night, and nothing good enough for her. It's a mercy she goes out of this to-morrow. I never see such an image."

"Tell me," implored Annalise, "tell me quick, before my mistress—"

"I'll write it for you," said Robin, taking the note-book from her. "You know you go into a cottage next week, so I'll put your new address." And he wrote it in a large round hand and gave it to her quickly, for Mrs. Pearce was listening to all this German and watching him write with a look that made him feel cheap. So cheap did it make him feel that he resisted for the present his desire to go on questioning Annalise, and putting his hands in his pockets sauntered away to the other end of the kitchen where Priscilla sat looking on. "I'm afraid that really was cheap of me," he thought ruefully, when he came once more into Priscilla's sweet presence; but he comforted himself with the reflection that no girl ought to be mysterious, and if this one chose to be so it was fair to cross her plans occasionally. Yet he went on feeling cheap; and when Tussie who was hurrying along with a cup of chocolate in each hand ran into him and spilt some on his sleeve the sudden rage with which he said "Confound you, Tussie," had little to do with the hot stuff soaking through to his skin and a great deal with the conviction that Tussie, despised from their common childhood for his weakness, smallness and ugliness, would never have done what he had just done and betrayed what the girl had chosen to keep secret from her maid.

"But why secret? Why? Why?" asked Robin, torn with desire to find out all about Priscilla.

"I'm going to do this often," said Priscilla, looking up at him with a pleased smile. "I never saw such easily amused little creatures. Don't you think it is beautiful, to give poor people a few happy moments sometimes?"

"Very beautiful," said Robin, his eyes on her face.

"It is what I mean to do in future," she said dreamily, her chin on her hand.

"It will be expensive," remarked Robin; for there were nearly two hundred children, and Priscilla had collected the strangest things in food on the long tables as a result of her method, when inviting, of asking each mother what her child best liked to eat and then ordering it with the lavishness of ignorance from Minehead.

"Oh, we shall live so simply ourselves that there will be enough left to do all I want. And it will be the most blessed change and refreshment, living simply. Fritzi hated the fuss and luxury quite as much as I did."

"Did he?" said Robin, holding his breath. The girl was evidently off her guard. He had not heard her call her uncle baldly Fritzi before; and what fuss and luxury could a German teacher's life have known?

"He it was who first made me see that the body is more than meat and the soul than raiment," mused Priscilla.

"Was he?"

"He pulled my soul out of the flesh-pots. I'm a sort of Israel come out of Egypt, but an Egypt that was altogether too comfortable."

"Too comfortable? Can one be too comfortable?"

"I was. I couldn't move or see or breathe for comfort. It was like a feather bed all over me."

"I wouldn't call that comfort," said Robin, for she paused, and he was afraid she was not going on. "It sounds much more like torture."

"So it was at last. And Fritzi helped me to shake it off. If he hadn't I'd have smothered slowly, and perhaps if I'd never known him I'd have done it as gracefully as my sisters did. Why, they don't know to this day that they are dead."

Robin was silent. He was afraid to speak lest anything he said should remind her of the part she ought to be playing. He had no doubt now at all that she was keeping a secret. A hundred questions were burning on his lips. He hated himself for wanting to ask them, for being so inquisitive, for taking advantage of the girl's being off her guard, but what are you to do with your inherited failings? Robin's mother was inquisitive and it had got into his blood, and I know of no moral magnesia that will purify these things away. "You said the other day," he burst out at last, quite unable to stop himself, "that you only had your uncle in the world. Are your sisters— are they in London?"

"In London?" Priscilla gazed at him a moment with a vague surprise. Then fright flashed into her eyes. "Did I not tell you they were dead? Smothered?" she said, getting up quickly, her face setting into the frown that had so chilled Tussie on the heath.

"But I took that as a parable."

"How can I help how you took it?"

And she instantly left him and went away round the tables, beginning those little pleasant observations to the children again that struck him as so strange.

Well did he know the sort of thing. He had seen Lady Shuttleworth do it fifty times to the tenants, to the cottagers, at flower-shows, bazaars, on all occasions of public hospitality or ceremony; but practised and old as Lady Shuttleworth was this girl seemed yet more practised. She was a finished artist in the work, he said to himself as he leaned against the wall, his handsome face flushed, his eyes sulky, watching her. It was enough to make any good-looking young man sulky, the mixture of mystery and aloofness about Miss Neumann-Schultz. Extraordinary as it seemed, up to this point he had found it quite impossible to indulge with her in that form of more or less illustrated dialogue known to Symford youths and maidens as billing and cooing. Very fain would Robin have billed and have cooed. It was a practice he excelled in. And yet though he had devoted himself for three whole days, stood on ladders, nailed up creepers, bought and carried rum, had a horrible scene with his mother because of her, he had not got an inch nearer things personal and cosy. Miss Neumann-Schultz thanked him quite kindly and graciously for his pains—oh, she was very gracious; gracious in the sort of way Lady Shuttleworth used to be when he came home for the holidays and she patted his head and uttered benignities—and having thanked, apparently forgot him till the next time she wanted anything.

"Fritzi," said Priscilla, when in the course of her progress down the room she met that burdened man, "I'm dreadfully afraid I've said some foolish things."

Fritzing put the plate of cake he was carrying down on a dresser and wiped his forehead. "Ma'am," he said looking worried, "I cannot watch you and administer food to these barbarians simultaneously. If your tongue is so unruly I would recommend complete silence."

"I've said something about my sisters."

"Sisters, ma'am?" said Fritzing anxiously.

"Does it matter?"

"Matter? I have carefully instructed the woman Pearce, who has certainly informed, as I intended she should inform, the entire village, that you were my brother's only child. Consequently, ma'am, you have no sisters."

Priscilla made a gesture of despair. "How fearfully difficult it is not to be straightforward," she said.

"Yes, ma'am, it is. Since we started on this adventure the whole race of rogues has become the object of my sincerest admiration. What wits, what quickness, what gifts—so varied and so deftly used—what skill in deception, what resourcefulness in danger, what self-command—"

"Yes but Fritzi what are we to do?"

"Do, ma'am? About your royal sisters? Would to heaven I had been born a rogue!"

"Yes, but as you were not—ought I to go back and say they're only half-sisters? Or step-sisters? Or sisters in law? Wouldn't that do?"

"With whom were you speaking?"

"Mr. Morrison."

"Ma'am, let me beg you to be more prudent with that youth than with any one. Our young friend Cæsar Augustus is I believe harmlessness itself compared with him. Be on your guard, ma'am. Curb that fatal feminine appendage, your tongue. I have remarked that he watches us. But a short time since I saw him eagerly conversing with your Grand Ducal Highness's maid. For me he has already laid several traps that I have only just escaped falling into by an extraordinary presence of mind and a nimbleness in dialectic almost worthy of a born rogue."

"Oh Fritzi," said the frightened Priscilla, laying her hand on his sleeve, "do go and tell him I didn't mean what I said."

Fritzing wiped his brow again. "I fail to understand," he said, looking at Priscilla with worried eyes, "what there is about us that can possibly attract any one's attention."

"Why, there isn't anything," said Priscilla, with conviction. "We've been most careful and clever. But just now—I don't know why—I began to think aloud."

"Think aloud?" exclaimed Fritzing, horrified. "Oh ma'am let me beseech you never again to do that. Better a thousand times not to think at all. What was it that your Grand Ducal Highness thought aloud?"

And Priscilla, shamefaced, told him as well as she could remember.

"I will endeavour to remedy it," said poor Fritzing, running an agitated hand through his hair.

Priscilla sighed, and stood drooping and penitent by the dresser while he went down the room to where Robin still leaned against the wall.

"Sir," said Fritzing—he never called Robin young man, as he did Tussie—"my niece tells me you are unable to distinguish truth from parable."

"What?" said Robin staring.

"You are not, sir, to suppose that when my niece described her sisters as dead that they are not really so."

"All right sir," said Robin, his eyes beginning to twinkle.

"The only portion of the story in which my niece used allegory was when she described them as having been smothered. These young ladies, sir, died in the ordinary way, in their beds."

"Feather beds, sir?" asked Robin briskly.

"Sir, I have not inquired into the nature of the beds," said Fritzing with severity.

"Is it not rather unusual," asked Robin, "for two young ladies in one family to die at once? Were they unhealthy young ladies?"

"Sir, they did not die at once, nor were they unhealthy. They were perfectly healthy until they—until they began to die."

"Indeed," said Robin, with an interest properly tinged with regret. "At least, sir," he added politely, after a pause in which he and Fritzing stared very hard at each other, "I trust I may be permitted to express my sympathy."

"Sir, you may." And bowing stiffly Fritzing returned to Priscilla, and with a sigh of relief informed her that he had made things right again.

"Dear Fritzi," said Priscilla looking at him with love and admiration, "how clever you are."

XIII

It was on the Tuesday, the day Priscilla and Fritzing left Baker's and moved into Creeper Cottage, that the fickle goddess who had let them nestle for more than a week beneath her wing got tired of them and shook them out. Perhaps she was vexed by their clumsiness at pretending, perhaps she thought she had done more than enough for them, perhaps she was an epicure in words and did not like a cottage called Creeper; anyhow she shook them out. And if they had had eyes to see they would not have walked into their new home with such sighs of satisfaction and such a comfortable feeling that now at last the era of systematic serenity and self-realization, beautifully combined with the daily exercise of charity, had begun; for waiting for them in Priscilla's parlour, established indeed in her easy-chair by the fire and warming her miserable toes on the very hob, sat grey Ill Luck horribly squinting.

Creeper Cottage, it will be remembered, consisted of two cottages, each with two rooms, an attic, and a kitchen, and in the back yard the further accommodation of a coal-hole, a pig-stye, and a pump. Thanks to Tussie's efforts more furniture had been got from Minehead. Tussie had gone in himself, after a skilful questioning of Fritzing had made him realize how little had been ordered, and had, with Fritzing's permission, put the whole thing into the hands of a Minehead firm. Thus there was a bed for Annalise and sheets for everybody, and the place was as decent as it could be made in the time. It was so tiny that it got done, after a great deal of urging from Tussie, by the Tuesday at midday, and Tussie himself had superintended the storing of wood in the coal-hole and the lighting of the fire that was to warm his divine lady and that Ill Luck found so comforting to her toes. The Shuttleworth horses had a busy time on the Friday, Saturday, and Monday, trotting up and down between Symford and Minehead; and the Shuttleworth servants and tenants, not being more blind than other people, saw very well that their Augustus had lost his heart to the lady from nowhere. As for Lady Shuttleworth, she only smiled a rueful smile and stroked her poor Tussie's hair in silence when, having murmured something about the horses being tired, he reproved her by telling her that it was everybody's duty to do what they could for strangers in difficulties.

Priscilla's side of Creeper Cottage was the end abutting on the churchyard, and her parlour had one latticed window looking south down the village street, and one looking west opening directly on to the churchyard. The long grass of the churchyard, its dandelions and daisies, grew right up beneath this window to her wall, and a tall tombstone half-blocked her view of the elm-trees and the church. Over this room, with the same romantic and gloomy outlook, was her bedroom. Behind her parlour was what had been the shoemaker's kitchen, but it had been turned into a temporary bathroom. True no water was laid on as yet, but the pump was just outside, and nobody thought there would be any difficulty about filling the bath every morning by means of the pump combined with buckets. Over the bathroom was the attic. This was Annalise's bedroom. Nobody thought there would be any difficulty about that either; nobody, in fact, thought anything about anything. It was a simple place, after the manner of attics, with a window in its sloping ceiling through which stars might be studied with great comfort as one lay in bed. A frugal mind, an earnest soul, would have liked the attic, would have found a healthy enjoyment in a place so plain and fresh, so swept in windy weather by the airs of heaven. A poet, too, would certainly have flooded any parts of it that seemed dark with the splendour of his own inner light; a nature-lover, again, would have quickly discovered the spiders that dwelt in its corners, and spent profitable hours on all fours observing them. But an Annalise—what was she to make of such a place? Is it not true that the less a person has inside him of culture and imagination the more he wants outside him of the upholstery of life? I think it is true; and if it is, then the vacancy of Annalise's mind may be measured by the fact that what she demanded of life in return for the negative services of not crying and wringing her hands was nothing less filled with food and sofas and servants than a grand ducal palace.

But neither Priscilla nor Fritzing knew anything of Annalise's mind, and if they had they would instantly have forgotten it again, of such extreme unimportance would it have seemed. Nor would I dwell on it myself if it were not that its very vacancy and smallness was the cause of huge upheavals in Creeper Cottage, and the stone that the builders ignored if they did not actually reject behaved as such stones sometimes do and came down upon the builders' heads and crushed them. Annalise, you see, was unable to appreciate peace, yet on the other hand she was very able to destroy the peace of other people; and Priscilla meant her cottage to be so peaceful—a temple, a holy place, within whose quiet walls sacred years were going to be spent in doing justly, in loving mercy, in walking humbly. True she had not as yet made a nearer acquaintance with its inconveniences, but anyhow she held the theory that inconveniences were things to be laughed at and somehow circumvented, and that they do not enter into the consideration of persons whose thoughts are absorbed by the burning desire to live out their ideals. "You can be happy in any place whatever," she remarked to Tussie on the Monday, when he was expressing fears as to her future comfort; "absolutely any place will do—a tub, a dingle, the top of a pillar—any place at all, if only your soul is on fire."

"Of course you can," cried Tussie, ready to kiss her feet.

"And look how comfortable my cottage seems," said Priscilla, "directly one compares it with things like tubs."

"Yes, yes," agreed Tussie, "I do see that it's enough for free spirits to live in. I was only wondering whether—whether bodies would find it enough."

"Oh bother bodies," said Priscilla airily.

But Tussie could not bring himself to bother bodies if they included her own; on the contrary, the infatuated young man thought it would be difficult sufficiently to cherish a thing so supremely precious and sweet. And each time he went home after having been in the frugal baldness of Creeper Cottage he hated the superfluities of his own house more and more, he accused himself louder and louder of being mean-spirited, effeminate, soft, vulgar, he loathed himself for living embedded in such luxury while she, the dear and lovely one, was ready cheerfully to pack her beauty into a tub if needs be, or let it be weather-beaten on a pillar for thirty years if by so doing she could save her soul alive. Tussie at this time became unable to see a sleek servant dart to help him take off his coat without saying something sharp to him, could not sit through a meal without making bitter comparisons between what they were eating and what the poor were probably eating, could not walk up his spacious staircase and along his lofty corridors without scowling; they, indeed, roused his contemptuous wrath in quite a special degree, the reason being that Priscilla's stairs, the stairs up and down which her little feet would have to clamber daily, were like a ladder, and she possessed no passages at all. But what of that? Priscilla could not see that it mattered, when Tussie drew her attention to it.

Both Fritzing's and her front door opened straight into their sitting-rooms; both their staircases walked straight from the kitchens up into the rooms above. They had meant to have a door knocked in the dividing wall downstairs, but had been so anxious to get away from Baker's that there was no time. In order therefore to get to Fritzing Priscilla would have either to go out into the street and in again at his front door, or go out at her back door and in again at his. Any meals, too, she might choose to have served alone would have to be carried round to her from the kitchen in Fritzing's half, either through the backyard or through the street.

Tussie thought of this each time he sat at his own meals, surrounded by deft menials, lapped as he told himself in luxury,—oh, thought Tussie writhing, it was base. His much-tried mother had to listen to many a cross and cryptic remark flung across the table from the dear boy who had always been so gentle; and more than that, he put his foot down once and for all and refused with a flatness that silenced her to eat any more patent foods. "Absurd," cried Tussie. "No wonder I'm such an idiot. Who could be anything else with his stomach full of starch? Why, I believe the stuff has filled my veins with milk instead of good honest blood."

"Dearest, I'll have it thrown out of the nearest window," said Lady Shuttleworth, smiling bravely in her poor Tussie's small cross face. "But what shall I give you instead? You know you won't eat meat."

"Give me lentils," cried Tussie. "They're cheap."

"Cheap?"

"Mother, I do think it offensive to spend much on what goes into or onto one's body. Why not have fewer things, and give the rest to the poor?"

"But I do give the rest to the poor; I'm always doing it. And there's quite enough for us and for the poor too."

"Give them more, then. Why," fumed Tussie, "can't we live decently? Hasn't it struck you that we're very vulgar?"

"No, dearest, I can't say that it has."

"Well, we are. Everything we have that is beyond bare necessaries makes us vulgar. And surely, mother, you do see that that's not a nice thing to be."

"It's a horrid thing to be," said his mother, arranging his tie with an immense and lingering tenderness.

"It's a difficult thing not to be," said Tussie, "if one is rich. Hasn't it struck you that this ridiculous big house, and the masses of things in it, and the whole place and all the money will inevitably end by crushing us both out of heaven?"

"No, I can't say it has. I expect you've been thinking of things like the eyes of needles and camels having to go through them," said his mother, still patting and stroking his tie.

"Well, that's terrifically true," mused Tussie, reflecting ruefully on the size and weight of the money-bags that were dragging him down into darkness. Then he added suddenly, "Will you have a small bed—a little iron one—put in my bedroom?"

"A small bed? But there's a bed there already, dear."

"That big thing's only fit for a sick woman. I won't wallow in it any longer."

"But dearest, all your forefathers wallowed, as you call it, in it. Doesn't it seem rather—a pity not to carry on traditions?"

"Well mother be kind and dear, and let me depart in peace from them. A camp bed,—that's what I'd like. Shall I order it, or will you? And did I tell you I've given Bryce the sack?"

"Bryce? Why, what has he done?"

"Oh he hasn't done anything that I know of, except make a sort of doll or baby of me. Why should I be put into my clothes and taken out of them again as though I hadn't been weaned yet?"

Now all this was very bad, but the greatest blow for Lady Shuttleworth fell when Tussie declared that he would not come of age. The cheerful face with which his mother had managed to listen to his other defiances went very blank at that; do what she would she could not prevent its falling. "Not come of age?" she repeated stupidly. "But my darling, you can't help yourself—you must come of age."

"Oh I know I can't help being twenty-one and coming into all this"— and he waved contemptuous arms—"but I won't do it blatantly."

"I—I don't understand," faltered Lady Shuttleworth.

"There mustn't be any fuss, mother."

"Do you mean no one is to come?"

"No one at all, except the tenants and people. Of course they are to have their fun—I'll see that they have a jolly good time. But I won't have our own set and the relations."

"Tussie, they've all accepted."

"Send round circulars."

"Tussie, you are putting me in a most painful position."

"Dear mother, I'm very sorry for that. I wish I'd thought like this sooner. But really the idea is so revolting to me—it's so sickening to think of all these people coming to pretend to rejoice over a worm like myself."

"Tussle, you are not a worm."

"And then the expense and waste of entertaining them—the dreariness, the boredom—oh, I wish I only possessed a tub—one single tub—or had the pluck to live like Lavengro in a dingle."

"It's quite impossible to stop it now," interrupted Lady Shuttleworth in the greatest distress; of Lavengro she had never heard.

"Yes you can, mother. Write and put it off."

"Write? What could I write? To-day is Tuesday, and they all arrive on Friday. What excuse can I make at the last moment? And how can a birthday be put off? My dearest boy, I simply can't." And Lady Shuttleworth, the sensible, the cheery, the resourceful, the perennially brave, wrung her hands and began quite helplessly to cry.

This unusual and pitiful sight at once conquered Tussie. For a moment he stood aghast; then his arms were round his mother, and he promised everything she wanted. What he said to her besides and what she sobbed back to him I shall not tell. They never spoke of it again; but for years they both looked back to it, that precious moment of clinging together with bursting hearts, her old cheek against his young one, her tears on his face, as to one of the most acutely sweet, acutely, painfully, tender experiences of their joint lives.

It will be conceded that Priscilla had achieved a good deal in the one week that had passed since she laid aside her high estate and stepped down among ordinary people for the purpose of being and doing good. She had brought violent discord into a hitherto peaceful vicarage, thwarted the hopes of a mother, been the cause of a bitter quarrel between her and her son, brought out by her mysteriousness a prying tendency in the son that might have gone on sleeping for ever, entirely upset the amiable Tussie's life by rending him asunder with a love as strong as it was necessarily hopeless, made his mother anxious and unhappy, and, what was perhaps the greatest achievement of all, actually succeeded in making that mother cry. For of course Priscilla was the ultimate cause of these unusual tears, as Lady Shuttleworth very well knew. Lady Shuttleworth was the deceased Sir Augustus's second wife, had married him when she was over forty and well out of the crying stage, which in the busy does not last beyond childhood, had lost him soon after Tussie's birth, had cried copiously and most properly at his funeral, and had not cried since. It was then undoubtedly a great achievement on the part of the young lady from nowhere, this wringing of tears out of eyes that had been dry for one and twenty years. But the list of what Priscilla had done does not end with this havoc among mothers. Had she not interrupted the decent course of Mrs. Jones's dying, and snatched her back to a hankering after the unfit? Had she not taught the entire village to break the Sabbath? Had she not made all its children either sick or cross under the pretence of giving them a treat? On the Monday she did something else that was equally well-meaning, and yet, as I shall presently relate, of disastrous consequences: she went round the village from cottage to cottage making friends with the children's mothers and leaving behind her, wherever she went, little presents of money. She had found money so extraordinarily efficacious in the comforting of Mrs. Jones that before she started she told Fritzing to fill her purse well, and in each cottage it was made somehow so clear how badly different things were wanted that the purse was empty before she was half round the village and she had to go back for a fresh supply. She was extremely happy that afternoon, and so were the visited mothers. They, indeed, talked of nothing else for the rest of the day, discussed it over their garden hedges, looked in on each other to compare notes, hurried to meet their husbands on their return from work to tell them about it, and were made at one stroke into something very like a colony of eager beggars. And in spite of Priscilla's injunction to Mrs. Jones to hide her five-pound note all Symford knew of that as well, and also of the five-pound note Mrs. Morrison had taken away. Nothing was talked of in Symford but Priscilla. She had in one week created quite a number of disturbances of a nature fruitful for evil in that orderly village; and when on the Tuesday she and Fritzing moved into Creeper Cottage they were objects of the intensest interest to the entire country side, and the report of their riches, their recklessness, and their eccentric choice of a dwelling had rolled over the intervening hills as far as Minehead, where it was the subject of many interesting comments in the local papers.

They got into their cottage about tea time; and the first thing Priscilla did was to exclaim at the pleasant sight of the wood fire and sit down in the easy-chair to warm herself. We know who was sitting in it already; and thus she was received by Bad Luck at once into her very lap, and clutched about securely by that unpleasant lady's cold and skinny arms. She looked up at Fritzing with a shiver to remark wonderingly that the room, in spite of its big fire and its smallness, was like ice, but her lips fell apart in a frozen stare and she gazed blankly past him at the wall behind his head. "Look," she whispered, pointing with a horrified forefinger. And Fritzing, turning quickly, was just in time to snatch a row of cheap coloured portraits from the wall and fling them face downwards under the table before Tussie came in to ask if he could do anything.

The portraits were those of all the reigning princes of Germany and had been put up as a delicate compliment by the representative of the Minehead furnishers, while Priscilla and Fritzing were taking leave of Baker's Farm; and the print Priscilla's eye had lighted on was the portrait of her august parent, smiling at her. He was splendid in state robes and orders, and there was a charger, and an obviously expensive looped-up curtain, and much smoke as of nations furiously raging together in the background, and outside this magnificence meandered the unmeaning rosebuds of Priscilla's cheap wallpaper. His smile seemed very terrible under the circumstances. Fritzing felt this, and seized him and flung him with a desperate energy under the table, where he went on smiling, as Priscilla remembered with a guilty shudder, at nothing but oilcloth. "I don't believe I'll sleep if I know he—he's got nothing he'd like better than oilcloth to look at," she whispered with an awestruck face to Fritzing as Tussie came in.

"I will cause them all to be returned," Fritzing assured her.

"What, have those people sent wrong things?" asked Tussie anxiously, who felt that the entire responsibility of this *ménage* was on his shoulders.

"Oh, only some cheap prints," said Priscilla hastily. "I think they're called oleographs or something."

"What impertinence," said Tussie hotly.

"I expect it was kindly meant, but I—I like my cottage quite plain."

"I'll have them sent back, sir," Tussie said to Fritzing, who was rubbing his hands nervously through his hair; for the sight of his grand ducal master's face smiling at him on whom he would surely never wish to smile again, and doing it, too, from the walls of Creeper Cottage, had given him a shock.

"You are ever helpful, young man," he said, bowing abstractedly and going away to put down his hat and umbrella; and Priscilla, with a cold feeling that she had had a bad omen, rang the handbell Tussie's thoughtfulness had placed on her table and ordered Annalise to bring tea.

Now Annalise had been standing on the threshold of her attic staring at it in an amazement too deep for words when the bell fetched her down. She appeared, however, before her mistress with a composed face, received the order with her customary respectfulness, and sought out Fritzing to inquire of him where the servants were to be found. "Her Grand Ducal Highness desires tea," announced Annalise, appearing in Fritzing's sitting-room, where he was standing absorbed in the bill from the furnishers that he had found lying on his table.

"Then take it in," said Fritzing impatiently, without looking up.

"To whom shall I give the order?" inquired Annalise.

"To whom shall you give the order?" repeated Fritzing, pausing in his study to stare at her, the bill in one hand and his pocket-handkerchief, with which he was mopping his forehead, in the other.

"Where," asked Annalise, "shall I find the cook?"

"Where shall you find the cook?" repeated Fritzing, staring still harder. "This house is so gigantic is it not," he said with an enormous sarcasm, "that no doubt the cook has lost himself. Have you perhaps omitted to investigate the coal-hole?"

"Herr Geheimrath, where shall I find the cook?" asked Annalise tossing her head.

"Fräulein, is there a mirror in your bedroom?"

"The smallest I ever saw. Only one-half of my face can I see reflected in it at a time."

"Fräulein, the half of that face you see reflected in it is the half of the face of the cook."

"I do not understand," said Annalise.

"Yet it is as clear as shining after rain. You, *mein liebes Kind*, are the cook."

It was now Annalise's turn to stare, and she stood for a moment doing it, her face changing from white to red while Fritzing turned his back and taking out a pencil made little sums on the margin of the bill. "Herr Geheimrath, I am not a cook," she said at last, swallowing her indignation.

"What, still there?" he exclaimed, looking up sharply. "Unworthy one, get thee quickly to the kitchen. Is it seemly to keep the Princess waiting?"

"I am not a cook," said Annalise defiantly. "I was not engaged as a cook, I never was a cook, and I will not be a cook."

Fritzing flung down the bill and came and glared close into Annalise's face. "Not a cook?" he cried. "You, a German girl, the daughter of poor parents, you are not ashamed to say it? You do not hide your head for shame? No—a being so useful, so necessary, so worthy of respect as a cook you are not and never will be. I'll tell you what you are,—I've told you once already, and I repeat it—you are a knave, my Fräulein, a knave, I say. And in those parts of your miserable nature where you are not a knave—for I willingly concede that no man or woman is bad all through—in those parts, I say, where your knavishness is intermittent, you are an absolute, unmitigated fool."

"I will not bear this," cried Annalise.

"Will not! Cannot! Shall not! Inept Negation, get thee to thy kitchen and seek wisdom among the pots."

"I am no one's slave," cried Annalise, "I am no one's prisoner."

"Hark at her! Who said you were? Have I not told you the only two things you are?"

"But I am treated as a prisoner, I am treated as a slave," sobbed Annalise.

"Unmannerly one, how dare you linger talking follies when your royal mistress is waiting for her tea? Run—run! Or must I show you how?"

"Her Grand Ducal Highness," said Annalise, not budging, "told me also to prepare the bath for her this evening."

"Well, what of that?" cried Fritzing, snatching up the bill again and adding up furiously. "Prepare it, then."

"I see no water-taps."

"Woman, there are none."

"How can I prepare a bath without water-taps?"

"O thou Inefficiency! Ineptitude garbed as woman! Must I then teach thee the elements of thy business? Hast thou not observed the pump? Go to it, and draw water. Cause the water to flow into buckets. Carry these buckets—need I go on? Will not Nature herself teach thee what to do with buckets?"

Annalise flushed scarlet. "I will not go to the pump," she said.

"What, you will not carry out her Grand Ducal Highness's orders?"

"I will not go to the pump."

"You refuse to prepare the bath?"

"I will not go to the pump."

"You refuse to prepare the tea?"

"I will not be a cook."

"You are rankly rebellious?"

"I will not sleep in the attic."

"What!"

"I will not eat the food."

"What!"

"I will not do the work."

"What!"

"I will go."

"Go?"

"*Go*," repeated Annalise, stamping her foot. "I demand my wages, the increased wages that were promised me, and I will go."

"And where, Impudence past believing, will you go, in a country whose tongue you most luckily do not understand?"

Annalise looked up into Fritzing's furious eyes with the challenge of him who flings down his trump card. "Go?" she cried, with a defiance that was blood-curdling in one so small and hitherto so silent, "I will first go to that young gentleman who speaks my language and I will tell him all, and then, with his assistance, I will go straight—but *straight*, do you hear?"—and she stamped her foot again—"to Lothen-Kunitz."

XIV

Early in this story I pointed out what to the intelligent must have been from the beginning apparent, that Annalise held Priscilla and Fritzing in the hollow of her hand. In the first excitement of the start she had not noticed it, but during those woeful days of disillusionment at Baker's she saw it with an ever-growing clearness; and since Sunday, since the day she found a smiling young gentleman ready to talk German to her and answer questions, she was perfectly aware that she had only to close her hand and her victims would squeeze into any shape she liked. She proposed to do this closing at the first moment of sheer intolerableness, and that moment seemed well reached when she entered Creeper Cottage and realized what the attic, the kitchen, and the pump really meant.

It is always a shock to find one's self in the company of a worm that turns, always a shock and an amazement; a spectacle one never, somehow, gets used to. But how dreadful does it become when one is in the power of the worm, and the worm is resentful, and ready to squeeze to any extent. Fritzing reflected bitterly that Annalise might quite well have been left at home. Quite well? A thousand times better. What had she done but whine during her passive period? And now that she was active, a volcano in full activity hurling forth hot streams of treachery on two most harmless heads, she, the insignificant, the base-born, the empty-brained, was actually going to be able to ruin the plans of the noblest woman on earth.

Thus thought Fritzing, mopping his forehead. Annalise had rushed away to her attic after flinging her defiance at him, her spirit ready to dare anything but her body too small, she felt, to risk staying within reach of a man who looked more like somebody who meant to shake her than any one she had ever seen. Fritzing mopped his forehead, and mopped and mopped again. He stood where she had left him, his eyes fixed on the ground, his distress so extreme that he was quite near crying. What was he to do? What was he to say to his Princess? How was he to stop the girl's going back to Kunitz? How was he to stop her going even so far as young Morrison? That she should tell young Morrison who Priscilla was would indeed be a terrible thing. It would end their being able to live in Symford. It would end their being able to live in England. The Grand Duke would be after them, and there would have to be another flight to another country, another start there, another search for a home, another set of explanations, pretences, fears, lies,—things of which he was so weary. But there was something else, something worse than any of these things, that made Fritzing mop his forehead with so extreme a desperation: Annalise had demanded the money due to her, and Fritzing had no money.

I am afraid Fritzing was never meant for a conspirator. Nature never meant him to be a plotter, an arranger of unpleasant surprises for parents. She never meant him to run away. She meant him, probably, to spend his days communing with the past in a lofty room with distempered walls and busts round them. That he should be forced to act, to decide, to be artful, to wrangle with maids, to make ends meet, to squeeze his long frame and explosive disposition into a Creeper Cottage where only an ill-fitting door separated him from the noise and fumes of the kitchen, was surely a cruel trick of Fate, and not less cruel because he had brought it on himself. That he should have thought he could run away as well as any man is merely a proof of his singleness of soul. A man who does that successfully is always, among a great many other things, a man who takes plenty of money with him and knows exactly where to put his hand on more when it is wanted. Fritzing had thought it better to get away quickly with little money than to wait and get away with more. He had seized all he could of his own that was not invested, and Priscilla had drawn her loose cash from the Kunitz bank; but what he took hidden in his gaiters after paying for Priscilla's outfit and bribing Annalise was not more than three hundred pounds; and what is three hundred pounds to a person who buys and furnishes cottages and scatters five-pound notes among the poor? The cottages were paid for. He had insisted on doing that at once, chiefly in order to close his dealings with Mr. Dawson; but Mr. Dawson had not let them go for less than a hundred and fifty for the two, in spite of Tussie's having said a hundred was enough. When Fritzing told Mr. Dawson what Tussie had said Mr. Dawson soon proved that Tussie could not possibly have meant it; and Fritzing, knowing how rich Priscilla really was and what vast savings he had himself lying over in Germany in comfortable securities, paid him without arguing and hastened from the hated presence. Then the journey for the three from Kunitz had been expensive; the stay at Baker's Farm had been, strange to say, expensive; Mrs. Jones's comforting had been expensive; the village mothers had twice emptied Priscilla's purse of ten pounds; and the treat to the Symford children had not been cheap. After paying for this—the Minehead confectioner turned out to be a man of little faith in unknown foreigners, and insisted on being paid at once—Fritzing had about forty pounds left. This, he had thought, would do for food and lights and things for a long while,—certainly till he had hit on a plan by which he would be able to get hold of the Princess's money and his own without betraying where they were; and here on his table, the second unpleasant surprise that greeted him on entering his new home (the first had been his late master's dreadful smile) was the bill for the furnishing of it. To a man possessed of only forty pounds any bill will seem tremendous. This one was for nearly two hundred; and at the end of the long list of items, the biggest of which was that bathroom without water that had sent Annalise out on strike, was the information that a remittance would oblige. A remittance! Poor Fritzing. He crushed the paper in his hand and made caustic mental comments on the indecency of these people, clamouring for their money almost before the last workman was out of the place, certainly before the smell of paint was out of it, and clamouring, too, in the face of the Shuttleworth countenance and support. He had not been a week yet in Symford, and had been so busy, so rushed, that he had put off thinking out a plan for getting his money over from Germany until he should be settled. Never had he imagined people would demand payment in this manner. Never, either, had he imagined the Princess would want so much money for the poor; and never, of course, had he imagined that there would be a children's treat within three days of their arrival. Least of all had he dreamed that Annalise would so soon need more bribing; for that was clearly the only thing to do. He saw it was the only thing, after he had stood for some time thinking and wiping the cold sweat from his forehead. She must be bribed, silenced, given in to. He must part with as much as he possibly could of that last forty pounds; as much, also, as he possibly could of his pride, and submit to have the hussy's foot on his neck. Some day, some day, thought Fritzing grinding his teeth, he would be even with her; and when that day came he promised himself that it should certainly begin with a sound shaking. "Truly," he reflected, "the foolish things of the world confound the wise, and the weak things of the world confound the things that are mighty." And he went out, and standing in the back yard beneath Annalise's window softly called to her. "Fräulein," called Fritzing, softly as a dove wooing its mate.

"Aha," thought Annalise, sitting on her bed, quick to mark the change; but she did not move.

"Fräulein," called Fritzing again; and it was hardly a call so much as a melodious murmur.

Annalise did not move, but she grinned.

"Fräulein, come down one moment," cooed Fritzing, whose head was quite near the attic window so low was Creeper Cottage. "I wish to speak to you. I wish to give you something."

Annalise did not move, but she stuffed her handkerchief into her mouth; for the first time since she left Calais she was enjoying herself.

"If," went on Fritzing after an anxious pause, "I was sharp with you just now—and I fear I may have been hasty—you should not take it amiss from one who, like Brutus, is sick of many griefs. Come down, Fräulein, and let me make amends."

The Princess's bell rang. At once habit impelled Annalise to that which Fritzing's pleadings would never have effected; she scrambled down the ladder, and leaving him still under her window presented herself before her mistress with her usual face of meek respect.

"I said tea," said Priscilla very distinctly, looking at her with slightly lifted eyebrows.

Annalise curtseyed and disappeared.

"How fearfully polite German maids are," remarked Tussie.

"In what way?" asked Priscilla.

"Those curtseys. They're magnificent."

"Don't English maids curtsey?"

"None that I've ever seen. Perhaps they do to royalties."

"Oh?" said Priscilla with a little jump. She was still so much unnerved by the unexpected meeting with her father on the wall of Creeper Cottage that she could not prevent the little jump.

"What would German maids do, I wonder, in dealing with royalties," said Tussie, "if they curtsey so beautifully to ordinary mistresses? They'd have to go down on their knees to a princess, wouldn't they?"

"How should I know?" said Priscilla, irritably, alarmed to feel she was turning red; and with great determination she began to talk literature.

Fritzing was lying in wait for Annalise, and caught her as she came into the bathroom.

"Fräulein," said the miserable man trying to screw his face into persuasiveness, "you cannot let the Princess go without tea."

"Yes I can," said Annalise.

He thrust his hands into his pockets to keep them off her shoulders.

"Make it this once, Fräulein, and I will hire a woman of the village to make it in future. And see, you must not leave the Princess's service, a service of such great honour to yourself, because I chanced to be perhaps a little—hasty. I will give you two hundred marks to console you for the slight though undoubted difference in the mode of living, and I will, as I said, hire a woman to come each day and cook. Will it not be well so?"

"No," said Annalise.

"No?"

Annalise put her hands on her hips, and swaying lightly from side to side began to sing softly. Fritzing gazed at this fresh development in her manners in silent astonishment. "*Jedermann macht mir die Cour, c'est l'amour, c'est l'amour,*" sang Annalise, her head one side, her eyes on the ceiling.

"*Liebes Kind,* are your promises of no value? Did you not promise to keep your mouth shut, and not betray the Princess's confidence? Did she not seek you out from all the others for the honour of keeping her secrets? And you will, after one week, divulge them to a stranger? You will leave her service? You will return to Kunitz? Is it well so?"

"*C'est l'amour, c'est l'amour,*" sang Annalise, swaying.

"Is it well so, Fräulein?" repeated Fritzing, strangling a furious desire to slap her.

"Did you speak?" inquired Annalise, pausing in her song.

"I am speaking all the time. I asked if it were well to betray the secrets of your royal mistress."

"I have been starved," said Annalise.

"You have had the same fare as ourselves."

"I have been called names."

"Have I not expressed—regret?"

"I have been treated as dirt."

"Well, well, I have apologized."

"If you had behaved to me as a maid of a royal lady should be behaved to, I would have faithfully done my part and kept silence. Now give me my money and I will go."

"I will give you your money—certainly, *liebes Kind.* It is what I am most desirous of doing. But only on condition that you stay. If you go, you go without it. If you stay, I will do as I said about the cook and will—" Fritzing paused—"I will endeavour to refrain from calling you anything hasty."

"Two hundred marks," said Annalise gazing at the ceiling, "is nothing."

"Nothing?" cried Fritzing. "You know very well that it is, for you, a great sum."

"It is nothing. I require a thousand."

"A thousand? What, fifty English sovereigns? Nay, then, but there is no reasoning with you," cried Fritzing in tones of real despair.

She caught the conviction in them and hesitated. "Eight hundred, then," she said.

"Impossible. And besides it would be a sin. I will give you twenty."

"Twenty? Twenty marks?" Annalise stared at him a moment then resumed her swaying and her song—"*Jedermann macht mir die Cour*"—sang Annalise with redoubled conviction.

"No, no, not marks—twenty pounds," said Fritzing, interrupting what was to him a most maddening music. "Four hundred marks. As much as many a German girl can only earn by labouring two years you will receive for doing nothing but hold your tongue."

Annalise closed her lips tightly and shook her head. "My tongue cannot be held for that," she said, beginning to sway again and hum.

Adjectives foamed on Fritzing's own, but he kept them back. "*Mädchen*," he said with the gentleness of a pastor in a confirmation class, "do you not remember that the love of money is the root of all evil? I do not recognize you. Since when have you become thus greedy for it?"

"Give me eight hundred and I will stop."

"I will give you six hundred," said Fritzing, fighting for each of his last precious pounds.

"Eight."

"Six."

"I said eight," said Annalise, stopping and looking at him with lifted eye-brows and exactly imitating the distinctness with which the Princess had just said "I said tea."

"Six is an enormous sum. Why, what would you do with it?"

"That is my affair. Perhaps buy food," she said with a malicious side-glance.

"I tell you there shall be a cook."

"A cook," said Annalise counting on her fingers,—"and a good cook, observe—not a cook like the Frau Pearce—a cook, then, no more rude names, and eight hundred marks. Then I stop. I suffer. I am silent."

"It cannot be done. I cannot give you eight."

"*C'est l'amour, c'est l'amour*.... The Princess waits for her tea. I will prepare it for her this once. I am good, you see, at heart. But I must have eight hundred marks. *Cest l'amo-o-o-o-our.*"

"I will give you seven," said Fritzing, doing rapid sums in his head. Seven hundred was something under thirty-five pounds. He would still have five pounds left for housekeeping. How long that would last he admitted to himself that probably only heaven knew, but he hoped that with economy it might be made to carry them over a fortnight; and surely by the end of a fortnight he would have hit on a way of getting fresh supplies from Germany? "I will give you seven hundred. That is the utter-most. I can give no more till I have written home for money. I have only a little more than that here altogether. See, I treat you like a reasonable being—I set the truth plainly before you. More than seven hundred I could not give if I would."

"Good," said Annalise, breaking off her music suddenly. "I will take that now and guarantee to be silent for fourteen days. At the end of that time the Herr Geheimrath will have plenty more money and will, if he still desires my services and my silence, give me the three hundred still due to me on the thousand I demand. If the Herr Geheimrath prefers not to, then I depart to my native country. While the fortnight lasts I will suffer all there is to suffer in silence. Is the Herr Geheimrath agreed?"

"Shameless one!" mentally shrieked Fritzing, "Wait and see what will happen to thee when my turn comes!" But aloud he only agreed. "It is well, Fräulein," he said. "Take in the Princess's tea, and then come to my sitting-room and I will give you the money. The fire burns in the kitchen. Utensils, I believe, are ready to hand. It should not prove a task too difficult."

"Perhaps the Herr Geheimrath will show me where the tea and milk is? And also the sugar, and the bread and butter if any?" suggested Annalise in a small meek voice as she tripped before him into the kitchen.

What could he do but follow? Her foot was well on his neck; and it occurred to him as he rummaged miserably among canisters that if the creature should take it into her head to marry him he might conceivably have to let her do it. As it was it was he and not Annalise who took the kettle out to the pump to fill it, and her face while he was doing it would have rejoiced her parents or other persons to whom she was presumably dear, it was wide with so enormous a satisfaction. Thus terrible is it to be in the power of an Annalise.

XV

The first evening in Creeper Cottage was unpleasant. There was a blazing wood fire, the curtains were drawn, the lamp shone rosily through its red shade, and when Priscilla stood up her hair dusted the oak beams of the ceiling, it was so low. The background, you see, was perfectly satisfactory; exactly what a cottage background should be on an autumn night when outside a wet mist is hanging like a grey curtain across the window panes; and Tussie arriving at nine o'clock to help consecrate the new life with Shakespeare felt, as he opened the door and walked out of the darkness into the rosy, cosy little room, that he need not after all worry himself with doubts as to the divine girl's being comfortable. Never did place appear more comfortable. It did not occur to him that a lamp with a red shade and the blaze of a wood fire will make any place appear comfortable so long as they go on shining, and he looked up at Priscilla—I am afraid he had to look up at her when they were both standing—with the broadest smile of genuine pleasure. "It *does* look jolly," he said heartily.

His pleasure was doomed to an immediate wiping out. Priscilla smiled, but with a reservation behind her smile that his sensitive spirit felt at once. She was alone, and there was no sign whatever either of her uncle or of preparations for the reading of Shakespeare.

"Is anything not quite right?" Tussie asked, his face falling at once to an anxious pucker.

Priscilla looked at him and smiled again, but this time the smile was real, in her eyes as well as on her lips, dancing in them together with the flickering firelight. "It's rather funny," she said. "It has never happened to me before. What do you think? I'm hungry."

"Hungry?"

"Hungry."

Tussie stared, arrested in the unwinding of his comforter.

"Really hungry. *Dreadfully* hungry. So hungry that I hate Shakespeare."

"But—"

"I know. You're going to say why not eat? It does seem simple. But you've no idea how difficult it really is. I'm afraid my uncle and I have rather heaps to learn. We forgot to get a cook."

"A cook? But I thought—I understood that curtseying maid of yours was going to do all that?"

"So did I. So did he. But she won't."

Priscilla flushed, for since Tussie left after tea she had had grievous surprises, of a kind that made her first indignant and then inclined to wince. Fritzing had not been able to hide from her that Annalise had rebelled and refused to cook, and Priscilla had not been able to follow her immediate impulse and dismiss her. It was at this point, when she realized this, that the wincing began. She felt perfectly sick at the thought, flashed upon her for the first time, that she was in the power of a servant.

"Do you mean to say," said Tussie in a voice hollow with consternation, "that you've had no dinner?"

"Dinner? In a cottage? Why of course there was no dinner. There never will be any dinner—at night, at least. But the tragic thing is there was no supper. We didn't think of it till we began to get hungry. Annalise began first. She got hungry at six o'clock, and said something to Fritz—my uncle about it, but he wasn't hungry himself then and so he snubbed her. Now he is hungry himself, and he's gone out to see if he can't find a cook. It's very stupid. There's nothing in the house. Annalise ate the bread and things she found. She's upstairs now, crying." And Priscilla's lips twitched as she looked at Tussie's concerned face, and she began to laugh.

He seized his hat. "I'll go and get you something," he said, dashing at the door.

"I can't think what, at this time of the night. The only shop shuts at seven."

"I'll make them open it."

"They go to bed at nine."

"I'll get them out of bed if I have to shie stones at their windows all night."

"Don't go without your coat—you'll catch a most frightful cold."

He put his arm through the door to take it, and vanished in the fog. He did not put on the coat in his agitation, but kept it over his arm. His comforter stayed in Priscilla's parlour, on the chair where he had flung it. He was in evening dress, and his throat was sore already with the cold that was coming on and that he had caught, as he expected, running races on the Sunday at Priscilla's children's party.

Priscilla went back to her seat by the fire, and thought very hard about things like bread. It would of course be impossible that she should have reached this state of famine only because one meal had been missed; but she had eaten nothing all day,—disliked the Baker's Farm breakfast too much even to look at it, forgotten the Baker's Farm dinner because she was just moving into her cottage, and at tea had been too greatly upset by the unexpected appearance of her father on the wall to care to eat the bread and butter Annalise brought in. Now she was in that state when you tremble and feel cold. She had told Annalise, about half-past seven, to bring her the bread left from tea, but Annalise had eaten it. At half-past eight she had told Annalise to bring her the sugar, for she had read somewhere that if you eat enough sugar it takes away the desire even of the hungriest for other food, but Annalise, who had eaten the sugar as well, said that the Herr Geheimrath must have eaten it. It certainly was not there, and neither was the Herr Geheimrath to defend himself; since half-past seven he had been out looking for a cook, his mind pervaded by the idea that if only he could get a cook food would follow in her wake as naturally as flowers follow after rain. Priscilla fretting in her chair that he should stay away so long saw very clearly that no cook could help them. What is the use of a cook in a house where there is nothing to cook? If only Fritzing would come back quickly with a great many loaves of bread! The door was opened a little way and somebody's knuckles knocked. She thought it was Tussie, quick and clever as ever, and in a voice full of welcome told him to come in; upon which in stepped Robin Morrison very briskly, delighted by the warmth of the invitation. "Why now this *is* nice," said Robin, all smiles.

Priscilla did not move and did not offer to shake hands, so he stood on the hearthrug and spread out his own to the blaze, looking down at her with bright, audacious eyes. He thought he had not yet seen her so beautiful. There was an extraordinary depth and mystery in her look, he thought, as it rested for a moment on his face, and she had never yet dropped her eyelashes as she now did when her eyes met his. We know she was very hungry, and there was no strength in her at all. Not only did her eyelashes drop, but her head as well, and her hands hung helplessly, like drooping white flowers, one over each arm of the chair.

"I came in to ask Mr. Neumann-Schultz if there's anything I can do for you," said Robin.

"Did you? He lives next door."

"I know. I knocked there first, but he didn't answer so I thought he must be here."

Priscilla said nothing. At any other time she would have snubbed Robin and got rid of him. Now she merely sat and drooped.

"Has he gone out?"

"Yes."

Her voice was very low, hardly more than a whisper. Those who know the faintness of hunger at this stage will also know the pathos that steals into the voice of the sufferer when he is unwillingly made to speak; it becomes plaintive, melodious with yearning, the yearning for food. But if you do not know this, if you have yourself just come from dinner, if you are half in love and want the other person to be quite in love, if you are full of faith in your own fascinations, you are apt to fall into Robin's error and mistake the nature of the yearning. Tussie in Robin's place would have doubted the evidence of his senses, but then Tussie was very modest. Robin doubted nothing. He saw, he heard, and he thrilled; and underneath his thrilling, which was real enough to make him flush to the roots of his hair, far down underneath it was the swift contemptuous comment, "They're all alike."

Priscilla shut her eyes. She was listening for the first sound of Tussie's or Fritzing's footfall, the glad sound heralding the approach of something to eat, and wishing Robin would go away. He was kind at times and obliging, but on the whole a nuisance. It was a great pity there were so many people in the world who were nuisances and did not know it. Somebody ought to tell them,—their mothers, or other useful persons of that sort. She vaguely decided that the next time she met Robin and was strengthened properly by food she would say a few things to him from which recovery would take a long while.

"Are you—not well?" Robin asked, after a silence during which his eyes never left her and hers were shut; and even to himself his voice sounded deeper, more intense than usual.

"Oh yes," murmured Priscilla with a little sigh.

"Are you—happy?"

Happy? Can anybody who is supperless, dinnerless, breakfastless, be happy, Priscilla wondered? But the question struck her as funny, and the vibrating tones in which it was asked struck her as rather funny too, and she opened her eyes for a moment to look up at Robin with a smile of amusement—a smile that she could not guess was turned by the hunger within her into something wistful and tremulous. "Yes," said Priscilla in that strange pathetic voice, "I—think so." And after a brief glance at him down went her weary eyelids again.

The next thing that happened was that Robin, who was trembling, kissed her hand. This she let him do with perfect placidity. Every German woman is used to having her hand kissed. It is kissed on meeting, it is kissed on parting, it is kissed at a great many odd times in between; she holds it up mechanically when she comes across a male acquaintance; she is never surprised at the ceremony; the only thing that surprises her is if it is left out. Priscilla then simply thought Robin was going. "What a mercy," she said to herself, glancing at him a moment through her eyelashes. But Robin was not used to hand-kissing and saw things in a very different light. He felt she made no attempt to draw her hand away, he heard her murmuring something inarticulate—it was merely Good-bye—he was hurled along to his doom; and stooping over her the unfortunate young man kissed her hair.

Priscilla opened her eyes suddenly and very wide. I don't know what folly he would have perpetrated next, or what sillinesses were on the tip of his tongue, or what meaning he still chose to read in her look, but an instant afterwards he was brought down for ever from the giddy heights of his illusions: Priscilla boxed his ears.

I am sorry to have to record it. It is always sweeter if a woman does not box ears. The action is shrewish, benighted, mediæval, nay, barbarous; and this box was a very hard one indeed, extraordinarily hard for so little a hand and so fasting a girl. But we know she had twice already been on the verge of doing it; and the pent-up vigour of what the policeman had not got and what the mother in the train had not got was added I imagine to what Robin got. Anyhow it was efficacious. There was an exclamation—I think of surprise, for surely a young man would not have minded the pain?—and he put his hand up quickly to his face. Priscilla got up just as quickly out of her chair and rang the handbell furiously, her eyes on his, her face ablaze. Annalise must have thrown herself down the ladder, for they hardly seemed to have been standing there an instant face to face, their eyes on a level, he scarlet, she white, both deadly silent, before the maid was in the room.

"This person has insulted me," said Priscilla, turning to her and pointing at Robin. "He never comes here again. Don't let me find you forgetting that," she added, frowning at the girl; for she remembered they had been seen talking eagerly together at the children's treat.

"I never"—began Robin.

"Will you go?"

Annalise opened the door for him. He went out, and she shut it behind him. Then she walked sedately across the room again, looking sideways at the Princess, who took no notice of her but stood motionless by the table gazing straight before her, her lips compressed, her face set in a kind of frozen white rage, and having got into the bathroom Annalise began to run.

She ran out at the back door, in again at Fritzing's back door, out at his front door into the street, and caught up Robin as he was turning down the lane to the vicarage. "What have you done?" she asked him breathlessly, in German.

"Done?" Robin threw back his head and laughed quite loud.

"Sh—sh," said Annalise, glancing back fearfully over her shoulder.

"Done?" said Robin, subduing his bitter mirth. "What do you suppose I've done? I've done what any man would have in my place—encouraged, almost asked to do it. I kissed your young lady, *liebes Fräulein*, and she pretended not to like it. Now isn't that what a sensible girl like you would call absurd?"

But Annalise started back from the hand he held out to her in genuine horror. "What?" she cried, "What?"

"What? What?" mocked Robin. "Well then, what? Are you all such prudes in Germany? Even you pretending, you little hypocrite?"

"Oh," cried Annalise hysterically, pushing him away with both her hands, "what have you done? *Elender Junge*, what have you done?"

"I think you must all be mad," said Robin angrily. "You can't persuade me that nobody ever kisses anybody over in Germany."

"Oh yes they do—oh yes they do," cried Annalise, wringing her hands, "but neither there nor anywhere else—in England, anywhere in the world—do the sons of pastors—the sons of pastors—" She seemed to struggle for breath, and twisted and untwisted her apron round her hands in a storm of agitation while Robin, utterly astonished, stared at her—"Neither there nor anywhere else do they—the sons of pastors—kiss—kiss royal princesses."

It was now Robin's turn to say "What?"

XVI

He went up to Cambridge the next morning. Term had not begun, but he went; a Robin with all the briskness gone out of him, and if still with something of the bird left only of a bird that is moulting. His father was mildly surprised, but applauded the apparent desire for solitary study. His mother was violently surprised, and tried hard to get at his true reasons. She saw with the piercing eye of a relation—that eye from which hardly anything can ever be hidden—that something had happened and that the something was sobering and unpleasant. She could not imagine what it was, for she did not know he had been to Creeper Cottage the night before and all the afternoon and at dinner he had talked and behaved as usual. Now he did not talk at all, and his behaviour was limited to a hasty packing of portmanteaus. Determined to question him she called him into the study just before he started, and shut the door.

"I must go mater," he said, pulling out his watch; he had carefully avoided her since breakfast though she had laid many traps for him.

"Robin, I want to tell you that I think you splendid."

"Splendid? What on earth for? You were telling me a very different sort of thing a day or two ago."

"I am sorry now for what I said on Sunday."

"I don't think a mother ought ever to say she's sorry," said Robin gloomily.

"Not if she is?"

"She oughtn't to say so."

"Well dear let us be friends. Don't go away angry with me. I do appreciate you so much for going. You are my own dear boy." And she put her hands on his shoulders.

He took out his watch again. "I say, I must be off."

"Don't suppose a mother doesn't see and understand."

"Oh I don't suppose anything. Good-bye mater."

"I think it so splendid of you to go, to turn your back on temptation, to unwind yourself from that wretched girl's coils."

"Coils?"

"My Robin"—she stroked his cheek, the same cheek, as it happened, Priscilla had smitten—"my Robin must not throw himself away. I am ambitious where you are concerned, my darling. It would have broken my heart for you to have married a nobody—perhaps a worse than nobody."

Robin, who was staring at her with an indescribable expression on his face, took her hands off his shoulders. "Look here mater," he said—and he was seized by a desire to laugh terrifically—"there is nothing in the world quite so amusing as the way people will talk wisely of things they don't in the faintest degree understand. They seem to feel wise in proportion to their ignorance. I expect you think that's a funny speech for me to make. I can tell you I don't think it half as funny as yours was. Good-bye. I shall miss my train you know if you keep me, and then I'd be exposed again to those—what was the word? ah, yes—coils. Coils!" He burst into loud laughter. "Good-bye mater."

She was staring at him blankly. He hastily brushed her forehead with his moustache and hurried to the door, his face full of strange mirth. "I say," he said, putting in his head again, "there's just one thing I'd like to say."

She made an eager step towards him. "Do say it my darling—say all that is in your heart."

"Oh it's not much—it's only God help poor Tuss." And that was the last of him. She heard him chuckling all down the passage; but long before his fly had reached Ullerton he had left off doing that and was moulting again.

It rained that day in Somersetshire, a steady, hopeless rain that soaked many a leaf off the trees before its time and made the year look suddenly quite old. From the windows of Creeper Cottage you could see the water running in rivulets down the hill into the deserted village, and wreaths of mist hanging about the downs beyond. The dripping tombstone that blocked Priscilla's window grew danker and blacker as the day went by. The fires in the cottage burnt badly, for the wood had somehow got wet. The oilcloth and the wall-papers looked very dismal in the grey daylight. Rain came in underneath the two front doors and made puddles that nobody wiped away.

Priscilla had got up very late, after a night spent staring into the darkness, and then had sent for Fritzing and told him what Robin had done. The unhappy man's horror will be easily imagined. She was in bed the night before when he came in, quite cured of her hunger and only wanting to be alone with her wrath. Fritzing had found no one in the parlour but Tussie clasping an immense biscuit-tin in his arms, with a face so tragic that

Fritzing thought something terrible must have happened. Tussie had returned joyfully, laden with biscuits and sardines, to find the girl standing straight and speechless by the table, her face rigid, her eyes ablaze. She had not so much as glanced at the biscuits; she had not said a single word; her look rested on him a moment as though she did not see him and then she went into the next room and upstairs to bed. He knew she went upstairs to bed for in Creeper Cottage you could hear everything.

Fritzing coming in a few minutes later without the cook he had hoped to find, was glad enough of Tussie's sardines and biscuits—they were ginger biscuits—and while he ate them, abstractedly and together, Tussie looked on and wondered in spite of his wretchedness what the combination could possibly taste like. Then, after a late breakfast on the Wednesday morning, Priscilla sent for Fritzing and told him what Robin had done. The burdened man, so full already of anxieties and worries, was shattered by the blow. "I have always held duelling in extreme contempt," he said when at last he could speak, "but now I shall certainly fight."

"Fight? You? Fritzi, I've only told you because I—I feel so unprotected here and you must keep him off if he ever tries to come again. But you shall not fight. What, first he is to insult me and then hurt or kill my Fritzi? Besides, nobody ever fights duels in England."

"That remains to be seen. I shall now go to his house and insult him steadily for half an hour. At the expiration of that time he will probably be himself anxious to fight. We might go to France—"

"Oh Fritzi don't be so dreadful. Don't go to him—leave him alone—nobody must ever know—"

"I shall now go and insult him," repeated Fritzing with an inflexibility that silenced her.

And she saw him a minute later pass her window under his umbrella, splashing indifferently through all the puddles, battle and destruction in his face.

Robin, however, was at Ullerton by the time Fritzing got to the vicarage. He waved the servant aside when she told him he had gone, and insisted on penetrating into the presence of the young man's father. He waved Mrs. Morrison aside too when she tried to substitute herself for the vicar, and did at last by his stony persistency get into the good man's presence. Not until the vicar himself told him that Robin had gone would Fritzing believe it. "The villain has fled," he told Priscilla, coming back drenched in body but unquenchable in spirit. "Your chastisement, ma'am, was very effectual."

"If he's gone, then don't let us think about him any more."

"Nay, ma'am, I now set out for Cambridge. If I may not meet him fairly in duel and have my chance of honourably removing him from a world that has had enough of him, I would fain in my turn box his ears."

But Priscilla caught him by both arms. "Why, Fritzi," she cried, "he might remove you and not you him—and from a world that hasn't had nearly enough of you. Fritzi, you cannot leave me. I won't let you go. I wish I had never told you. Don't let us talk of it ever again. It is hateful to me. I—I can't bear it." And she looked into his face with something very like tears in her eyes.

Of course Fritzing stayed. How could he go away even for one hour, even in search of a cook, when such dreadful things happened? He was bowed down by the burden of his responsibilities. He went into his sitting-room and spent the morning striding up and down it between the street door and the door into the kitchen,—a stride and a half one way, and a stride and a half back back again,—doing what all evildoers have to do sooner or later, cudgelling his brains for a way out of life's complications: and every now and then the terribleness of what had happened to his Princess, his guarded Princess, his unapproachable one, came over him with a fresh wave of horror and he groaned aloud.

In the kitchen sat the Shuttleworth kitchenmaid, a most accomplished young person, listening to the groans and wondering what next. Tussie had sent her, with fearful threats of what sort of character she would get if she refused to go. She had at once given notice, but had been forced all the same to go, being driven over in a dog-cart in the early morning rain by a groom who made laboured pleasantries at her expense. She could cook very well, almost as well as that great personage the Shuttleworth cook, but she could only cook if there were things to be cooked; and what she found at Creeper Cottage was the rest of the ginger biscuits and sardines. Well, I will not linger over that. Priscilla did get breakfast somehow, the girl, after trying vainly to strike sparks of helpfulness out of Annalise, going to the store and ordering what was necessary. Then she washed up, while Annalise tripped in and out for the express purpose, so it seemed, of turning up her nose; then she sat and waited and wondered what next. For a long time she supposed somebody would send for her to come and talk about luncheon; but nobody did. She heard the ceaseless stridings in the next room, and every now and then the groans. The rain on the kitchen window did not patter more ceaselessly than the footsteps strode up and down, and the groans got very much on to the girl's nerves. At last she decided that no person who was groaning like that would ever want to order luncheon, and she had better go to the young lady. She went out accordingly and knocked at Priscilla's door. Priscilla was in her chair by the fire, lost in troublous thought. She looked vaguely at the kitchenmaid for a moment, and then asked her to go away. "I'm busy," explained Priscilla, whose hands were folded in her lap.

"Please miss, what do you wish for luncheon?"

"Who are you?"

"I'm the—assistant cook at the 'All, miss. Lady Shuttleworth's assistant cook. Sir Augustus desired me to cook for you to-day."

"Then please do it."

"Yes miss. What do you wish for luncheon?"

"Nothing."

"Yes miss. And the gentleman—don't he want nothing neither?"

"He'll probably tell you when he does."

"Yes miss. It's as well to know a little beforehand, ain't it, miss. There's nothing in the—a-hem—'ouse, and I suppose I'd have to buy something."

"Please do."

"Yes miss. Perhaps if you'd tell me what the gentleman likes I could go out and get it."

"But I don't know what he likes. And wouldn't you get wet? Send somebody."

"Yes miss. Who?"

Priscilla gazed at her a moment. "Ah yes—" she said, "I forgot. I'm afraid there isn't anybody. I think you had better ask my uncle what he wants, and then if you would—I'm very sorry you should have such bad weather—but if you don't mind, would you go and buy the things?"

"Yes miss."

The girl went away, and Priscilla began for the first time to consider the probability of her having in the near future to think of and order three meals every day of her life; and not only three meals, but she dimly perceived there would be a multitude of other dreary things to think of and order,—their linen, for instance, must be washed, and how did one set about that? And would not Fritzing's buttons presently come off and have to be sewn on again? His socks, when they went into holes, could be thrown out of the window and new ones bought, but even Priscilla saw that you could not throw a whole coat out of a window because its buttons had come off. There would, then, have to be some mending done for Fritzing, and Annalise would certainly not be the one to do it. Was the simple life a sordid life as well? Did it only look simple from outside and far away? And was it, close, mere drudging? A fear came over her that her soul, her precious soul, for whose sake she had dared everything, instead of being able to spread its wings in the light of a glorious clear life was going to be choked out of existence by weeds just as completely as at Kunitz.

The Shuttleworth kitchenmaid meanwhile, who was not hindered at every turn by a regard for her soul, made her way to Fritzing as she had been told and inquired of him what she should cook for his dinner. No man likes to be interrupted in his groanings; and Fritzing, who was not hungry and was startled by the sudden appearance of a stranger in his room asking him intimate questions, a person of whose presence in the cottage he had been unaware, flew at her. "Woman, what have I to do with you?" he cried, stopping in his walk and confronting her with surprising fierceness. "Is it seemly to burst in on a man like this? Have you no decency? No respect for another's privacy? Begone, I command you—begone! Begone!" And he made the same movements with his hands that persons do when they shoo away fowls or other animals in flocks.

This was too much for the Shuttleworth kitchenmaid. The obligations, she considered, were all on the side of Creeper Cottage, and she retreated in amazement and anger to the kitchen, put on her hat and mackintosh, and at once departed, regardless of the rain and the consequences, through two miles of dripping lanes to Symford Hall. What would have happened to her there if she had been discovered by Tussie I do not know, but I imagine it would have been something bad. She was saved, however, by his being in bed, clutched by the throat by a violent cold; and there he lay helpless, burning and shivering and throbbing, the pains of his body increased a hundredfold by the distraction of his mind about Priscilla. Why, Tussie asked himself over and over again, had she looked so strange the night before? Why had she gone starving to bed? What was she doing to-day? Was the kitchenmaid taking proper care of her? Was she keeping warm and dry this shocking weather? Had she slept comfortably the first night in her little home? Poor Tussie. It is a grievous thing to love any one too much; a grievous, wasteful, paralyzing thing; a tumbling of the universe out of focus, a bringing of the whole world down to the mean level of one desire, a shutting out of wider, more beautiful feelings, a wrapping of one's self in a thick garment of selfishness, outside which all the dear, tender, modest, everyday affections and friendships, the wholesome, ordinary loves, the precious loves of use and wont, are left to shiver and grow cold. Tussie's mother sat outside growing very cold indeed. Her heart was stricken within her. She, most orderly of women, did not in the least mind, so occupied was she with deeper cares, that her household was in rebellion, her cook who had been with her practically all her life leaving because she had been commanded by Tussie, before he had to fall back on the kitchenmaid, to proceed forthwith to Creeper Cottage and stay there indefinitely; her kitchenmaid, also a valued functionary, leaving; Bryce, Tussie's servant who took such care of him and was so clever in sickness, gone suddenly in his indignation at having to go at all,—all these things no longer mattered. Nor did it matter that the coming of age festivities were thrown into hopeless confusion by Tussie's illness, that the guests must all be telegraphed to and put off, that the whole village would be aghast at such a disappointment, that all her plans and preparations had been wasted. As the first day and night of illness dragged slowly past she grew to be nothing but one great ache of yearning over her sick boy, a most soul-rending yearning to do what she knew was for ever impossible, to put her arms so close round him, so close, so carefully, so tenderly, that nothing, no evil, no pain, could get through that clasp of love to hurt him any more.

"Why don't you take better care of your only son?" said the doctor grimly after he had seen Tussie that evening, who by that time was in a very pitiable condition.

Lady Shuttleworth stared at him, wide-eyed and speechless.

"It's absurd, you know, to let him get into this state. I've often warned you. He can't be allowed to play ducks and drakes with himself like other young men. He's got no strength to fall back upon. I consider you are directly responsible for this illness. Why do you let him go out at night this time of year? Why do you let him over-exert himself? I suppose," said the doctor, who had brought Tussie into the world and was as brutal as he was clever, besides being at that moment extremely angry, "I suppose you want to lose him, eh?"

How could she explain to him what she knew to be true, that the one person responsible for Tussie's illness was Priscilla? She therefore only stared, wide-eyed and speechless; and indeed her heart was very nearly broken.

XVII

About three o'clock that afternoon Priscilla saw quite clearly what she had dimly perceived in the morning, that if there was to be domestic peace in Creeper Cottage she must bestir herself. She did not like bestirring herself; at least, not in such directions. She would go out and help the poor, talk to them, cheer them, nurse their babies even and stir their porridge, but she had not up to this point realized her own needs, and how urgent they could be and how importunate. It was hunger that cleared her vision. The first time she was hungry she had been amused. Now when it happened again she was both surprised and indignant. "Can one's wretched body *never* keep quiet?" she thought impatiently, when the first twinges dragged her relentlessly out of her dejected dreaming by the fire. She remembered the cold tremblings of the night before, and felt that that state would certainly be reached again quite soon if she did not stop it at once. She rang for Annalise. "Tell the cook I will have some luncheon after all," she said.

"The cook is gone," said Annalise, whose eyes were more aggressively swollen than they had yet been.

"Gone where?"

"Gone away. Gone for ever."

"But why?" asked Priscilla, really dismayed.

"The Herr Geheimrath insulted her. I heard him doing it. No woman of decency can permit such a tone. She at once left. There has been no dinner to-day. There will be, I greatly fear, n—o—o—supp—pper." And Annalise gave a loud sob and covered her face with her apron.

Then Priscilla saw that if life was to roll along at all it was her shoulder that would have to be put to the wheel. Fritzing's shoulder was evidently not a popular one among the lower classes. The vision of her own doing anything with wheels was sufficiently amazing, but she did not stop to gaze upon it. "Annalise," she said, getting up quickly and giving herself a little shake, "fetch me my hat and coat. I'm going out."

Annalise let her apron drop far enough to enable her to point to the deluge going on out of doors. "Not in this weather?" she faltered, images of garments soaked in mud and needing much drying and brushing troubling her.

"Get me the things," said Priscilla.

"Your Grand Ducal Highness will be wet through."

"Get me the things. And don't cry quite so much. Crying really is the most shocking waste of time."

Annalise withdrew, and Priscilla went round to Fritzing. It was the first time she had been round to him. He was sitting at his table, his head in his hands, staring at the furnisher's bill, and he started to see her coming in unexpectedly through the kitchen, and shut the bill hastily in a drawer.

"Fritzi, have you had anything to eat to-day?"

"Certainly. I had an excellent breakfast."

"Nothing since?"

"I have not yet felt the need."

"You know the cook Lady Shuttleworth sent has gone again?"

"What, that woman who burst in upon me was Lady Shuttleworth's cook?"

"Yes. And you frightened her so she ran home."

"Ma'am, she overstepped the limits of my patience."

"Dear Fritzi, I often wonder where exactly the limits of your patience are. With me they have withdrawn into infinite space—I've never been able to reach them. But every one else seems to have a knack—well, somebody must cook. You tell me Annalise won't. Perhaps she really can't. Anyhow I cannot mention it to her, because it would be too horrible to have her flatly refusing to do something I told her to do and yet not be able to send her away. But somebody must cook, and I'm going out to get the somebody. Hush"—she put up her hand as he opened his mouth to speak—"I know it's raining. I know I'll get wet. Don't let us waste time protesting. I'm going."

Fritzing was conscience-stricken. "Ma'am," he said, "you must forgive me for unwittingly bringing this bother upon you. Had I had time for reflection I would not have been so sharp. But the woman burst upon me. I knew not who she was. Sooner than offend her I would have cut out my tongue, could I have foreseen you would yourself go in search in the rain of a substitute. Permit me to seek another."

"No, no—you have no luck with cooks," said Priscilla smiling. "I'm going. Why I feel more cheerful already—just getting out of that chair makes me feel better."

"Were you not cheerful before?" inquired Fritzing anxiously.

"Not very," admitted Priscilla. "But then neither were you. Don't suppose I didn't see you with your head in your hands when I came in. Cheerful people never seize their heads in that way. Now Fritzi I know what's worrying you—it's that absurd affair last night. I've left off thinking about it. I'm going to be very happy again, and so must you be. We won't let one mad young man turn all our beautiful life sour, will we?"

He bent down and kissed her hand. "Permit me to accompany you at least," he begged. "I cannot endure—"

But she shook her head; and as she presently walked through the rain holding Fritzing's umbrella,—none had been bought to replace hers, broken on the journey—getting muddier and more draggled every minute, she felt that now indeed she had got down to elementary conditions, climbed right down out of the clouds to the place where life lies unvarnished and uncomfortable, where Necessity spends her time forcing you to do all the things you don't like, where the whole world seems hungry and muddy and wet. It was an extraordinary experience for her, this slopping through the mud with soaking shoes, no prospect of a meal, and a heart that insisted on sinking in spite of her attempts to persuade herself that the situation was amusing. It did not amuse her. It might have amused somebody else,—the Grand Duke, for instance, if he could have watched her now (from, say, a Gothic window, himself dry and fed and taken care of), being punished so naturally and inevitably by the weapons Providence never allows to rust, those weapons that save parents and guardians so much personal exertion if only they will let things take their course, those sharp, swift consequences that attend the actions of the impetuous. I might, indeed, if this were a sermon and there were a congregation unable to get away, expatiate on the habit these weapons have of smiting with equal fury the just and the unjust; how you only need to be a little foolish, quite a little foolish, under conditions that seem to force it upon you, and down they come, sure and relentless, and you are smitten with a thoroughness that leaves you lame for years; how motives are nothing, circumstances are nothing; how the motives may have been aflame with goodness, the circumstances such that any other course was impossible; how all these things don't matter in the least,—you are and shall be smitten. But this is not a sermon. I have no congregation. And why should I preach to a reader who meanwhile has skipped?

It comforted Priscilla to find that almost the whole village wanted to come and cook for her, or as the women put it "do" for her. Their cooking powers were strictly limited, and they proposed to make up for this by doing for her very completely in other ways; they would scrub, sweep, clean windows, wash,—anything and everything they would do. Would they also sew buttons on her uncle's clothes? Priscilla asked anxiously. And they were ready to sew buttons all over Fritzing if buttons would make him happy. This eagerness was very gratifying, but it was embarrassing as well. The extremely aged and the extremely young were the only ones that refrained from offering their services. Some of the girls were excluded as too weedy; some of the mothers because their babies were too new; some of the wives because their husbands were too exacting; but when Priscilla counted up the names she had written down she found there were twenty-five. For a moment she was staggered. Then she rose to the occasion and got out of the difficulty with what she thought great skill, arranging, as it was impossible to disappoint twenty-four of these, that they should take it in turn, each coming for one day until all had had a day and then beginning again with the first one. It seemed a brilliant plan. Life at Creeper Cottage promised to be very varied. She gathered them together in the village shop to talk it over. She asked them if they thought ten shillings a day and food would be enough. She asked it hesitatingly, afraid lest she were making them an impossibly frugal offer. She was relieved at the cry of assent; but it was followed after a moment by murmurs from the married women, when they had had time to reflect, that it was unfair to pay the raw young ones at the same rate as themselves. Priscilla however turned a deaf ear to their murmurings. "The girls may not," she said, raising her hand to impose silence, "be able to get through as much as you do in a day, but they'll be just as tired when evening comes. Certainly I shall give them the same wages." She made them draw lots as to who should begin, and took the winner home with her then and there; she too, though the day was far spent, was to have her ten shillings. "What, have you forgotten your New Testaments?" Priscilla cried, when more murmurs greeted this announcement. "Don't you remember the people who came at the eleventh hour to labour in the vineyard and got just the same as the others? Why should I try to improve on parables?" And there was something about Priscilla, an air, an authority, that twisted the women of Symford into any shape of agreement she chose. The twenty-four went their several ways. The twenty-fifth ran home to put on a clean apron, and got back to the shop in time to carry the eggs and butter and bread Priscilla had bought. "I forgot to bring any money," said Priscilla when the postmistress—it was she who kept the village shop—told her how much it came to. "Does it matter?"

"Oh don't mention it, Miss Neumann-Schultz," was the pleasant answer of that genteel and trustful lady; and she suggested that Priscilla should take with her a well-recommended leg of mutton she had that day for sale as well. Priscilla shuddered at the sight of it and determined never to eat legs of mutton again. The bacon, too, piled up on the counter, revolted her. The only things that looked as decent raw as when they were cooked were eggs; and on eggs she decided she and Fritzing would in future live. She broke off a piece of the crust of the bread Mrs. Vickerton was wrapping up and ate it, putting great pressure on herself to do it carelessly, with a becoming indifference.

"It's good bread," said Mrs. Vickerton, doing up her parcel.

"Where in the world do you get it from?" asked Priscilla enthusiastically. "The man must be a genius."

"The carrier brings it every day," said Mrs. Vickerton, pleased and touched by such appreciation. "It's a Minehead baker's."

"He ought to be given an order, if ever man ought."

"An order? For you regular, Miss Neumann-Schultz?"

"No, no,—the sort you pin on your breast," said Priscilla.

"Ho," smiled Mrs. Vickerton vaguely, who did not follow; she was so genteel that she could never have enough of aspirates. And Priscilla, giving the parcel to her breathless new help, hurried back to Creeper Cottage.

Now this help, or char-girl—you could not call her a charwoman she was manifestly still so very young—was that Emma who had been obliged to tell the vicar's wife about Priscilla's children's treat and who did not punctually return books. I will not go so far as to say that not to return books punctually is sinful, though deep down in my soul I think it is, but anyhow it is a symptom of moral slackness. Emma was quite good so long as she was left alone. She could walk quite straight so long as there were no stones in the way and nobody to pull her aside. If there were stones, she instantly stumbled; if somebody pulled, she instantly went. She was weak, amiable, well-intentioned. She had a widowed father who was unpleasant and who sometimes beat her on Saturday nights, and on Sunday mornings sometimes, if the fumes of the Cock and Hens still hung about him, threw things at her before she went to church. A widowed father in Emma's class is an ill being to live with. The vicar did his best to comfort her. Mrs. Morrison talked of the commandments and of honouring one's father and mother and of how the less there was to honour the greater the glory of doing it; and Emma was so amiable that she actually did manage to honour him six days out of the seven. At the same time she could not help thinking it would be nice to go away to a place where he wasn't. They were extremely poor; almost the poorest family in the village, and the vision of possessing ten shillings of her very own was a dizzy one. She had a sweetheart, and she had sent him word by a younger sister of the good fortune that had befallen her and begged him to come up to Creeper Cottage that evening and help her carry the precious wages safely home; and at nine o'clock when her work was done she presented herself all blushes and smiles before Priscilla and shyly asked her for them.

Priscilla was alone in her parlour reading. She referred her, as her habit was, to Fritzing; but Fritzing had gone out for a little air, the rain having cleared off, and when the girl told her so Priscilla bade her come round in the morning and fetch the money.

Emma's face fell so woefully at this—was not her John at that moment all expectant round the corner?—that Priscilla smiled and got up to see if she could find some money herself. In the first drawer she opened in Fritzing's sitting-room was a pocket-book, and in this pocket-book Fritzing's last five-pound note. There was nothing else except the furnisher's bill. She pushed that on one side without looking at it; what did bills matter? Bills never yet had mattered to Priscilla. She pushed it on one side and searched for silver, but found none. "Perhaps you can change this?" she said, holding out the note.

"The shop's shut now, miss," said Laura, gazing with round eyes at the mighty sum.

"Well then take it, and bring me the change in the morning."

Emma took it with trembling fingers—she had not in her life touched so much money—and ran out into the darkness to where her John was waiting. Symford never saw either of them again. Priscilla never saw her change. Emma went to perdition. Priscilla went back to her chair by the fire. She was under the distinct and comfortable impression that she had been the means of making the girl happy. "How easy it is, making people happy," thought Priscilla placidly, the sweetest smile on her charming mouth.

XVIII

Bad luck, it will be seen, dogged the footsteps of Priscilla. Never indeed for a single hour after she entered Creeper Cottage did the gloomy lady cease from her attentions. The place was pervaded by her thick and evil atmosphere. Fritzing could not go out for an airing without something of far-reaching consequence happening while he was away. It was of course Bad Luck that made the one girl in Symford who was easily swayed by passing winds of temptation draw the lot that put the five-pound note into her hands; if she had come to the cottage just one day later, or if the rain had gone on just half an hour longer and kept Fritzing indoors, she would, I have no doubt whatever, be still in Symford practising every feeble virtue either on her father or on her John, by this time probably her very own John. As it was she was a thief, a lost soul, a banished face for ever from the ways of grace.

Thus are we all the sport of circumstance. Thus was all Symford the sport of Priscilla. Fritzing knew nothing of his loss. He had not told Priscilla a word of his money difficulties, his idea being to keep every cloud from her life as long and as completely as possible. Besides, how idle to talk of these things to some one who could in no way help him with counsel or suggestions. He had put the money in his drawer, and the thought that it was still unchanged and safe comforted him a little in the watches of the sleepless nights.

Nothing particular happened on the Thursday morning, except that the second of the twenty-five kept on breaking things, and Priscilla who was helping Fritzing arrange the books he had ordered from London remarked at the fifth terrific smash, a smash so terrific as to cause Creeper Cottage to tremble all over, that more crockery had better be bought.

"Yes," said Fritzing, glancing swiftly at her with almost a guilty glance.

He felt very keenly his want of resourcefulness in this matter of getting the money over from Germany, but he clung to the hope that a few more wakeful nights would clear his brain and show him the way; and meanwhile there was always the five-pound note in the drawer.

"And Fritzi, I shall have to get some clothes soon," Priscilla went on, dusting the books as he handed them to her.

"Clothes, ma'am?" repeated Fritzing, straightening himself to stare at her.

"Those things you bought for me in Gerstein—they're delicious, they're curiosities, but they're not clothes. I mean always to keep them. I'll have them put in a glass case, and they shall always be near me when we're happy again."

"Happy again, ma'am?"

"Settled again, I mean," quickly amended Priscilla.

She dusted in silence for a little, and began to put the books she had dusted in the shelves. "I'd better write to Paris," she said presently.

Fritzing jumped. "Paris, ma'am?"

"They've got my measurements. This dress can't stand much more. It's the one I've worn all the time. The soaking it got yesterday was very bad for it. You don't see such things, but if you did you'd probably get a tremendous shock."

"Ma'am, if you write to Paris you must give your own name, which of course is impossible. They will send nothing to an unknown customer in England called Neumann-Schultz."

"Oh but we'd send the money with the order. That's quite easy, isn't it?"

"Perfectly easy," said Fritzing in an oddly exasperated voice; at once adding, still more snappily, "Might I request your Grand Ducal Highness to have the goodness not to put my Æschylus—a most valuable edition—head downwards on the shelf? It is a manner of treating books often to be observed in housemaids and similar ignorants. But you, ma'am, have been trained by me I trust in other and more reverent ways of handling what is left to us of the mighty spirits of the past."

"I'm sorry," said Priscilla, hastily turning the Æschylus right side up again; and by launching forth into a long and extremely bitter dissertation on the various ways persons of no intellectual conscience have of ill-treating books, he got rid of some of his agitation and fixed her attention for the time on questions less fraught with complications than clothes from Paris.

About half-past two they were still sitting over the eggs and bread and butter that Priscilla ordered three times a day and that Fritzing ate with unquestioning obedience, when the Shuttleworth victoria stopped in front of the cottage and Lady Shuttleworth got out. Fritzing, polite man, hastened to meet her, pushing aside the footman and offering his arm. She looked at him vaguely, and asked if his niece were at home.

"Certainly," said Fritzing, leading her into Priscilla's parlour. "Shall I inquire if she will receive you?"

"Do," said Lady Shuttleworth, taking no apparent notice of the odd wording of this question. "Tussie isn't well," she said the moment Priscilla appeared, fixing her eyes on her face but looking as though she hardly saw her, as though she saw past her, through her, to something beyond, while she said a lesson learned by rote.

"Isn't he? Oh I'm sorry," said Priscilla.

"He caught cold last Sunday at your treat. He oughtn't to have run those races with the boys. He can't—stand—much."

Priscilla looked at her questioningly. The old lady's face was quite set and calm, but there had been a queer catch in her voice at the last words.

"Why does he do such things, then?" asked Priscilla, feeling vaguely distressed.

"Ah yes, my dear—why? That is a question for you to answer, is it not?"

"For me?"

"On Tuesday night," continued Lady Shuttleworth, "he was ill when he left home to come here. He would come. It was a terrible night for a delicate boy to go out. And he didn't stay here, I understand. He went out to buy something after closing time, and stood a long while trying to wake the people up."

"Yes," said Priscilla, feeling guilty, "I—that was my fault. He went for me."

"Yes my dear. Since then he has been ill. I've come to ask you if you'll drive back with me and see if—if you cannot persuade him that you are happy. He seems to be much—troubled."

"Troubled?"

"He seems to be afraid you are not happy. You know," she added with a little quavering smile, "Tussie is very kind. He is very unselfish. He takes everybody's burdens on his shoulders. He seems to be quite haunted by the idea that your life here is unendurably uncomfortable, and it worries him dreadfully that he can't get to you to set things straight. I think if he were to see you, and you were very cheerful, and—and smiled, my dear, it might help to get him over this."

"Get him over this?" echoed Priscilla. "Is he so ill?"

Lady Shuttleworth looked at her and said nothing.

"Of course I'll come," said Priscilla, hastily ringing the bell.

"But you must not look unhappy," said Lady Shuttleworth, laying her hand on the girl's arm, "that would make matters ten times worse. You must promise to be as gay as possible."

"Yes, yes—I'll be gay," promised Priscilla, while her heart became as lead within her at the thought that she was the cause of poor Tussie's sufferings. But was she really, she asked herself during the drive? What had she done but accept help eagerly offered? Surely it was very innocent to do that? It was what she had been doing all her life, and people had been delighted when she let them be kind to her, and certainly had not got ill immediately afterwards. Were you never to let anybody do anything for you lest while they were doing it they should get wet feet and things, and then their colds would be upon your head? She was very sorry Tussie should be ill, dreadfully sorry. He was so kind and good that it was impossible not to like him. She did like him. She liked him quite as well as most young men and much better than many. "I'm afraid you are very unhappy," she said suddenly to Lady Shuttleworth, struck by the look on her face as she leaned back, silent, in her corner.

"I do feel rather at my wits' end," said Lady Shuttleworth. "For instance, I'm wondering whether what I'm doing now isn't a great mistake."

"What you are doing now?"

"Taking you to see Tussie."

"Oh but I promise to be cheerful. I'll tell him how comfortable we are. He'll see I look well taken care of."

"But for all that I'm afraid he may—he may—"

"Why, we're going to be tremendously taken care of. Even he will see that. Only think—I've engaged twenty-five cooks."

"Twenty-five cooks?" echoed Lady Shuttleworth, staring in spite of her sorrows. "But isn't my kitchenmaid—?"

"Oh she left us almost at once. She couldn't stand my uncle. He is rather difficult to stand at first. You have to know him quite a long while before you can begin to like him. And I don't think kitchenmaids ever would begin."

"But my dear, twenty-five cooks?"

And Priscilla explained how and why she had come by them; and though Lady Shuttleworth, remembering the order till now prevailing in the village and the lowness of the wages, could not help thinking that here was a girl more potent for mischief than any girl she had ever met, yet a feeble gleam of amusement did, as she listened, slant across the inky blackness of her soul.

Tussie was sitting up in bed with a great many pillows behind him, finding immense difficulty in breathing, when his mother, her bonnet off and every trace of having been out removed, came in and said Miss Neumann-Schultz was downstairs.

"Downstairs? Here? In this house?" gasped Tussie, his eyes round with wonder and joy.

"Yes. She—called. Would you like her to come up and see you?"

"Oh mother!"

Lady Shuttleworth hurried out. How could she bear this, she thought, stumbling a little as though she did not see very well. She went downstairs with the sound of that Oh mother throbbing in her ears.

Tussie's temperature, high already, went up by leaps during the few minutes of waiting. He gave feverish directions to the nurse about a comfortable chair being put exactly in the right place, about his pillows being smoothed, his medicine bottles hidden, and was very anxious that the flannel garment he was made to wear when ill, a garment his mother called a nightingale—not after the bird but the lady—and that was the bluest flannel garment ever seen, should be arranged neatly over his narrow chest.

The nurse looked disapproving. She did not like her patients to be happy. Perhaps she was right. It is always better, I believe, to be cautious and careful, to husband your strength, to be deadly prudent and deadly dull. As you would poison, so should you avoid doing what the poet calls living too much in your large hours. The truly prudent never have large hours; nor should you, if you want to be comfortable. And you get your reward, I am told, in living longer; in having, that is, a few more of those years that cluster round the end, during which you are fed and carried and washed by persons who generally grumble. Who wants to be a flame, doomed to be blown out by the same gust of wind that has first fanned it to its very brightest? If you are not a flame you cannot, of course, be blown out. Gusts no longer shake you. Tempests pass you by untouched. And if besides you have the additional advantage of being extremely smug, extremely thick-skinned, you shall go on living till ninety, and not during the whole of that time be stirred by so much as a single draught.

Priscilla came up determined to be so cheerful that she began to smile almost before she got to the door. "I've come to tell you how splendidly we're getting on at the cottage," she said taking Tussie's lean hot hand, the shell of her smile remaining but the heart and substance gone out of it, he looked so pitiful and strange.

"Really? Really?" choked Tussie, putting the other lean hot hand over hers and burning all the coolness out of it.

The nurse looked still more disapproving. She had not heard Sir Augustus had a *fiancée*, and even if he had this was no time for philandering. She too had noticed the voice in which he had said Oh mother, and she saw by his eyes that his temperature had gone up. Who was this shabby young lady? She felt sure that no one so shabby could be his *fiancée*, and she could only conclude that Lady Shuttleworth must be mad.

"Nurse, I'm going to stay here a little," said Lady Shuttleworth. "I'll call you when I want you."

"I think, madam, Sir Augustus ought not—" began the nurse.

"No, no, he shall not. Go and have forty winks, nurse."

And the nurse had to go; people generally did when Lady Shuttleworth sent them.

"Sit down—no don't—stay a moment like this," said Tussie, his breath coming in little jerks,—"unless you are tired? Did you walk?"

"I'm afraid you are very ill," said Priscilla, leaving her hand in his and looking down at him with a face that all her efforts could not induce to smile.

"Oh I'll be all right soon. How good of you to come. You've not been hungry since?"

"No, no," said Priscilla, stroking his hands with her free hand and giving them soothing pats as one would to a sick child.

"Really not? I've thought of that ever since. I've never got your face that night out of my head. What had happened? While I was away—what had happened?"

"Nothing—nothing had happened," said Priscilla hastily. "I was tired. I had a mood. I get them, you know. I get angry easily. Then I like to be alone till I'm sorry."

"But what had made you angry? Had I—?"

"No, never. You have never been anything but good and kind. You've been our protecting spirit since we came here."

Tussie laughed shrilly, and immediately was seized by a coughing fit. Lady Shuttleworth stood at the foot of the bed watching him with a face from which happiness seemed to have fled for ever. Priscilla grew more and more wretched, caught, obliged to stand there, distractedly stroking his hands in her utter inability to think of anything else to do.

"A nice protecting spirit," gasped Tussie derisively, when he could speak. "Look at me here, tied down to this bed for heaven knows how long, and not able to do a thing for you."

"But there's nothing now to do. We're quite comfortable. We are really. Do, do believe it."

"Are you only comfortable, or are you happy as well?"

"Oh, we're *very* happy," said Priscilla with all the emphasis she could get into her voice; and again she tried, quite unsuccessfully, to wrench her mouth into a smile.

"Then, if you're happy, why do you look so miserable?"

He was gazing up into her face with eyes whose piercing brightness would have frightened the nurse. There was no shyness now about Tussie. There never is about persons whose temperature is 102.

"Miserable?" repeated Priscilla. She tried to smile; looked helplessly at Lady Shuttleworth; looked down again at Tussie; and stammering "Because you are so ill and it's all my fault," to her horror, to her boundless indignation at herself, two tears, big and not to be hidden, rolled down her face and dropped on to Tussie's and her clasped hands.

Tussie struggled to sit up straight. "Look, mother, look—" he cried, gasping, "my beautiful one—my dear and lovely one—my darling—she's crying—I've made her cry—now never tell me I'm not a brute again—see, see what I've done!"

"Oh"—murmured Priscilla, in great distress and amazement. Was the poor dear delirious? And she tried to get her hands away.

But Tussie would not let them go. He held them in a clutch that seemed like hot iron in both his, and dragging himself nearer to them covered them with wild kisses.

Lady Shuttleworth was appalled. "Tussie," she said in a very even voice, "you must let Miss Neumann-Schultz go now. You must be quiet again now. Let her go, dear. Perhaps she'll—come again."

"Oh mother, leave me alone," cried Tussie, lying right across his pillows, his face on Priscilla's hands. "What do you know of these things? This is my darling—this is my wife—dream of my spirit—star of my soul—"

"Never in this world!" cried Lady Shuttleworth, coming round to the head of the bed as quickly as her shaking limbs would take her.

"Yes, yes, come here if you like, mother—come close—listen while I tell her how I love her. I don't care who hears. Why should I? If I weren't ill I'd care. I'd be tongue-tied—I'd have gone on being tongue-tied for ever. Oh I bless being ill, I bless being ill—I can say anything, anything—"

"Tussie, don't say it," entreated his mother. "The less you say now the more grateful you'll be later on. Let her go."

"Listen to her!" cried Tussie, interrupting his kissing of her hands to look up at Priscilla and smile with a sort of pitying wonder, "Let you go? Does one let one's life go? One's hope of salvation go? One's little precious minute of perfect happiness go? When I'm well again I shall be just as dull and stupid as ever, just such a shy fool, not able to speak—"

"But it's a gracious state"—stammered poor Priscilla.

"Loving you? Loving you?"

"No, no—not being able to speak. It's always best—"

"It isn't. It's best to be true to one's self, to show honestly what one feels, as I am now—as I am now—" And he fell to kissing her hands again.

"Tussie, this isn't being honest," said Lady Shuttleworth sternly, "it's being feverish."

"Listen to her! Was ever a man interrupted like this in the act of asking a girl to marry him?"

"Tussie!" cried Lady Shuttleworth.

"Ethel, will you marry me? Because I love you so? It's an absurd reason—the most magnificently absurd reason, but I know there's no other why you should—"

Priscilla was shaken and stricken as she had never yet been; shaken with pity, stricken with remorse. She looked down at him in dismay while he kissed her hands with desperate, overwhelming love. What was she to do? Lady Shuttleworth tried to draw her away. What was she to do? If Tussie was overwhelmed with love, she was overwhelmed with pity.

"Ethel—Ethel—" gasped Tussie, kissing her hands, looking up at her, kissing them again.

Pity overcame her, engulfed her. She bent her head down to his and laid her cheek an instant on the absurd flannel nightingale, tenderly, apologetically.

"Ethel—Ethel," choked Tussie, "will you marry me?"

"Dear Tussie," she whispered in a shaky whisper, "I promise to answer you when you are well. Not yet. Not now. Get quite well, and then if you still want an answer I promise to give you one. Now let me go."

"Ethel," implored Tussie, looking at her with a wild entreaty in his eyes, "will you kiss me? Just once—to help me to live—"

And in her desire to comfort him she stooped down again and did kiss him, soberly, almost gingerly, on the forehead.

He let her hands slide away from between his and lay back on his pillows in a state for the moment of absolute beatitude. He shut his eyes, and did not move while she crept softly out of the room.

"What have you done?" asked Lady Shuttleworth trembling, when they were safely in the passage and the door shut behind them.

"I can't think—I can't think," groaned Priscilla, wringing her hands. And, leaning against the balusters, then and there in that most public situation she began very bitterly to cry.

XIX

Priscilla went home dazed. All her suitors hitherto had approached her ceremoniously, timidly, through the Grand Duke; and we know they had not approached very near. But here was one, timid enough in health, who was positively reckless under circumstances that made most people meek. He had proposed to her arrayed in a blue flannel nightingale, and Priscilla felt that headlong self-effacement could go no further. "He must have a great soul," she said to herself over and over again during the drive home, "a great, *great* soul." And it seemed of little use wiping her tears away, so many fresh ones immediately took their place.

She ached over Tussie and Tussie's mother. What had she done? She felt she had done wrong; yet how, except by just existing? and she did feel she couldn't help doing that. Certainly she had made two kind hearts extremely miserable,—one was miserable now, and the other didn't yet know how miserable it was going to be. She ought to have known, she ought to have thought, she ought to have foreseen. She of all persons in the world ought to have been careful with young men who believed her to be of their own class. Contrition and woe took possession of Priscilla's soul. She knew it was true that she could not help existing, but she knew besides, far back in a remote and seldom investigated corner of her mind, a corner on which she did not care to turn the light of careful criticism, that she ought not to be existing in Symford. It was because she was there, out of her proper sphere, in a place she had no business to be in at all, that these strange and heart-wringing scenes with young men occurred. And Fritzing would notice her red eyes and ask what had happened; and here within two days was a second story to be told of a young man unintentionally hurried to his doom. Would Fritzing be angry? She never knew beforehand. Would he, only remembering she was grand ducal, regard it as an insult and want to fight Tussie? The vision of poor Tussie, weak, fevered, embedded in pillows, swathed in flannel, receiving bloodthirsty messages of defiance from Fritzing upset her into more tears. Fritzing, she felt at that moment, was a trial. He burdened her with his gigantic efforts to keep her from burdens. He burdened her with his inflated notions of how burdenless she ought to be. He was admirable, unselfish, devoted; but she felt it was possible to be too admirable, too unselfish, too devoted. In a word Priscilla's mind was in a state of upheaval, and the only ray of light she saw anywhere—and never was ray more watery—was that Tussie, for the moment at least, was content. The attitude of his mother, on the other hand, was distressing and disturbing. There had been no more My dears and other kind ways. She had watched her crying on the stairs in stony silence, had gone down with her to the door in stony silence, and just at the last had said in an unmistakably stony voice, "All this is very cruel."

Priscilla was overwhelmed by the difficulties of life. The world was too much with her, she felt, a very great deal too much. She sent the Shuttleworth carriage away at the entrance to the village and went in to sit with Mrs. Jones a little, so that her eyes might lose their redness before she faced Fritzing; and Mrs. Jones was so glad to see her, so full of praises of her unselfish goodness in coming in, that once again Priscilla was forced to be ashamed of herself and of everything she did.

"I'm not unselfish, and I'm not good," she said, smoothing the old lady's coverlet.

Mrs. Jones chuckled faintly. "Pretty dear," was her only comment.

"I don't think I'm pretty and I know I'm not a dear," said Priscilla, quite vexed.

"Ain't you then, deary," murmured Mrs. Jones soothingly.

Priscilla saw it was no use arguing, and taking up the Bible that always lay on the table by the bed began to read aloud. She read and read till both were quieted,—Mrs. Jones into an evidently sweet sleep, she herself into peace. Then she left off and sat for some time watching the old lady, the open Bible in-her lap, her soul filled with calm words and consolations, wondering what it could be like being so near death. Must it not be beautiful, thought Priscilla, to slip away so quietly in that sunny room, with no sound to break the peace but the ticking of the clock that marked off the last minutes, and outside the occasional footstep of a passer-by still hurrying on life's business? Wonderful to have done with everything, to have it all behind one, settled, lived through, endured. The troublous joys as well as the pains, all finished; the griefs and the stinging happinesses, all alike lived down; and now evening, and sleep. In the few days Priscilla had known her the old lady had drawn visibly nearer death. Lying there on the pillow, so little and light that she hardly pressed it down at all, she looked very near it indeed. And how kind Death was, rubbing away the traces of what must have been a sordid existence, set about years back with the usual coarse pleasures and selfish hopes,—how kind Death was, letting all there was of spirit shine out so sweetly at the end. There was an enlarged photograph of Mrs. Jones and her husband over the fireplace, a photograph taken for their silver wedding; she must have been about forty-five; how kind Death was, thought Priscilla, looking from the picture to the figure on the bed. She sighed a little, and got up. Life lay before her, an endless ladder up each of whose steep rungs she would have to clamber; in every sort of weather she would have to clamber, getting more battered, more blistered with every rung.... She looked wistfully at the figure on the bed, and sighed a little. Then she crept out, and softly shut the door.

She walked home lost in thought. As she was going up the hill to her cottage Fritzing suddenly emerged from it and indulged in movements so strange and complicated that they looked like nothing less than a desperate dancing on the doorstep. Priscilla walked faster, staring in astonishment. He made strange gestures, his face was pale, his hair rubbed up into a kind of infuriated mop.

"Why, what in the world—" began the amazed Priscilla, as soon as she was near enough.

"Ma'am, I've been robbed," shouted Fritzing; and all Symford might have heard if it had happened to be listening.

"Robbed?" repeated Priscilla. "What of?"

"Of all my money, ma'am. Of all I had—of all we had—to live on."

"Nonsense, Fritzi," said Priscilla; but she did turn a little paler. "Don't let us stand out here," she added; and she got him in and shut the street door.

He would have left it open and would have shouted his woes through it as through a trumpet down the street, oblivious of all things under heaven but his misfortune. He tore open the drawer of the writing-table. "In this drawer—in the pocket-book you see in this drawer—in this now empty pocket-book, did I leave it. It was there yesterday. It was there last night. Now it is gone. Miscreants from without have visited us. Or perhaps, viler still, miscreants from within. A miscreant, I do believe, capable of anything—Annalise—"

"Fritzi, I took a five-pound note out of that last night, if that's what you miss."

"You, ma'am?"

"To pay the girl who worked here her wages. You weren't here. I couldn't find anything smaller."

"*Gott sei Dank! Gott sei Dank!*" cried Fritzing, going back to German in his joy. "Oh ma'am, if you had told me earlier you would have spared me great anguish. Have you the change?"

"Didn't she bring it?"

"Bring it, ma'am?"

"I gave it to her last night to change. She was to bring it round this morning. Didn't she?"

Fritzing stared aghast. Then he disappeared into the kitchen. In a moment he was back again. "She has not been here," he said, in a voice packed once more with torment.

"Perhaps she has forgotten."

"Ma'am, how came you—"

"Now you're going to scold me."

"No, no—but how is it possible that you should have trusted—"

"Fritzi, you *are* going to scold me, and I'm so tired. What else has been taken? You said all your money—"

He snatched up his hat. "Nothing else, ma'am, nothing else. I will go and seek the girl." And he clapped it down over his eyes as he always did in moments of great mental stress.

"What a fuss," thought Priscilla wearily. Aloud she said, "The girl here to-day will tell you where she lives. Of course she has forgotten, or not been able to change it yet." And she left him, and went out to get into her own half of the house.

Yes, Fritzi really was a trial. Why such a fuss and such big words about five pounds? If it were lost and the girl afraid to come and say so, it didn't matter much; anyhow nothing like so much as having one's peace upset. How foolish to be so agitated and talk of having been robbed of everything. Fritzing's mind, she feared, that large, enlightened mind on whose breadth and serenity she had gazed admiringly ever since she could remember gazing at all, was shrinking to dimensions that would presently exactly match the dimensions of Creeper Cottage. She went upstairs disheartened and tired, and dropping down full length on her sofa desired Annalise to wash her face.

"Your Grand Ducal Highness has been weeping," said Annalise, whisking the sponge in and out of corners with a skill surprising in one who had only practised the process during the last ten days.

Priscilla opened her eyes to stare at her in frankest surprise, for never yet had Annalise dared make a remark unrequested. Annalise, by beginning to wash them, forced her to shut them again.

Priscilla then opened her mouth to tell her what she thought of her. Immediately Annalise's swift sponge stopped it up.

"Your Grand Ducal Highness," said Annalise, washing Priscilla's mouth with a thoroughness and an amount of water suggestive of its not having been washed for months, "told me only yesterday that weeping was a terrible—*schreckliche*—waste of time. Therefore, since your Grand Ducal Highness knows that and yet herself weeps, it is easy to see that there exists a reason for weeping which makes weeping inevitable."

"Will you—" began Priscilla, only to be stopped instantly by the ready sponge.

"Your Grand Ducal Highness is unhappy. 'Tis not to be wondered at. Trust a faithful servant, one whose life-blood is at your Grand Ducal Highness's disposal, and tell her if it is not then true that the Herr Geheimrath has decoyed you from your home and your Grossherzoglicher Herr Papa?"

"Will you—"

Again the pouncing sponge.

"My heart bleeds—indeed it bleeds—to think of the Herr Papa's sufferings, his fears, his anxieties. It is a picture on which I cannot calmly look. Day and night—for at night I lie sleepless on my bed—I am inquiring of myself what it can be, the spell that the Herr Geheimrath has cast over your Grand Ducal—"

"Will you—"

Again the pouncing sponge; but this time Priscilla caught the girl's hand, and holding it at arm's length sat up. "Are you mad?" she asked, looking at Annalise as though she saw her for the first time.

Annalise dropped the sponge and clasped her hands. "Not mad," she said, "only very, very devoted."

"No. Mad. Give me a towel."

Priscilla was so angry that she did not dare say more. If she had said a part even of what she wanted to say all would have been over between herself and Annalise; so she dried her face in silence, declining to allow it to be touched. "You can go," she said, glancing at the door, her face pale with suppressed wrath but also, it must be confessed, very clean; and when she was alone she dropped once again on to the sofa and buried her head in the cushion. How dared Annalise? How dared she? How dared she? Priscilla asked herself over and over again, wincing, furious. Why had she not thought of this, known that she would be in the power of any servant they chose to bring? Surely there was no limit, positively none, to what the girl might do or say? How was she going to bear her about her, endure the sight and sound of that veiled impertinence? She buried her head very deep in the cushion, vainly striving to blot out the world and Annalise in its feathers, but even there there was no peace, for suddenly a great noise of doors going and legs striding penetrated through its stuffiness and she heard Fritzing's voice very loud and near—all sounds in Creeper Cottage were loud and near—ordering Annalise to ask her Grand Ducal Highness to descend.

"I won't," thought Priscilla, burying her head deeper. "That poor Emma has lost the note and he's going to fuss. I won't descend."

Then came Annalise's tap at her door. Priscilla did not answer. Annalise tapped again. Priscilla did not answer, but turning her head face upwards composed herself to an appearance of sleep.

Annalise tapped a third time. "The Herr Geheimrath wishes to speak to your Grand Ducal Highness," she called through the door; and after a pause opened it and peeped in. "Her Grand Ducal Highness sleeps," she informed Fritzing down the stairs, her nose at the angle in the air it always took when she spoke to him.

"Then wake her! Wake her!" cried Fritzing.

"Is it possible something has happened?" thought Annalise joyfully, her eyes gleaming as she willingly flew back to Priscilla's door,—anything, anything, she thought, sooner than the life she was leading.

Priscilla heard Fritzing's order and sat up at once, surprised at such an unprecedented indifference to her comfort. Her heart began to beat faster; a swift fear that Kunitz was at her heels seized her; she jumped up and ran out.

Fritzing was standing at the foot of the stairs.

"Come down, ma'am," he said; "I must speak to you at once."

"What's the matter?" asked Priscilla, getting down the steep little stairs as quickly as was possible without tumbling.

"Hateful English tongue," thought Annalise, to whom the habit the Princess and Fritzing had got into of talking English together was a constant annoyance and disappointment.

Fritzing preceded Priscilla into her parlour, and when she was in he shut the door behind her. Then he leaned his hands on the table to steady himself and confronted her with a twitching face. Priscilla looked at him appalled. Was the Grand Duke round the corner? Lingering, perhaps, among the very tombs just outside her window? "What is it?" she asked faintly.

"Ma'am, the five pounds has disappeared for ever."

"Really Fritzi, you are too absurd about that wretched five pounds," cried Priscilla, blazing into anger.

"But it was all we had."

"All we—?"

"Ma'am, it was positively our last penny."

"I—don't understand."

He made her understand. With paper and pencil, with the bills and his own calculations, he made her understand. His hands shook, but he went through with it item by item, through everything they had spent from the moment they left Kunitz. They were in such a corner, so tightly jammed, that all efforts to hide it and pretend there was no corner seemed to him folly. He now saw that such efforts always had been folly, and that he ought to have seen to it that her mind on this important point was from the first perfectly clear; then nothing would have happened. "You have had the misfortune, ma'am, to choose a fool for your protector in this adventure," he said bitterly, pushing the papers from him as though he loathed the sight of them.

Priscilla sat dumfoundered. She was looking quite straight for the first time at certain pitiless aspects of life. For the first time she was face to face with the sternness, the hardness, the relentlessness of everything that has to do with money so soon as one has not got any. It seemed almost incredible to her that she who had given so lavishly to anybody and everybody, who had been so glad to give, who had thought of money when she thought of it at all as a thing to be passed on, as a thing that soiled one unless it was passed on, but that, passed on, became strangely glorified and powerful for good—it seemed incredible that she should be in need of it herself, and unable to think of a single person who would give her some. And what a little she needed: just to tide them over the next week or two till they had got theirs from home; yet even that little, the merest nothing compared to what she had flung about in the village, was as unattainable as though it had been a fortune. "Can we—can we not borrow?" she said at last.

"Yes ma'am, we can and we must. I will proceed this evening to Symford Hall and borrow of Augustus."

"No," said Priscilla; so suddenly and so energetically that Fritzing started.

"No, ma'am?" he repeated, astonished. "Why, he is the very person. In fact he is our only hope. He must and shall help us."

"No," repeated Priscilla, still more energetically.

"Pray ma'am," said Fritzing, shrugging his shoulders, "are these women's whims—I never comprehended them rightly and doubt if I ever shall—are they to be allowed to lead us even in dangerous crises? To lead us to certain shipwreck, ma'am? The alternatives in this case are three. Permit me to point them out. Either we return to Kunitz—"

"Oh," shivered Priscilla, shrinking as from a blow.

"Or, after a brief period of starvation and other violent discomfort, we are cast into gaol for debt—"

"Oh?" shivered Priscilla, in tones of terrified inquiry.

"Or, I borrow of Augustus."

"No," said Priscilla, just as energetically as before.

"Augustus is wealthy. Augustus is willing. Ma'am, I would stake my soul that he is willing."

"You shall not borrow of him," said Priscilla. "He—he's too ill."

"Well then, ma'am," said Fritzing with a gesture of extreme exasperation, "since you cannot be allowed to be cast into gaol there remains but Kunitz. Like the dogs of the Scriptures we will return—"

"Why not borrow of the vicar?" interrupted Priscilla. "Surely he would be glad to help any one in difficulties?"

"Of the vicar? What, of the father of the young man who insulted your Grand Ducal Highness and whom I propose to kill in duel my first leisure moment? Ma'am, there are depths of infamy to which even a desperate man will not descend."

Priscilla dug holes in the tablecloth with the point of the pencil. "I can't conceive," she said, "why you gave Annalise all that money. So *much*."

"Why, ma'am, she refused, unless I did, to prepare your Grand Ducal Highness's tea."

"Oh Fritzi!" Priscilla looked up at him, shaking her head and smiling through all her troubles. Was ever so much love and so much folly united in one wise old man? Was ever, for that matter, so expensive a tea?

"I admit I permitted the immediate, the passing, moment to blot out the future from my clearer vision on that occasion."

"On that occasion? Oh Fritzi. What about all the other occasions? When you gave me all I asked for—for the poor people, for my party. You must have suffered tortures of anxiety. And all by yourself. Oh Fritzi. It was dear of you—perfectly, wonderfully, dear. But you ought to have been different with me from the beginning—treated me exactly as you would have treated a real niece—"

"Ma'am," cried Fritzing, jumping up, "this is waste of time. Our case is very urgent. Money must be obtained. You must allow me to judge in this matter, however ill I have acquitted myself up to now. I shall start at once for Symford Hall and obtain a loan of Augustus."

Priscilla pushed back her chair and got up too. "My dear Fritzi, please leave that unfortunate young man out of the question," she said, flushing. "How can you worry a person who is ill in bed with such things?"

"His mother is not ill in bed and will do quite as well. I am certainly going."

"You are not going. I won't have you ask his mother. I—forbid you to do anything of the sort. Oh Fritzi," she added in despair, for he had picked up the hat and stick he had flung down on coming in and was evidently not going to take the least notice of her commands—"oh Fritzi, you can't ask Tussie for money. It would kill him to know we were in difficulties."

"Kill him, ma'am? Why should it kill him?" shouted Fritzing, exasperated by such a picture of softness.

"It wouldn't only kill him—it would be simply too dreadful besides," said Priscilla, greatly distressed. "Why, he asked me this afternoon—wasn't going to tell you, but you force me to—he asked me this very afternoon to marry him, and the dreadful part is that I'm afraid he thinks—he hopes— that I'm going to."

XX

The only inhabitant of Creeper Cottage who slept that night was Annalise. Priscilla spent it walking up and down her bedroom, and Fritzing on the other side of the wall spent it walking up and down his. They could hear each other doing it; it was a melancholy sound. Once Priscilla was seized with laughter—a not very genial mirth, but still laughter—and had to fling herself on her bed and bury her face in the pillows lest Fritzing should hear so blood-curdling a noise. It was when their steps had fallen steadily together for several turns and the church clock, just as she was noticing this, had struck three. Not for this, to tramp up and down their rooms all night, not for this had they left Kunitz. The thought of all they had dreamed life in Creeper Cottage was going to be, of all they had never doubted it was going to be, of peaceful nights passed in wholesome slumber, of days laden with fruitful works, of evenings with the poets, came into her head and made this tormented marching suddenly seem intensely droll. She laughed into her pillow till the tears rolled down her face, and the pains she had to take to keep all sounds from reaching Fritzing only made her laugh more.

It was a windy night, and the wind sighed round the cottage and rattled the casements and rose every now and then to a howl very dreary to hear. While Priscilla was laughing a great gust shook the house, and involuntarily she raised her head to listen. It died away, and her head dropped back on to her arms again, but the laughter was gone. She lay solemn enough, listening to Fritzing's creakings, and thought of the past day and of the days to come till her soul grew cold. Surely she was a sort of poisonous weed, fatal to every one about her? Fritzing, Tussie, the poor girl Emma—oh, it could not be true about Emma. She had lost the money, and was trying to gather courage to come and say so; or she had simply not been able to change it yet. Fritzing had jumped to the conclusion, because nothing had been heard of her all day at home, that she had run away with it. Priscilla twisted herself about uneasily. It was not the loss of the five pounds that made her twist, bad though that loss was in their utter poverty; it was the thought that if Emma had really run away she, by her careless folly, had driven the girl to ruin. And then Tussie. How dreadful that was. At three in the morning, with the wailing wind rising and falling and the room black with the inky blackness of a moonless October night, the Tussie complication seemed to be gigantic, of a quite appalling size, threatening to choke her, to crush all the spring and youth out of her. If Tussie got well she was going to break his heart; if Tussie died it would be her fault. No one but herself was responsible for his illness, her own selfish, hateful self. Yes, she was a poisonous weed; a baleful, fatal thing, not fit for great undertakings, not fit for a noble life, too foolish to depart successfully from the lines laid down for her by other people; wickedly careless; shamefully shortsighted; spoiling, ruining, everything she touched. Priscilla writhed. Nobody likes being forced to recognize that they are poisonous weeds. Even to be a plain weed is grievous to one's vanity, but to be a weed and poisonous as well is a very desperate thing to be. She passed a dreadful night. It was the worst she could remember.

And the evening too—how bad it had been; though contrary to her expectations Fritzing showed no desire to fight Tussie. He was not so unreasonable as she had supposed; and besides, he was too completely beaten down by the ever-increasing weight and number of his responsibilities to do anything in regard to that unfortunate youth but be sorry for him. More than once that evening he looked at Priscilla in silent wonder at the amount of trouble one young woman could give. How necessary, he thought, and how wise was that plan at which he used in his ignorance to rail, of setting an elderly female like the Disthal to control the actions and dog the footsteps of the Priscillas of this world. He hated the Disthal and all women like her, women with mountainous bodies and minimal brains—bodies self-indulged into shapelessness, brains neglected into disappearance; but the nobler and simpler and the more generous the girl the more did she need some such mixture of fleshliness and cunning constantly with her. It seemed absurd, and it seemed all wrong; yet surely it was so. He pondered over it long in dejected musings, the fighting tendency gone out of him completely for the time, so dark was his spirit with the shadows of the future.

They had borrowed the wages—it was a dreadful moment—for that day's cook from Annalise. For their food they decided to run up a bill at the store; but every day each fresh cook would have to be paid, and every day her wages would have to be lent by Annalise. Annalise lent superbly; with an air as of giving freely, with joy. All she required was the Princess's signature to a memorandum drawn up by herself by which she was promised the money back, doubled, within three months. Priscilla read this, flushed to her hair, signed, and ordered her out of the room. Annalise, who was beginning to enjoy herself, went upstairs singing. In the parlour Priscilla broke the pen she had signed with into quite small pieces and flung them on to the fire,—a useless demonstration, but then she was a quick-tempered young lady. In the attic Annalise sat down and wrote a letter breathing lofty sentiments to the Countess Disthal in Kunitz, telling her she could no longer keep silence in the face of a royal parent's anxieties and she was willing to reveal the address of the Princess Priscilla and so staunch the bleeding of a noble heart if the Grand Duke would forward her or forward to her parents on her behalf the sum of twenty thousand marks. Gladly would she render this service, which was at the same time her duty, for nothing, if she had not the future to consider and an infirm father. Meanwhile she gave the Symford post-office as an address, assuring the Countess that it was at least fifty miles from the Princess's present hiding-place, the address of which would only be sent on the conditions named. Then, immensely proud of her cleverness, she trotted down to the post-office, bought stamps, and put the letter herself in the box.

That evening she sang in the kitchen, she sang in the bath-room, she sang in the attic and on the stairs to the attic. What she sang, persistently, over and over again, and loudest outside Fritzing's door, was a German song about how beautiful it is at evening when the bells ring one to rest, and the refrain at the end of each verse was ding-dong twice repeated. Priscilla rang her own bell, unable to endure it, but Annalise did not consider this to be one of those that are beautiful and did not answer it till it had been rung three times.

"Do not sing," said Priscilla, when she appeared.

"Your Grand Ducal Highness objects?"

Priscilla turned red. "I'll give no reasons," she said icily. "Do not sing."

"Yet it is a sign of a light heart. Your Grand Ducal Highness did not like to see me weep—she should the more like to hear me rejoice."

"You can go."

"My heart to-night is light, because I am the means of being of use to your Grand Ducal Highness, of showing my devotion, of being of service."

"Do me the service of being quiet."

Annalise curtseyed and withdrew, and spent the rest of the evening bursting into spasmodic and immediately interrupted song,—breaking off after a few bars with a cough of remembrance and apology. When this happened Fritzing and Priscilla looked at each other with grave and meditative eyes; they knew how completely they were in her power.

Fritzing wrote that night to the friend in London who had engaged the rooms for him at Baker's Farm, and asked him to lend him fifty pounds for a week,—preferably three hundred (this would cover the furnisher's bill), but if he could lend neither five would do. The friend, a teacher of German, could as easily have lent the three hundred as the five, so poor was he, so fit an object for a loan himself; but long before his letter explaining this in words eloquent of regret (for he was a loyal friend) reached Fritzing, many things had happened to that bewildered man to whom so many things had happened already, and caused him to forget both his friend and his request.

This, then, was how the afternoon and evening of Thursday were passed; and on Friday morning, quite unstrung by their sleepless night, Priscilla and Fritzing were proposing to go up together on to the moor, there to seek width and freshness, be blown upon by moist winds, and forget for a little the crushing narrowness and perplexities of Creeper Cottage, when Mrs. Morrison walked in. She opened the door first and then, when half of her was inside, knocked with her knuckles, which were the only things to knock with on Priscilla's simple door.

Priscilla was standing by the fire dressed to go out, waiting for Fritzing, and she stared at this apparition in great and unconcealed surprise. What business, said Priscilla's look more plainly than any words, what business had people to walk into other people's cottages in such a manner? She stood quite still, and scrutinized Mrs. Morrison with the questioning expression she used to find so effective in Kunitz days when confronted by a person inclined to forget which, exactly, was his proper place. But Mrs. Morrison knew nothing of Kunitz, and the look lost half its potency without its impressive background. Besides, the lady was not one to notice things so slight as looks; to keep her in her proper place you would have needed sledge-hammers. She came in without thinking it necessary to wait to be asked to, nodded something that might perhaps have represented a greeting and of which Priscilla took no notice, and her face was the face of somebody who is angry.

"How wearing for the vicar," thought Priscilla, "to have a wife who is angry at ten o'clock in the morning."

"I've come in the interests——" began Mrs. Morrison, whose voice was quite as angry as her face.

"I'm just going out," said Priscilla.

"——Of religion and morality."

"Are they distinct?" asked Priscilla, drawing on her gloves.

"You can imagine that nothing would make me pay you a visit but the strongest sense of the duty I owe to my position in the parish."

"Why should I imagine it?"

"Of course I expect impertinence."

"I'm afraid you've come here to be rude."

"I shall not be daunted by anything you may say from doing my duty."

"Will you please do it, then, and get it over?"

"The duties of a clergyman's wife are often very disagreeable."

"Probably you've got hold of a perfectly wrong idea of what yours really are."

"It is a new experience for me to be told so by a girl of your age."

"I am not telling you. I only suggest."

"I was prepared for rudeness."

"Then why did you come?"

"How long are you going to stay in this parish?"

"You don't expect me to answer that?"

"You've not been in it a fortnight, and you have done more harm than most people in a lifetime."

"I'm afraid you exaggerate."

"You have taught it to drink."

"I gave a dying old woman what she most longed for."

"You've taught it to break the Sabbath."

"I made a great many little children very happy."

"You have ruined the habits of thrift we have been at such pains to teach and encourage for twenty-five years."

"I helped the poor when they asked me to."

"And now what I want to know is, what has become of the Hancock girl?"

"Pray who, exactly, is the Hancock girl?"

"That unfortunate creature who worked here for you on Wednesday."

Priscilla's face changed. "Emma?" she asked.

"Emma. At this hour the day before yesterday she was as good a girl as any in the village. She was good, and dutiful, and honest. Now what is she and where is she?"

"Has she—isn't she in her home?"

"She never went home."

"Then she did lose the money?"

"Lose it? She has stolen it. Do you not see you have deliberately made a thief out of an honest girl?"

Priscilla gazed in dismay at the avenging vicar's wife. It was true then, and she had the fatal gift of spoiling all she touched.

"And worse than that—you have brought a good girl to ruin. He'll never marry her now."

"He?"

"Do you not know the person she was engaged to has gone with her?"

"I don't know anything."

"They walked from here to Ullerton and went to London. Her father came round to us yesterday after your uncle had been to him making inquiries, and it is all as clear as day. Till your uncle told him, he did not know about the money, and had been too—not well enough that day to notice Emma's not having come home. Your uncle's visit sobered him. We telegraphed to the police. They've been traced to London. That's all. Except," and she glared at Priscilla with all the wrath of a prophet whose denunciations have been justified, "except that one more life is ruined."

"I'm very sorry—very, very sorry," said Priscilla, so earnestly, so abjectly even, that her eyes filled with tears. "I see now how thoughtless it was of me."

"Thoughtless!"

"It was inexcusably thoughtless."

"Thoughtless!" cried Mrs. Morrison again.

"If you like, it was criminally thoughtless."

"Thoughtless!" cried Mrs. Morrison a third time.

"But it wasn't more than thoughtless. I'd give anything to be able to set it right. I am most truly grieved. But isn't it a little hard to make me responsible?"

Mrs. Morrison stared at her as one who eyes some strange new monster. "How amazingly selfish you are," she said at last, in tones almost of awe.

"Selfish?" faltered Priscilla, who began to wonder what she was not.

"In the face of such total ruin, such utter shipwreck, to be thinking of what is hard on you. You! Why, here you are with a safe skin, free from the bitter anxieties and temptations poor people have to fight with, with so much time unoccupied that you fill it up with mischief, with more money than you know what to do with"—Priscilla pressed her hands together—"sheltered, free from every care"—Priscilla opened her lips but shut them again—"and there is that miserable Emma, hopeless, branded, for ever an outcast because of you,—only because of you, and you think of yourself and talk of its being hard."

Priscilla looked at Mrs. Morrison, opened her mouth to say something, shut it, opened it again, and remarked very lamely that the heart alone knows its own bitterness.

"Psha," said Mrs. Morrison, greatly incensed at having the Scriptures, her own speciality, quoted at her. "I'd like to know what bitterness yours has known, unless it's the bitterness of a bad conscience. Now I've come here to-day"—she raised her voice to a note of warning—"to give you a chance. To make you think, by pointing out the path you are treading. You are young, and it is my duty to let no young person go downhill without one warning word. You have brought much evil on our village—why you, a stranger, should be bent on making us all unhappy I can't imagine. You hypocritically try to pretend that what plain people call evil is really good. But your last action, forcing Emma Hancock to be a thief and worse, even you cannot possibly defend. You have much on your conscience—far, far more than I should care to have on mine. How wicked to give all that money to Mrs. Jones. Don't you see you are tempting people who know she is defenceless to steal it from her? Perhaps even murder her? I saved her from that—you did not reckon with me, you see. Take my advice—leave Symford, and go back to where you came from"—Priscilla started—"and get something to do that will keep you fully occupied. If you don't, you'll be laying up a wretched, perhaps a degraded future for yourself. Don't suppose,"—her voice grew very loud—"don't suppose we are fools here and are not all of us aware of the way you have tried to lure young men on"—Priscilla started again—"in the hope, of course, of getting one of them to marry you. But your intentions have been frustrated luckily, in the one case by Providence flinging your victim on a bed of sickness and in the other by your having altogether mistaken the sort of young fellow you were dealing with."

Mrs. Morrison paused for breath. This last part of her speech had been made with an ever accumulating rage. Priscilla stood looking at her, her eyebrows drawn down very level over her eyes.

"My son is much too steady and conscientious, besides being too much accustomed to first-rate society, to stoop to anything so vulgar—"

"As myself?" inquired Priscilla.

"As a love-affair with the first stray girl he picks up."

"Do you mean me?"

"He saw through your intentions, laughed at them, and calmly returned to his studies at Cambridge."

"I boxed his ears."

"What?"

"I boxed his ears."

"You?"

"I boxed his ears. That's why he went. He didn't go calmly. It wasn't his studies."

"How dare you box—oh, this is too horrible—and you stand there and tell me so to my face?"

"I'm afraid I must. The tone of your remarks positively demands it. Your son's conduct positively demanded that I should box his ears. So I did."

"Of all the shameless—"

"I'm afraid you're becoming like him—altogether impossible."

"You first lure him on, and then—oh, it is shameful!"

"Have you finished what you came for?"

"You are the most brazen—"

"Hush. Do be careful. Suppose my uncle were to hear you? If you've finished won't you go?"

"Go? I shall not go till I have said my say. I shall send the vicar to you about Robin—such conduct is so—so infamous that I can't—I can't—I can't—"

"I'm sorry if it has distressed you."

"Distressed me? You are the most—"

"Really I think we've done, haven't we?" said Priscilla hurriedly, dreadfully afraid lest Fritzing should come in and hear her being called names.

"To think that you dared—to think that my—my noble boy—"

"He wasn't very noble. Mothers don't ever really know their sons, I think."

"Shameless girl!" cried Mrs. Morrison, so loud, so completely beside herself, that Priscilla hastily rang her bell, certain that Fritzing must hear and would plunge in to her rescue; and of all things she had learned to dread Fritzing's plunging to her rescue. "Open the door for this lady," she said to Annalise, who appeared with a marvellous promptitude; and as Mrs. Morrison still stood her ground and refused to see either Annalise or the door Priscilla ended the interview by walking out herself, with great dignity, into the bathroom.

XXI

And now I have come to a part of my story that I would much rather not write. Always my inclination if left alone is to sit in the sun and sing of things like crocuses, of nothing less fresh and clean than crocuses. The engaging sprightliness of crocuses; their dear little smell, not to be smelled except by the privileged few; their luminous transparency—I am thinking of the white and the purple; their kind way of not keeping hearts sick for Spring waiting longer than they can just bear; how pleasant to sit with a friend in the sun, a friend who like myself likes to babble of green fields, and talk together about all things flowery. But Priscilla's story has taken such a hold on me, it seemed when first I heard it to be so full of lessons, that I feel bound to set it down from beginning to end for the use and warning of all persons, princesses and others, who think that by searching, by going far afield, they will find happiness, and do not see that it is lying all the while at their feet. They do not see it because it is so close. It is so close that there is a danger of its being trodden on or kicked away. And it is shy, and waits to be picked up. Priscilla, we know, went very far afield in search of hers, and having undertaken to tell of what befell her I must not now, only because I would rather, suppress any portion of the story. Besides, it is a portion vital to the catastrophe.

In Minehead, then, there lived at this time a murderer. He had not been found out yet and he was not a murderer by profession, for he was a bricklayer; but in his heart he was, and that is just as bad. He had had a varied career into the details of which I do not propose to go, had come three or four years before to live in the West of England because it was so far from all the other places he had lived in, had got work in Minehead, settled there respectably, married, and was a friend of that carrier who brought the bread and other parcels every day to the Symford store. At this time he was in money difficulties and his wife, of whom he was fond, was in an expensive state of health. The accounts of Priscilla's generosity and wealth had reached Minehead as I said some time ago, and had got even into the local papers. The carrier was the chief transmitter of news, for he saw Mrs. Vickerton every day and she was a woman who loved to talk; but those of the Shuttleworth servants who were often in Minehead on divers errands ratified and added to all he said, and embellished the tale besides with what was to them the most interesting part, the unmistakable signs their Augustus showed of intending to marry the young woman. This did not interest the murderer. Sir Augustus and the lady he meant to marry were outside his sphere altogether; too well protected, too powerful. What he liked to hear about was the money Priscilla had scattered among the cottagers, how much each woman had got, whether it had been spent or not, whether she had a husband, or grown-up children; and best of all he liked to hear about the money Mrs. Jones had got. All the village, and therefore Mrs. Vickerton and the carrier, knew of it, knew even the exact spot beneath the bolster where it was kept, knew it was kept there for safety from the depredations of the vicar's wife, knew the vicar's wife had taken away Priscilla's first present. The carrier knew too of Mrs. Jones's age, her weakness, her nearness to death. He remarked that such a sum wasn't of much use to an old woman certain to die in a few days, and that it might just as well not be hers at all for all the spending it got. The murderer, whose reputation in Minehead was so immaculate that not a single fly had ever dared blow on it, said kindly that no doubt just to have it in her possession was cheering and that one should not grudge the old their little bits of comfort; and he walked over to Symford that night, and getting there about one o'clock murdered Mrs. Jones. I will not enter into details. I believe it was quite simple. He was back by six next morning with the five pounds in his pocket, and his wife that day had meat for dinner.

That is all I shall say about the murderer, except that he was never found out; and nothing shall induce me to dwell upon the murder. But what about the effect it had on Priscilla? Well, it absolutely crushed her.

The day before, after Mrs. Morrison's visit, she had been wretched enough, spending most of it walking very fast, as driven spirits do, with Fritzing for miles across the bleak and blowy moor, by turns contrite and rebellious, one moment ready to admit she was a miserable sinner, the next indignantly repudiating Mrs. Morrison's and her own conscience's accusations, her soul much beaten and bent by winds of misgiving but still on its feet, still defiant, still sheltering itself when it could behind plain common sense which whispered at intervals that all that had happened was only bad luck. They walked miles that day; often in silence, sometimes in gusty talk—talk gusty with the swift changes of Priscilla's mood scudding across the leaden background of Fritzing's steadier despair—and they got back tired, hungry, their clothes splashed with mud, their minds no nearer light than when they started. She had, I say, been wretched enough; but what was this wretchedness to that which followed? In her ignorance she thought it the worst day she had ever had, the most tormented; and when she went to bed she sought comfort in its very badness by telling herself that it was over and could never come again. It could not. But Time is prolific of surprises; and on Saturday morning Symford woke with a shudder to the murder of Mrs. Jones.

Now such a thing as this had not happened in that part of Somersetshire within the memory of living man, and though Symford shuddered it was also proud and pleased. The mixed feeling of horror, pleasure, and pride was a thrilling one. It felt itself at once raised to a position of lurid conspicuousness in the county, its name would be in every mouth, the papers, perhaps even the London papers, would talk about it. At all times, in spite of the care and guidance it had had from the clergy and gentry, the account of a murder gave Symford more pure pleasure than any other form of entertainment; and now here was one, not at second-hand, not to be viewed through the cooling medium of print and pictures, but in its midst, before its eyes, at its very doors. Mrs. Jones went up strangely in its estimation. The general feeling was that it was an honour to have known her. Nobody worked that day. The school was deserted. Dinners were not cooked. Babies shrieked uncomforted. All Symford was gathered in groups outside Mrs. Jones's cottage, and as the day wore on and the news spread, visitors from the neighbouring villages, from Minehead and from Ullerton, arrived with sandwiches and swelled them.

Priscilla saw these groups from her windows. The fatal cottage was at the foot of the hill in full view both of her bedroom and her parlour. Only by sitting in the bathroom would she be able to get away from it. When the news was brought her, breathlessly, pallidly, by Annalise in the early morning with her hot water, she refused to believe it. Annalise knew no English and must have got hold of a horrible wrong tale. The old lady was dead no doubt, had died quietly in her sleep as had been expected, but what folly was all this about a murder? Yet she sat up in bed and felt rather cold as she looked at Annalise, for Annalise was very pallid. And then at last she had to believe it. Annalise had had it told her from beginning to end, with the help of signs, by the charwoman. She had learned more English in those few crimson minutes than in the whole of the time she had been in England. The charwoman had begun her demonstration by slowly drawing her finger across her throat from one ear to the other, and Annalise repeated the action for Priscilla's clearer comprehension. How Priscilla got up that day and dressed she never knew. Once at least during the process she stumbled back on to the bed and lay with her face on her arms, shaken by a most desperate weeping. That fatal charity; those fatal five-pound notes. Annalise, panic-stricken lest she who possessed so many should be the next victim, poured out the tale of the missing money, of the plain motive for the murder, with a convincingness, a naked truth, that stabbed Priscilla to the heart with each clinching word.

"They say the old woman must have cried out—must have been awakened, or the man would have taken the money without—"

"Oh don't—oh leave me—" moaned Priscilla.

She did not go downstairs that day. Every time Annalise tried to come in she sent her away. When she was talked to of food, she felt sick. Once she began to pace about the room, but the sight of those eager black knots of people down the street, of policemen and other important and official-looking persons going in and out of the cottage, drove her back to her bed and its sheltering, world-deadening pillow. Indeed the waters of life had gone over her head and swallowed her up in hopeless blackness. She acknowledged herself wrong. She gave in utterly. Every word Mrs. Morrison—a dreadful woman, yet dreadful as she was still a thousand times better than herself—every word she had said, every one of those bitter words at which she had been so indignant the morning before, was true, was justified. That day Priscilla tore the last shreds of self-satisfaction from her soul and sat staring at it with horrified eyes as at a thing wholly repulsive, dangerous, blighting. What was to become of her, and of poor Fritzing, dragged down by her to an equal misery? About one o'clock she heard Mrs. Morrison's voice below, in altercation apparently with him. At this time she was crying again; bitter, burning tears; those scorching tears that follow in the wake of destroyed illusions, that drop, hot and withering, on to the fragments of what was once the guiding glory of an ideal. She was brought so low, was so humbled, so uncertain of herself, that she felt it would bring her peace if she might go down to Mrs. Morrison and acknowledge all her vileness; tell her how wrong she had been, ask her forgiveness for her rudeness, beg her for pity, for help, for counsel. She needed some kind older woman,—oh she needed some kind older woman to hold out cool hands of wisdom and show her the way. But then she would have to make a complete confession of everything she had done, and how would Mrs. Morrison or any other decent woman look upon her flight from her father's home? Would they not turn away shuddering from what she now saw was a hideous selfishness and ingratitude? The altercation going on below rose rapidly in heat. Just at the end it grew so heated that even through the pillow Priscilla could hear its flaming conclusion.

"Man, I tell you your niece is to all intents and purposes a murderess, a double murderess," cried Mrs. Morrison. "Not only has she the woman's murder to answer for, but the ruined soul of the murderer as well."

Upon which there was a loud shout of "Hence! Hence!" and a great slamming of the street door.

For some time after this Priscilla heard fevered walking about in her parlour and sounds as of many and muffled imprecations; then, when they had grown a little more intermittent, careful footsteps came up her stairs, footsteps so careful, so determined not to disturb, that the stairs cracked and wheezed more than they had ever yet been known to do. Arrived at the top they paused outside her door, and Priscilla, checking her sobs, could hear how Fritzing stood there wrestling with his body's determination to breathe too loud. He stood there listening for what seemed to her an eternity. She almost screamed at last as the minutes passed and she knew he was still there, motionless, listening. After a long while he went away again with the same anxious care to make no noise, and she, with a movement of utter abandonment to woe, turned over and cried herself sick.

Till evening she lay there alone, and then the steps came up again, accompanied this time by the tinkle of china and spoons. Priscilla was sitting at the window looking on to the churchyard, staring into the dark with its swaying branches and few faint stars, and when she heard him outside the door listening again in anxious silence she got up and opened it.

Fritzing held a plate of food in one hand and a glass of milk in the other. The expression on his face was absurdly like that of a mother yearning over a sick child. "*Mein liebes Kind—mein liebes Kind,*" he stammered when she came out, so woebegone, so crushed, so utterly unlike any Priscilla of any one of her moods that he had ever seen before. Her eyes were red, her eyelids heavy with tears, her face was pinched and narrower, the corners of her mouth had a most piteous droop, her very hair, pushed back off her forehead, seemed sad, and hung in spiritless masses about her neck and ears. "*Mein liebes Kind,*" stammered poor Fritzing; and his hand shook so that he upset some of the milk.

Priscilla leaned against the door-post. She was feeling sick and giddy. "How dreadful this is," she murmured, looking at him with weary, woeful eyes.

"No, no—all will be well," said Fritzing, striving to be brisk. "Drink some milk, ma'am."

"Oh, I have been wicked."

"Wicked?"

Fritzing hastily put the plate and glass down on the floor, and catching up the hand hanging limply by her side passionately kissed it. "You are the noblest woman on earth," he said.

"Oh," said Priscilla, turning away her head and shutting her eyes for very weariness of such futile phrases.

"Ma'am, you are. I would swear it. But you are also a child, and so you are ready at the first reverse to suppose you have done with happiness for ever. Who knows," said Fritzing with a great show of bright belief in his own prophecy, the while his heart was a stone, "who knows but what you are now on the very threshold of it?"

"Oh," murmured Priscilla, too beaten to do anything but droop her head.

"It is insisting on the commonplace to remind you, ma'am, that the darkest hour comes before dawn. Yet it is a well-known natural phenomenon."

Priscilla leaned her head against the door-post. She stood there motionless, her hands hanging by her side, her eyes shut, her mouth slightly open, the very picture of one who has given up.

"Drink some milk, ma'am. At least endeavour to."

She took no heed of him.

"For God's sake, ma'am, do not approach these slight misadventures in so tragic a spirit. You have done nothing wrong whatever. I know you accuse yourself. It is madness to do so. I, who have so often scolded you, who have never spared the lash of my tongue when in past years I saw fair reason to apply it, I tell you now with the same reliable candour that your actions in this village and the motives that prompted them have been in each single case of a stainless nobility."

She took no heed of him.

He stooped down and picked up the glass. "Drink some milk, ma'am. A few mouthfuls, perhaps even one, will help to clear the muddied vision of your mind. I cannot understand," he went on, half despairing, half exasperated, "what reasons you can possibly have for refusing to drink some milk. It is a feat most easily accomplished."

She did not move.

"Do you perchance imagine that a starved and badly treated body can ever harbour that most precious gift of the gods, a clear, sane mind?"

She did not move.

He looked at her in silence for a moment, then put down the glass. "This is all my fault," he said slowly. "The whole responsibility for this unhappiness is on my shoulders, and I frankly confess it is a burden so grievous that I know not how to bear it."

He paused, but she took no notice.

"Ma'am, I have loved you."

She took no notice.

"And the property of love, I have observed, is often to mangle and kill the soul of its object."

She might have been asleep.

"Ma'am, I have brought you to a sorry pass. I was old, and you were young. I experienced, you ignorant. I deliberate, you impulsive. I a man, you a woman. Instead of restraining you, guiding you, shielding you from yourself, I was most vile, and fired you with desires for freedom that under the peculiar circumstances were wicked, set a ball rolling that I might have foreseen could never afterwards be stopped, put thoughts into your head that never without me would have entered it, embarked you on an enterprise in which the happiness of your whole life was doomed to shipwreck."

She stirred a little, and sighed a faint protest.

"This is very terrible to me—of a crushing, killing weight. Let it not also have to be said that I mangled your very soul, dimmed your reason, impaired the sweet sanity, the nice adjustment of what I know was once a fair and balanced mind."

She raised her head slowly and looked at him. "What?" she said. "Do you think—do you think I'm going mad?"

"I think it very likely, ma'am," said Fritzing with conviction.

A startled expression crept into her eyes.

"So much morbid introspection," he went on, "followed by hours of weeping and fasting, if indulged in long enough will certainly have that result. A person who fasts a sufficient length of time invariably parts piecemeal with valuable portions of his wits."

She stretched out her hand.

He mistook the action and bent down and kissed it.

"No," said Priscilla, "I want the milk."

He snatched it up and gave it to her, watching her drink with all the relief, the thankfulness of a mother whose child's sickness takes a turn for the better. When she had finished she gave him back the glass. "Fritzi," she said, looking at him with eyes wide open now and dark with anxious questioning, "we won't reproach ourselves then if we can help it—"

"Certainly not, ma'am—a most futile thing to do."

"I'll try to believe what you say about me, if you promise to believe what I say about you."

"Ma'am, I'll believe anything if only you will be reasonable."

"You've been everything to me—that's what I want to say. Always, ever since I can remember."

"And you, ma'am? What have you not been to me?"

"And there's nothing, nothing you can blame yourself for."

"Ma'am—"

"You've been too good, too unselfish, and I've dragged you down."

"Ma'am—"

"Well, we won't begin again. But tell me one thing—and tell me the truth—oh Fritzi tell me the truth as you value your soul—do you anywhere see the least light on our future? Do you anywhere see even a bit, a smallest bit of hope?"

He took her hand again and kissed it; then lifted his head and looked at her very solemnly. "No, ma'am," he said with the decision of an unshakable conviction, "upon my immortal soul I do not see a shred."

XXII

Let the reader now picture Priscilla coming downstairs the next morning, a golden Sunday morning full of Sabbath calm, and a Priscilla leaden-eyed and leaden-souled, her shabby garments worn out to a symbol of her worn out zeals, her face the face of one who has forgotten peace, her eyes the eyes of one at strife with the future, of one for ever asking "What next?" and shrinking with a shuddering "Oh please not that," from the bald reply.

Out of doors Nature wore her mildest, most beneficent aspect. She very evidently cared nothing for the squalid tragedies of human fate. Her hills were bathed in gentle light. Her sunshine lay warm along the cottage fronts. In the gardens her hopeful bees, cheated into thoughts of summer, droned round the pale mauves and purples of what was left of starworts. The grass in the churchyard sparkled with the fairy film of gossamers. Sparrows chirped. Robins whistled. And humanity gave the last touch to the picture by ringing the church bells melodiously to prayer.

Without doubt it was a day of blessing, supposing any one could be found willing to be blest. Let the reader, then, imagine this outward serenity, this divine calmness, this fair and light-flooded world, and within the musty walls of Creeper Cottage Priscilla coming down to breakfast, despair in her eyes and heart.

They breakfasted late; so late that it was done to the accompaniment, strangely purified and beautified by the intervening church walls and graveyard, of Mrs. Morrison's organ playing and the chanting of the village choir. Their door stood wide open, for the street was empty. Everybody was in church. The service was, as Mrs. Morrison afterwards remarked, unusually well attended. The voluntaries she played that day were Dead Marches, and the vicar preached a conscience-shattering sermon upon the text "Lord, who is it?"

He thought that Mrs. Jones's murderer must be one of his parishioners. It was a painful thought, but it had to be faced. He had lived so long shut out from gossip, so deaf to the ever-clicking tongue of rumour, that he had forgotten how far even small scraps can travel, and that the news of Mrs. Jones's bolster being a hiding-place for her money should have spread beyond the village never occurred to him. He was moved on this occasion as much as a man who has long ago given up being moved can be, for he had had a really dreadful two days with Mrs. Morrison, dating from the moment she came in with the news of the boxing of their only son's ears.

He had, as the reader will have gathered, nothing of it having been recorded, refused to visit and reprimand Priscilla for this. He had found excuses for her. He had sided with her against his son. He had been as wholly, maddeningly obstinate as the extremely good sometimes are. Then came Mrs. Jones's murder. He was greatly shaken, but still refused to call upon Priscilla in connection with it, and pooh-poohed the notion of her being responsible for the crime as definitely as an aged saint of habitually grave speech can be expected to pooh-pooh at all. He said she was not responsible. He said, when his wife with all the emphasis apparently inseparable from the conversation of those who feel strongly, told him that he owed it to himself, to his parish, to his country, to go and accuse her, that he owed no man anything but to love one another. There was nothing to be done with the vicar. Still these scenes had not left him scathless, and it was a vicar moved to the utmost limits of his capacity in that direction who went into the pulpit that day repeating the question "Who is it?" so insistently, so appealingly, with such searching glances along the rows of faces in the pews, that the congregation, shuffling and uncomfortable, looked furtively at each other with an ever growing suspicion and dislike. The vicar as he went on waxing warmer, more insistent, observed at least a dozen persons with guilt on every feature. It darted out like a toad from the hiding-place of some private ooze at the bottom of each soul into one face after the other; and there was a certain youth who grew so visibly in guilt, who had so many beads of an obviously guilty perspiration on his forehead, and eyes so guiltily starting from their sockets, that only by a violent effort of self-control could the vicar stop himself from pointing at him and shouting out then and there "Thou art the man!"

Meanwhile the real murderer had hired a waggonette and was taking his wife for a pleasant country drive.

It was to pacify Fritzing that Priscilla came down to breakfast. Left to herself she would by preference never have breakfasted again. She even drank more milk to please him; but though it might please him, no amount of milk could wash out the utter blackness of her spirit. He, seeing her droop behind the jug, seeing her gazing drearily at nothing in particular, jumped up and took a book from the shelves and without more ado began to read aloud. "It is better, ma'am," he explained briefly, glancing at her over his spectacles, "than that you should give yourself over to gloom."

Priscilla turned vague eyes on to him. "How can I help gloom?" she asked.

"Yes, yes, that may be. But nobody should be gloomy at breakfast. The entire day is very apt, in consequence, to be curdled."

"It will be curdled anyhow," said Priscilla, her head sinking on to her chest.

"Ma'am, listen to this."

And with a piece of bread and butter in one hand, from which he took occasional hurried bites, and the other raised in appropriate varying gesticulation, Fritzing read portions of the Persae of Æschylus to her, first in Greek for the joy of his own ear and then translating it into English for the edification of hers. He, at least, was off after the first line, sailing golden seas remote and glorious, places where words were lovely and deeds heroic, places most beautiful and brave, most admirably, most restfully unlike Creeper Cottage. He rolled out the sentences, turning them on his tongue, savouring them, reluctant to let them go. She sat looking at him, wondering how he could possibly even for an instant forget the actual and the present.

"'Xerxes went forth, Xerxes perished, Xerxes mismanaged all things in the depths of the sea—'" declaimed Fritzing.

"He must have been like us," murmured Priscilla.

"'O for Darius the scatheless, the protector! No woman ever mourned for deed of his—'"

"What a nice man," sighed Priscilla. "'O for Darius!'"

"Ma'am, if you interrupt how can I read? And it is a most beautiful passage."

"But we do want a Darius badly," moaned Priscilla.

"'The ships went forth, the grey-faced ships, like to each other as bird is to bird, the ships and all they carried perished, the ships perished by the hand of the Greeks. The king, 'tis said, escapes, but hardly, by the plains of Thrace and the toilsome ways, and behind him he leaves his first-fruits— sailors unburied on the shores of Salamis. Then grieve, sting yourselves to grief, make heaven echo, howl like dogs for the horror, for they are battered together by the terrible waters, they are shredded to pieces by the voiceless children of the Pure. The house has no master—'"

"Fritzi, I wish you'd leave off," implored Priscilla. "It's quite as gloomy as anything I was thinking."

"But ma'am the difference is that it is also beautiful, whereas the gloom at present enveloping us is mere squalor. 'The voiceless children of the Pure—' how is that, ma'am, for beauty?"

"I don't even know what it means," sighed Priscilla.

"Ma'am, it is an extremely beautiful manner of alluding to fish."

"I don't care," said Priscilla.

"Ma'am, is it possible that the blight of passing and outward circumstance has penetrated to and settled upon what should always be of a sublime inaccessibility, your soul?"

"I don't care about the fish," repeated Priscilla listlessly. Then with a sudden movement she pushed back her chair and jumped up. "Oh," she cried, beating her hands together, "don't talk to me of fish when I can't see an inch—oh not a single inch into the future!"

Fritzing looked at her, his finger on the page. Half of him was still at the bottom of classic seas with the battered and shredded sailors. How much rather would he have stayed there, have gone on reading Æschylus a little, have taken her with him for a brief space of serenity into that moist refuge from the harassed present, have forgotten at least for one morning the necessity, the dreariness of being forced to face things, to talk over, to decide. Besides, what could he decide? The unhappy man had no idea. Nor had Priscilla. To stay in Symford seemed impossible, but to leave it seemed still more so. And sooner than go back disgraced to Kunitz and fling herself at paternal feet which would in all probability immediately spurn her, Priscilla felt she would die. But how could she stay in Symford, surrounded by angry neighbours, next door to Tussie, with Robin coming back for vacations, with Mrs. Morrison hating her, with Lady Shuttleworth hating her, with Emma's father hating her, with the blood of Mrs. Jones on her head? Could one live peacefully in such an accursed place? Yet how could they go away? Even if they were able to compose their nerves sufficiently to make new plans they could not go because they were in debt.

"Fritzi," cried Priscilla with more passion than she had ever put into speech before, "life's too much for me—I tell you life's too much for me!" And with a gesture of her arms as though she would sweep it all back, keep it from surging over her, from choking her, she ran out into the street to get into her own room and be alone, pulling the door to behind her for fear he should follow and want to explain and comfort, leaving him with his Æschylus in which, happening to glance sighing, he, enviable man, at once became again absorbed, and running blindly, headlong, as he runs who is surrounded and accompanied by a swarm of deadly insects which he vainly tries to out-distance, she ran straight into somebody coming from the opposite direction, ran full tilt, was almost knocked off her feet, and looking up with the impatient anguish of him who is asked to endure his last straw her lips fell apart in an utter and boundless amazement; for the person she had run against was that Prince—the last of the series, distinguished from the rest by his having quenched the Grand Duke's irrelevant effervescence by the simple expedient of saying Bosh—who had so earnestly desired to marry her.

XXIII

"Hullo," said the Prince, who spoke admirable English.

Priscilla could only stare.

His instinct was to repeat the exclamation which he felt represented his feelings very exactly, for her appearance—clothes, expression, everything—astonished him, but he doubted whether it would well bear repeating. "Is this where you are staying?" he inquired instead.

"Yes," said Priscilla.

"May I come in?"

"Yes," said Priscilla.

He followed her into her parlour. He looked at her critically as she walked slowly before him, from head to foot he looked at her critically; at every inch of the shabby serge gown, at the little head with its badly arranged hair, at the little heel that caught in an unmended bit of braid, at the little shoe with its bow of frayed ribbon, and he smiled broadly behind his moustache. But when she turned round he was perfectly solemn.

"I suppose," said the Prince, putting his hands in his pockets and gazing about the room with an appearance of cheerful interest, "this is what one calls a snug little place."

Priscilla stood silent. She felt as though she had been shaken abruptly out of sleep. Her face even now after the soul-rending time she had been having, in spite of the shadows beneath the eyes, the droop at the corners of the mouth, in spite, too, it must be said of the flagrantly cottage fashion in which Annalise had done her hair, seemed to the Prince so extremely beautiful, so absolutely the face of his dearest, best desires, so limpid, apart from all grace of colouring and happy circumstance of feature, with the light of a sweet and noble nature, so manifestly the outward expression of an indwelling lovely soul, that his eyes, after one glance round the room, fixed themselves upon it and never were able to leave it again.

For a minute or two she stood silent, trying to collect her thoughts, trying to shake off the feeling that she was being called back to life out of a dream. It had not been a dream, she kept telling herself—bad though it was it had not been a dream but the reality; and this man dropped suddenly in to the middle of it from another world, he was the dream, part of the dream she had rebelled against and run away from a fortnight before.

Then she looked at him, and she knew she was putting off her soul with nonsense. Never was anybody less like a dream than the Prince; never was anybody more squarely, more certainly real. And he was of her own kind, of her own world. He and she were equals. They could talk together plainly, baldly, a talk ungarnished and unretarded by deferences on the one side and on the other a kindness apt to become excessive in its anxiety not to appear to condescend. The feeling that once more after what seemed an eternity she was with an equal was of a singular refreshment. During those few moments in which they stood silent, facing each other, in spite of her efforts to keep it out, in spite of really conscientious efforts, a great calm came in and spread over her spirit. Yet she had no reason to feel calm she thought, struggling. Was there not rather cause for an infinity of shame? What had he come for? He of all people. The scandalously jilted, the affronted, the run away from. Was it because she had been looking so long at Fritzing that this man seemed so nicely groomed? Or at Tussie, that he seemed so well put together? Or at Robin, that he seemed so modest? Was it because people's eyes—Mrs. Morrison's, Lady Shuttleworth's—had been so angry lately whenever they rested on her that his seemed so very kind? No; she did remember thinking them that, even being struck by them, when she saw him first in Kunitz. A dull red crept into her face when she remembered that day and what followed. "It isn't very snug," she said at last, trying to hide by a careful coldness of speech all the strange things she was feeling. "When it rains there are puddles by the door. The door, you see, opens into the street."

"I see," said the Prince.

There was a silence.

"I don't suppose you really do," said Priscilla, full of strange feelings.

"My dear cousin?"

"I don't know if you've come to laugh at me?"

"Do I look as if I had?"

"I dare say you think—because you've not been through it yourself—that it—it's rather ridiculous."

"My dear cousin," protested the Prince.

Her lips quivered. She had gone through much, and she had lived for two days only on milk.

"Do you wipe the puddles up, or does old Fritzing?"

"You see you *have* come to laugh."

"I hope you'll believe that I've not. Must I be gloomy?"

"How do you know Fritzing's here?"

"Why everybody knows that."

"Everybody?" There was an astonished pause. "How do you know we're here—here, in Creeper Cottage?"

"Creeper Cottage is it? I didn't know it had a name. Do you have so many earwigs?"

"How did you know we were in Symford?"

"Why everybody knows that."

Priscilla was silent. Again she felt she was being awakened from a dream.

"I've met quite a lot of interesting people since I saw you last," he said. "At least, they interested me because they all knew you."

"Knew me?"

"Knew you and that old scound—the excellent Fritzing. There's an extremely pleasant policeman, for instance, in Kunitz—"

"Oh," said Priscilla, starting and turning red. She could not think of that policeman without crisping her fingers.

"He and I are intimate friends. And there's a most intelligent person—really a most helpful, obliging person—who came with you from Dover to Ullerton."

"With us?"

"I found the conversation, too, of the ostler at the Ullerton Arms of immense interest."

"But what—"

"And last night I slept at Baker's Farm, and spent a very pleasant evening with Mrs. Pearce."

"But why—"

"She's an instructive woman. Her weakest point, I should say, is her junkets."

"I wonder why you bother to talk like this—to be sarcastic."

"About the junkets? Didn't you think they were bad?"

"Do you suppose it's worth while to—to kick somebody who's down? And so low down? So completely got to the bottom?"

"Kick? On my soul I assure you that the very last thing I want to do is to kick you."

"Then why do you do it?"

"I don't do it. Do you know what I've come for?"

"Is my father round the corner?"

"Nobody's round the corner. I've muzzled your father. I've come quite by myself. And do you know why?"

"No," said Priscilla, shortly, defiantly; adding before he could speak, "I can't imagine." And adding to that, again before he could speak, "Unless it's for the fun of hunting down a defenceless quarry."

"I say, that's rather picturesque," said the Prince with every appearance of being struck.

Priscilla blushed. In spite of herself every word they said to each other made her feel more natural, farther away from self-torment and sordid fears, nearer to that healthy state of mind, swamped out of her lately, when petulance comes more easily than meekness. The mere presence of the Prince seemed to set things right, to raise her again in her own esteem. There was undoubtedly something wholesome about the man, something everyday and reassuring, something dependable and sane. The first smile for I don't know how long came and cheered the corners of her mouth. "I'm afraid I've grown magniloquent since—since—"

"Since you ran away?"

She nodded. "Fritzing, you know, is most persistently picturesque. I think it's catching. But he's wonderful," she added quickly,—"most wonderful in patience and goodness."

"Oh everybody knows he's wonderful. Where is the great man?"

"In the next room. Do you want him?"

"Good Lord, no. You've not told me what you suppose I've come for."

"I did. I told you I couldn't imagine."

"It's for a most saintly, really nice reason. Guess."

"I can't guess."

"Oh but try."

Priscilla to her extreme disgust felt herself turning very red. "I suppose to spy out the nakedness of the land," she said severely.

"Now you're picturesque again. You must have been reading a tremendous lot lately. Of course you would, with that learned old fossil about. No my dear, I've come simply to see if you are happy."

She looked at him, and her flush slowly died away.

"Simply to convince myself that you are happy."

Her eyes filling with tears she thought it more expedient to fix them on the table-cloth. She did fix them on it, and the golden fringe of eyelashes that he very rightly thought so beautiful lay in long dusky curves on her serious face. "It's extraordinarily nice of you if—if it's true," she said.

"But it is true. And if you are, if you tell me you are and I'm able to believe it, I bow myself out, dear cousin, and shall devote any energies I have left after doing that to going on muzzling your father. He shall not, I promise you, in any way disturb you. Haven't I kept him well in hand up to this?"

She raised her eyes to his. "Was it you keeping him so quiet?"

"It was, my dear. He was very restive. You've no notion of all the things he wanted to do. It wanted a pretty strong hand, and a light one too, I can tell you. But I was determined you should have your head. That woman Disthal—"

Priscilla started.

"You don't like her?" inquired the Prince sympathetically.

"No."

"I was afraid you couldn't. But I didn't know how to manage that part. She's in London."

Priscilla started again. "I thought—I thought she was in bed," she said.

"She was, but she got out again. Your—departure cured her."

"Didn't you tell me nobody was round the corner?"

"Well, you don't call London round the corner? I wouldn't let her come any nearer to you. She's waiting there quite quietly."

"What is she waiting for?" asked Priscilla quickly.

"Come now, she's your lady in waiting you know. It seems natural enough she should wait, don't it?"

"No," said Priscilla, knitting her eyebrows.

"Don't frown. She had to come too. She's brought some of your women and a whole lot"—he glanced at the blue serge suit and put his hand up to his moustache—"a whole lot of clothes."

"Clothes?" A wave of colour flooded her face. She could not help it at the moment any more than a starving man can help looking eager when food is set before him. "Oh," she said, "I hope they're the ones I was expecting from Paris?"

"I should think it very likely. There seem to be a great many. I never saw so many boxes for one little cousin."

Priscilla made a sudden movement with her hands. "You can't think," she said, "how tired I am of this dress."

"Yes I can," the Prince assured her.

"I've worn it every day."

"You must have."

"Every single day since the day I—I—"

"The day you ran away from me."

She blushed. "I didn't run away from you. At least, not exactly. You were only the last straw."

"A nice thing for a man to be."

"I ran because—because—oh, it's a long story, and I'm afraid a very foolish one."

A gleam came into the Prince's eyes. He took a step nearer her, but immediately thinking better of it took it back again. "Perhaps," he said pleasantly, "only the beginning was foolish, and you'll settle down after a bit and get quite fond of Creeper Cottage."

She looked at him startled.

"You see my dear it was rather tremendous what you did. You must have been most fearfully sick of things at Kunitz. I can well understand it. You couldn't be expected to like me all at once. And if I had to have that Disthal woman at my heels wherever I went I'd shoot myself. What you've done is much braver really than shooting one's self. But the question is do you like it as much as you thought you would?"

Priscilla gave him a swift look, and said nothing.

"If you don't, there's the Disthal waiting for you with all those charming frocks, and all you've got to do is to put them on and go home."

"But I can't go home. How can I? I am disgraced. My father would never let me in."

"Oh I'd arrange all that. I don't think you'd find him angry if you followed my advice very carefully. On the other hand, if you like this and want to stay on there's nothing more to be said. I'll say good-bye, and promise you shall be left in peace. You shall be left to be happy entirely in your own way."

Priscilla was silent.

"You don't—look happy," he said, scrutinizing her face.

She was silent.

"You've got very thin. How did you manage that in such a little while?"

"We've muddled things rather," she said with an ashamed sort of smile. "On the days when I was hungry there wasn't anything to eat, and then when there were things I wasn't hungry."

The Prince looked puzzled. "Didn't that old scamp—I mean didn't the excellent Fritzing bring enough money?"

"He thought he did, but it wasn't enough."

"Is it all gone?"

"We're in debt."

Again he put his hand up to his moustache. "Well I'll see to all that, of course," he said gravely. "And when that has been set right you're sure you'll like staying on here?"

She summoned all her courage, and looked at him for an instant straight in the face. "No," she said.

"No?"

"No."

There was another silence. He was standing on the hearthrug, she on the other side of the table; but the room was so small that by putting out his hand he could have touched her. A queer expression was in his eyes as he looked at her, an expression entirely at variance with his calm and good-natured talk, the exceedingly anxious expression of a man who knows his whole happiness is quivering in the balance. She did not see it, for she preferred to look at the table-cloth.

"Dreadful things have happened here," she said in a low voice.

"What sort?"

"Horrid sorts. Appalling sorts."

"Tell me."

"I couldn't bear to."

"But I think I know."

She looked at him astonished.

"Mrs. Pearce—"

"She told you?"

"What she knew she told me. Perhaps there's something she doesn't know."

Priscilla remembered Robin, and blushed.

"Yes, she told me about that," said the Prince nodding.

"About what?" asked Priscilla, startled.

"About the squire intending to marry you."

"Oh," said Priscilla.

"It seems hard on him, don't it? Has it struck you that such things are likely to occur pretty often to Miss Maria-Theresa Ethel Neumann-Schultz?"

"I'm afraid you really have come only to laugh," said Priscilla, her lips quivering.

"I swear it's only to see if you are happy."

"Well, see then." And throwing back her head with a great defiance she looked at him while her eyes filled with tears; and though they presently brimmed over, and began to drop down pitifully one by one, she would not flinch but went on looking.

"I see," said the Prince quietly. "And I'm convinced. Of course, then, I shall suggest your leaving this."

"I want to."

"And putting yourself in the care of the Disthal."

Priscilla winced.

"Only her temporary care. Quite temporary. And letting her take you back to Kunitz."

Priscilla winced again.

"Only temporarily," said the Prince.

"But my father would never—"

"Yes my dear, he will. He'll be delighted to see you. He'll rejoice."

"Rejoice?"

"I assure you he will. You've only got to do what I tell you."

"Shall you—come too?"

"If you'll let me."

"But then—but then—"

"Then what, my dear?"

She looked at him, and her face changed slowly from white to red and red to white again. Fritzing's words crossed her mind—"If you marry him you will be undoubtedly eternally lost," and her very soul cried out that they were folly. Why should she be eternally lost? What cobwebs were these, cobwebs of an old brain preoccupied with shadows, dusty things to be swept away at the first touch of Nature's vigorous broom? Indeed she thought it far more likely that she would be eternally found. But she was ashamed of herself, ashamed of all she had done, ashamed of the disgraceful way she had treated this man, terribly disillusioned, terribly out of conceit with herself, and she stood there changing colour, hanging her head, humbled, penitent, every shred of the dignity she had been trained to gone, simply somebody who has been very silly and is very sorry.

The Prince put out his hand.

She pretended not to see it.

The Prince came round the table. "You know," he said, "our engagement hasn't been broken off yet?"

Her instinct was to edge away, but she would not stoop to edging. "Was it ever made?" she asked, not able to induce her voice to rise above a whisper.

"Practically."

There was another silence.

"Why, then—" began Priscilla, for the silence had come to be more throbbing, more intolerably expressive than any speech.

"Yes?" encouraged the Prince, coming very close.

She turned her head slowly. "Why, then—" said Priscilla again, her face breaking into a smile, half touched, half mischievous, wholly adorable.

"I think so too," said the Prince; and he shut her mouth with a kiss.

"And now," said the Prince some time afterwards, "let us go to that old sinner Fritzing."

Priscilla hung back, reluctant to deal this final blow to the heart that had endured so many. "He'll be terribly shocked," she said.

But the Prince declared it had to be done; and hand in hand they went out into the street, and opening Fritzing's door stood before him.

He was still absorbed in his Æschylus, had been sitting absorbed in the deeds of the dead and departed, of the long dead Xerxes, the long dead Darius, the very fish, voiceless but voracious, long since as dead as the most shredded of the sailors,—he had been sitting absorbed in these various corpses all the while that in the next room, on the other side of a few inches of plaster and paper, so close you would have thought his heart must have burned within him, so close you would have thought he must be scorched, the living present had been pulsing and glowing, beating against the bright bars of the future, stirring up into alertness a whole row of little red-headed souls till then asleep, souls with golden eyelashes, souls eager to come and be princes and princesses of—I had almost revealed the mighty nation's name. A shadow fell across his book, and looking up he saw the two standing before him hand in hand.

Priscilla caught her breath: what white anguish was going to flash into his face when he grasped the situation? Judge then of her amazement, her hesitation whether to be pleased or vexed, to laugh or cry, when, grasping it, he leaped to his feet and in tones of a most limitless, a most unutterable relief, shouted three times running "*Gott sei Dank!*"

CONCLUSION

So that was the end of Priscilla's fortnight,—according to the way you look at it glorious or inglorious. I shall not say which I think it was; whether it is better to marry a prince, become in course of time a queen, be at the head of a great nation, be surfeited with honour, wealth, power and magnificence till the day when Death with calm, indifferent fingers strips everything away and leaves you at last to the meek simplicity of a shroud; or whether toilsome paths, stern resistances, buffetings bravely taken, battles fought inch by inch, an ideal desperately clung to even though in clinging you are slain, is not rather the part to be chosen of him whose soul would sit attired with stars. Anyhow the goddess laughed, the goddess who had left Priscilla in the lurch, when she heard the end of the adventure; and her unpleasant sister, having nothing more to do in Creeper Cottage, gathered up her rags and grinned too as she left it. At least her claws had lacerated much over-tender flesh during her stay; and though the Prince had interrupted the operation and forced her for the moment to inactivity, she was not dissatisfied with what had been accomplished.

Priscilla, it will readily be imagined, made no farewell calls. She disappeared from Symford as suddenly as she had appeared; and Mrs. Morrison, coming into Creeper Cottage on Monday afternoon to unload her conscience yet more, found only a pleasant gentleman, a stranger of mellifluous manners, writing out cheques. She had ten minutes talk with him, and went home very sad and wise. Indeed from that day, her spirit being the spirit of the true snob, the hectorer of the humble, the devout groveller in the courtyards of the great, she was a much-changed woman. Even her hair felt it, and settled down unchecked to greyness. She no longer cared to put on a pink tulle bow in the afternoons, which may or may not be a sign of grace. She ceased to suppose that she was pretty. When the accounts of Priscilla's wedding filled all the papers she became so ill that she had to go to bed and be nursed. Sometimes to the vicar's mild surprise she hesitated before expressing an opinion. Once at least she of her own accord said she had been wrong. And although she never told any one of the conversation with the gentleman writing cheques, when Robin came home for Christmas and looked at her he knew at once what she knew.

As for Lady Shuttleworth, she got a letter from Priscilla; quite a long one, enclosing a little one for Tussie to be given him if and when his mother thought expedient. Lady Shuttleworth was not surprised by what she read. She had suspected it from the moment Priscilla rose up the day she called on her at Baker's Farm and dismissed her. Till her marriage with the late Sir Augustus she had been lady-in-waiting to one of the English princesses, and she could not be mistaken on such points. She knew the sort of thing too well. But she never forgave Priscilla. How could she? Was the day of Tussie's coming of age, that dreadful day when he was nearest death, a day a mother could ever forget? It had all been most wanton, most cruel. We know she was full of the milk of human kindness: on the subject of Priscilla it was unmixed gall.

As for Tussie,—well, you cannot have omelettes without breaking eggs, and Tussie on this occasion was the eggs. It is a painful part to play. He found it exquisitely painful, and vainly sought comfort in the consolation that it had been Priscilla's omelette. The consolation proved empty, and for a long while he suffered every sort of torment known to the sensitive. But he got over it. People do. They will get over anything if you give them time, and he being young had plenty of it. He lived it down as one lives down every sorrow and every joy; and when in the fulness of time, after a series of years in which he went about listlessly in a soft felt hat and an unsatisfactory collar, he married, it was to Priscilla's capital that he went for his honeymoon. She, hearing he was there, sent for them both and was kind.

As for Annalise, she never got her twenty thousand marks. On the contrary, the vindictive Grand Duke caused her to be prosecuted for blackmailing, and she would undoubtedly have languished in prison if Priscilla had not interfered and sent her back to her parents. Like Mrs. Morrison, she is chastened. She does not turn up her nose so much. She does not sing. Indeed her songs ceased from the moment she caught sight through a crack in the kitchen door of the Prince's broad shoulders filling up Fritzing's sitting-room. From that moment Annalise swooned from one depth of respect and awe to the other. She became breathlessly willing, meek to vanishing point. But Priscilla could not forget all she had made her suffer; and the Prince, who had thought of everything, suddenly producing her head woman from some recess in Baker's Farm, where she too had spent the night, Annalise was superseded, her further bitter fate being to be left behind at Creeper Cottage in the charge of the gentleman with the cheque-book—who as it chanced was a faddist in food and would allow nothing more comforting than dried fruits and nuts to darken the doors— till he should have leisure to pack her up and send her home.

As for Emma, she was hunted out by that detective who travelled down into Somersetshire with the fugitives and who had already been so useful to the Prince; and Priscilla, desperately anxious to make amends wherever she could, took her into her own household, watching over her herself, seeing to it that no word of what she had done was ever blown about among the crowd of idle tongues, and she ended, I believe, by marrying a lacquey,— one of those splendid persons with white silk calves who were so precious in the sight of Annalise. Indeed I am not sure that it was not the very lacquey Annalise had loved most and had intended to marry herself. In this story at least, the claims of poetic justice shall be strictly attended to; and Annalise had sniffed outrageously at Emma.

As for the Countess Disthal, she married the doctor and was sorry ever afterwards; but her sorrow was as nothing compared with his.

As for Fritzing, he is *Hofbibliothekar* of the Prince's father's court library; a court more brilliant than and a library vastly inferior to the one he had fled from at Kunitz. He keeps much in his rooms, and communes almost exclusively with the dead. He finds the dead alone truly satisfactory. Priscilla loves him still and will always love him, but she is very busy and has little time to think. She does not let him give her children lessons; instead he plays with them, and grows old and patient apace.

And now having finished my story, there is nothing left for me to do but stand aside and watch Priscilla and her husband walking hand-in-hand farther and farther away from me up a path which I suppose is the path of glory, into something apparently golden and rosy, something very glowing and full of promise, that turns out on closer scrutiny to be their future. It certainly seems radiant enough to the superficial observer. Even I, who have looked into her soul and known its hungers, am a little dazzled. Let it not however be imagined that a person who has been truthful so long as myself is going to lapse into easy lies at the last, and pretend that she was uninterruptedly satisfied and happy for the rest of her days. She was not; but then who is?